UNFURLED: HEROING IS A TOUGH GIG

UNLIKELY HERO SERIES BOOK 1

ERIC PADILLA

Cover Art by Damonza (https://damonza.com/)

ISBN-13: 978-1-943531-03-5

❀ Created with Vellum

To Ryan,

We are all heroic in our own way. Let your light shine in the way that is yours alone. I love you, son.

1

On my sixteenth birthday, I saw a person die. Until then, I dreamed about being a superhero like the ones on the news. You know, the guy who did unbelievably cool things with his incredible powers. The guy with the sweet costume, the person everyone adored. Everyone except villains, that is. The baddies feared him.

My fantasies were ripped to shreds that day.

I was walking home from school—no one should have to go to school on their birthday!—and I passed a group of older kids. They were seniors, judging by their "I'm too cool for you" faces and their "I have less than a year to go and I'm outta here" attitudes. I pretended not to notice them. It was usually safer that way.

I was what you might call easy pickings. Bullies? Yeah, I'm familiar with the species. Intimately. I was never what might be considered the athletic type. In fact, if there were an anti-athletic nation, I'd be their king. At five feet nine inches, with maybe another couple of inches to grow yet, I could look most of the other kids in my high school in the eye, but even the shorter kids outweighed me. By a lot.

I weighed just over one hundred pounds. Fully clothed. Soaking wet. I've been told I look like a stork, but not nearly as cute.

So there I was, walking home—alone. Did I mention I was alone? Well, I was—and I passed by these older kids. Four of them gathered around something I couldn't see. Following my protocol for avoiding seniors, I went wide of them, walking the edge of the sidewalk opposite the bit of grass they stood on.

As I passed the group, a loud bang startled me so much my neck cracked as my head whipped around toward the sound. I thought maybe they were playing with fireworks. It had to be at least an M80. No firecracker was that loud. I automatically looked toward the group and saw it.

The blood.

One of the kids, a heavyset boy I'd seen around the campus at school, had fallen to the ground. Blood poured from his head, more blood than I thought could come from that part of the body. It wasn't spurting like when characters in movies get an arm or leg cut off. It just leaked out. A deep red stain spread across the grass underneath him.

One of the others, the only girl in the group, screamed hysterically. I stared at her for what seemed like a very long time, trying to make sense of her face, of what had happened. The scene looked like I was watching it in one of those funhouse mirrors, all elongated and stretched. I noticed she breathed quickly and thought she would probably hyperventilate soon if she didn't get it under control. Funny what things pass through your head when you're in shock.

As my vision returned to normal, details became clear.

One of the other boys held a gun with two fingers as if it would bite him. It dangled from the handle, a tiny wisp of smoke coming out of the barrel.

Now, I'm no doctor or any kind of expert—unless video games count—but even I could tell the kid was dead. That quickly. He was standing one moment, and then parts of his brain leaked onto the grass the next. The surrounding people buffeted me on all sides, rushing in to see what had happened. It all seemed like it was happening to someone else. Luckily, the crowd pushed me aside instead of trampling me. The next thing I remember was walking in my front door, going straight to my room, and throwing myself on my bed. I still don't remember the walk home.

"Daniel?" My mom called to me from the kitchen. "Is that you?"

I didn't answer. I seemed to have forgotten how to speak. A shadow fell on me from my doorway. "Daniel? How was school? What's wrong? Are you getting sick?"

"I...I'm...there was—" She ran to my side, put her hand on my forehead. Her brow furrowed as she looked in my eyes. "What is it?"

I still couldn't put two thoughts together. I closed my eyes, but when I did, I saw that kid—what was his name? I couldn't remember—lying on the grass with his body in a strange position, blood leaking out of him. My eyes snapped open again to dispel the picture. Her eyes widened, and her mouth set like it did every time she prepared to cure whatever afflicted me, whether that meant serious illness or a skinned knee.

The tears burst out of me. I couldn't control them. I began to breathe like the girl had earlier, fast panting breaths that did nothing to get the oxygen I needed into my lungs. Sobbing uncontrollably, I felt light-headed and my vision of the watery world narrowed to tunnels.

I don't know how long I blubbered. I only remember my mother holding me and patting my back like she was burping me, trying to calm me. I hovered on the verge of passing out, but I never did. Instead, I floated, separated from my body and from the rest of the world. While I cried like a small child after his first spanking, my mind jumped from pictures of the gun accident, the body, the other kids, to logical analysis of what had happened. It was comforting in a way.

I cried for a long time, finally tapering off to soft sobbing and then intermittent bouts of crying. My mother still held me, wiping the mop of my hair out of my face, kissing my forehead.

"Mom!" my brother Tim yelled as he slammed the front door. "Mom?"

His feet thudded on the stairs, and then he burst into my room. He looked at me and cocked his head. Shaking it, he looked to my mother.

"Mom, some high school kids were playing with a gun and one of them got his head blown off. There are police and reporters and everything out there, just a few blocks away. Mom? What's up with Danny?"

The situation must have thrown him off because he wasn't acting like the little jerk he normally was. Normally he would tease me for sure, with me crying like that.

I had to see a school psychologist that evening. I guess they needed to make sure I wasn't going to go crazy. It was okay, though. Mrs. Phillips was a kind, older lady. I didn't mind talking to her. Much. She asked gentle questions and I cried a little, but not as much as I expected. I had probably cried out when I had the meltdown in my room earlier.

Somehow, talking about it in follow-up visits made me feel better. Within a week, the memory shrank to a ball of uncomfortableness somewhere in the back of my mind, coming out to let me know it was still there once in a while, but not taking center stage.

"How has what you observed changed you, Daniel?" Mrs. Phillips asked in one of our last sessions.

"Changed me?"

"Yes. When traumatic things happen to us, we very often change in some way. Our attitude shifts, we adopt another opinion, we learn something we didn't really consider before. How has what you witnessed changed you?"

I hadn't thought of that before. Changed me. Hmmm. "I think I never understood before how fragile things are."

"What do you mean by that?" she said, pushing the glasses up on her nose and focusing her eyes on me more intently.

My face heated. "You know. One silly mistake, one choice, and it could all end. It's a little scary."

"I see," she said. "How does that make you feel? What will your new understanding mean for you?"

"Geez, I don't know. I'm just a kid." I scrubbed my hand through my hair and stopped speaking to think. She looked down at her notebook, allowing me time to finish my thought. A moment later, I said, "I guess it will make me think more carefully about the decisions I make, what things are really important. Stuff like that."

"Stuff that is important?" The way she snapped her head toward me in surprise, I either said something completely stupid or something very deep. Or maybe she had been falling asleep, and the sound of my voice after the pause startled her.

"Yeah. There are things in life sometimes that we have to

do that might be dangerous, and we have to decide whether the danger is worth it. Like if I became a cop or a firefighter. Some things aren't worth the risk, though. Like playing with guns when you don't know how to do so safely. Does that sound stupid?"

The question seemed to take her aback. Maybe she was too used to younger kids who didn't ask questions back. "No, of course not, Daniel. It is never silly when you express how you feel or what you think. In fact, it is an appropriate and, if I may say so, *adult* thing to say. It is also a promising sign that you are accepting what happened to you, recognizing a lesson it can teach you about life, and at least thinking of modifying your own viewpoint because of it."

I started having my fantasies again about being a superhero, with a slight change. Instead of acclaim and adoration, my dreams focused on helping people, saving them. I didn't ever want to see someone die again.

MY SEVENTEENTH BIRTHDAY PASSED, and the edge on the memories of the death I had seen dulled, as the psychologist suggested it would. Nothing else in my life changed. A birthday was only a day like any other, right? I'd given up thinking it was special.

On that particular day, I didn't feel like going straight home from school. If I had friends, I'd have hung out with them, but going to the psychologist after the shooting marked me as even more of a "weird kid" than before. There were others, of course, but for me the label seemed to stick more readily.

I had been feeling different in the last few weeks. I'm not sure exactly how to describe it other than to say that I felt something wasn't normal, sort of off. Walking, it almost seemed as if it was someone else's feet touching the ground, like I wasn't even part of this world. I felt like the victim of some kind of out-of-body experience. It was weird.

Instead of heading home to do the same thing I did every day—watching TV, poking around on the internet, or reading one of my many comics or adventure novels—I turned down a street I'd never taken before.

It was a dead-end street, stopping at a field that separated the houses nearby from a stand of trees the kids called "the woods." I walked along the street toward the field, oblivious to what was going on around me, whether there were people or pets, cars, or anything else. What was going on with me, anyway? Hormones. Maybe it was hormones. In his Life Science class, Mr. Peterson always talked about the *changes* kids my age were going through. Everything, it seemed, was related to hormone changes. They were the bane of teen existence. I shook my head as if I could rattle the problem loose and walked on.

It was a blistering sixty degrees, an unseasonably warm, late January day in my city, Sueño, Arizona. The sky contained only a few wispy clouds. It was one of those perfect days, the ones where you can go outside and do anything from running around and climbing trees to swimming. Well, maybe not swimming, but most anything else. I took in a deep breath and sighed it out.

Movement off to my right, at the edge of the field, caught my attention. People clustered near the edge of the trees. What were they doing?

I counted them—seven. I recognized some of them from school, all seniors, and a couple kids I thought had already graduated. They surrounded someone, but I couldn't see who from where I was. I moved closer, walking into the field and to the side to get a different angle. I honestly didn't even think about whether or not they could see me. Like I said, my thinking hadn't been normal.

I finally got a clear view of the person in the middle. I recognized the girl from school, an outcast, like me. Glasses dominated her skinny face. Her dark brown hair was put up into some kind of tangled bun and stuffed into the ugliest hat I had ever seen. Her clothes didn't fit well, either, hanging off her like hand-me-downs she hadn't yet grown into. She shuffled back and forth in her clunky black shoes, but the circle tightened and she couldn't escape.

It didn't look good for her. I had been bullied before, a lot, though not as much since my growth spurt. I remembered the feeling well, and it made me sad to see her in that position. I looked around for anyone else to help, someone I could ask to go and extract her from the circle. There was no one.

It occurred to me that I was standing in the middle of a field, looking right at all those bullies. If even one of them turned around and saw me, they'd run me down and give me the same as that girl was about to get. I had to leave. My heart went out to her, but I couldn't fight six bigger boys. The best course of action was to go find someone who could do something. Where was a cop when you needed one?

One of the bigger boys slapped the backpack the girl had been holding like a shield out of her hands. The others laughed as another pushed her hard, knocking her down. I couldn't hear their taunts, but I'd heard the like before. Not for the first time in my life, I wished I were bigger, stronger, more athletic. In short, I wished I were a hero. Instead, I was a coward who would leave a girl to be pushed around. I felt like a jerk.

As I turned to leave, the girl saw me. She was crying, trying to get up. All the boys were busy giving each other high fives and fist bumps, so they didn't see where her eyes were pointed. I did, though. I did. The sadness and pleading in those eyes made my own eyes water. I shrugged, trying to convey that I'd only get myself beat up as well if I tried to help. The disappointment in those eyes tore into my soul. I turned and started walking away, feeling like I was the one who deserved to be beaten up.

"We're going to make you feel really good," one of the boys said in a voice that carried across the field so it echoed clearly in my ears. I looked back to see him licking his lips and leering at her.

"Yeah," another chimed in. "Come on, we'll show you what you've been missing." He grabbed the girl's arm and easily pulled her to her feet. Then he turned toward the trees and started dragging her into them.

The girl tried to scream, but a rough hand over her mouth ended it before the sound had a chance to escape.

Oh no. They couldn't have meant... No, they wouldn't do that. Would they? I was halfway to them before I realized it. I couldn't stop, though. I was committed. Letting someone be pushed around was one thing, but this? This was way beyond anything I had ever thought to see.

I launched myself at the guy holding her. My shoulder struck his hip, and he stumbled away. The next closest boy got my backpack in his face, swung with as much force as I could muster. I turned to the girl. "Run!" I said, whirling to face the other four, who were closing in on me.

No, make that six. The one I pushed had turned and stalked back toward me, and the one I hit with the backpack had recovered too.

"RUN!" I shouted at the girl. This time she did as I said.

She made it about four steps before one of the boys grabbed her.

"Whoa, there," he sneered. "We're not done with you. You'll watch us beat your boyfriend up, and then you have a date over there with us." He pointed toward the trees.

The girl kicked at her captor, but he hugged her to his chest, wrapping his arms around hers and keeping her from moving. He leaned his head down to whisper something to her, or to try to kiss her, and she head-butted him, causing him to curse her and throw her to the ground. I had to turn my attention to the three getting ready to cream me, so I only glimpsed the boy straddling her, sitting on her to keep her still while his friends took care of me. We all figured it wouldn't take long.

The first boy pushed me hard toward his buddies. My neck whipped to the side, making my vision spin, disorienting me. A fist that came out of nowhere hammered my forehead and stopped me cold. I guess it was lucky I was moving because if that punch had hit me in the mouth or nose, it would have broken something. Tiny flashes of light danced around the edges of my vision, and the world narrowed to a dark tunnel. Time slowed as I fell toward the ground. I didn't feel the pain yet, but I was sure I would soon.

The world grew dim except for the sparkles of light that seemed to be following me to the ground. Knocked out on the first punch. Some great hero I was.

Time snapped back into normal motion. Blades of grass prickled against my cheeks. My ears rang with a high-pitched sound, like one of the tuning forks I had heard in music class. It was not unpleasant. Maybe if I pretended I had been knocked out, they would leave me alone. A hard kick to my ribs told me that wouldn't be how it happened.

Through the ringing, I heard the girl trying to scream through the hand covering her mouth. Out of the corner of my eye, through the fading blackness, I saw her squirming to get free.

Another foot cocked back and started coming toward me. I couldn't lie there and let them kick me. I'd be bleeding internally before they stopped. As the foot came in, I rolled away from it. It still made contact, but not as hard as the first. The others hadn't reached me yet. It seemed like it had been a long time since the first boy punched me, but I guess it had only been a few seconds.

I wobbled to my feet. Why was the ground so uneven? And moving? Was it an earthquake? I stood there shakily, watching all five remaining boys—the other one still sat on the girl—coming at me, the closest with blood trickling from his nose. Uh-oh. That was the guy I hit with the backpack. He didn't look happy.

Frantically, I looked around for anything that could help...or anyone. There was no one else around and not so much as a stick on the ground. I could still run; I was good at that. They probably wouldn't be able to catch me. If I did, though, the girl would be alone. If I went for help, I'd never get back before they had done the things they promised to her. I gritted my teeth, put my fists up, and hoped I wouldn't die. Maybe she could get away from the boy sitting on her and would be smart enough to make a run for it.

The bloody-nosed boy slowed down, surprise lighting up his eyes. Of all things he might have expected, me standing my ground and acting like I would fight probably wasn't one of them. He glanced to the left and then to the right and saw that his buddies were with him. Then, he clenched his jaw and came at me.

I remember exactly what happened next, but I don't understand why or how it happened. I have thought about it a lot.

Bloody-nose threw a punch at me with his right hand. It was a good punch—for a kid—with the weight of his whole body behind it. The thing is, it seemed really slow. I mean *really* slow.

I had something like five seconds to react to it as it inched toward me. I know. I counted. As it made its way to my face, I calmly—did I think I was invincible like Superman?—moved to the right a half step, reached up, and grabbed his fist out of the air with my left hand. It surprised me as much as it did him.

Not knowing what else to do, I slapped him. It was pathetic, as uncoordinated and slow as a blow from a child. I didn't even aim. I just swung my open right hand at him, hoping to do something. It did that.

My palm smacked against his left shoulder. Luckily I had let go of his fist, because my slap sent him hurtling off, crashing into two of the others, all of them ending up in a heap on the ground.

I looked down at my hands. One stopped a punch in mid-swing—and it didn't even sting—and one sent a much bigger boy flying several feet. As I stared, the biggest guy, the one who had seemed to be the leader, swung at me.

It's funny, looking back. Though he moved slowly, too, I wasn't paying attention, too shocked by what had just happened. So, when the slow punch came in, I didn't react. I didn't need to.

I heard a cracking sound and felt a light thump against my stomach. The boy in front of me bent over, holding his hand in the other, and howled like someone had hit him with a metal pipe. Our eyes met and his held fear. Real fear, like I'm-going-to-die kind of fear. They widened when my right arm shot out and pushed him high on the chest, just below the shoulder, on the collar bone. I heard another crack, and he flew backward off his feet, landing awkwardly on the grass. He skidded for a few feet before coming to rest.

No one spoke. I looked around to see all the other boys staring at me in disbelief. None were moving. Even the one sitting on the girl had stopped all motion.

I recovered from my surprise more quickly than the others. I put on my most fierce look—I had no practice with fierce looks, so I'm not sure how effective it was—and my eyes bored into those of the boy still sitting on the girl.

"Get off her!" I was surprised yet again when he jumped off her immediately. He didn't even try to stop the kick she aimed at his shin as she got up.

The spell broken, all six turned and ran, two of them limping and one other running awkwardly, one arm cradled in the other. My shoulders slumped, and I let out what seemed to be the first breath I had taken all day.

I shook all over, hardly able to stand. Still, I forced my feet to shuffle to the girl's backpack, its contents spilled across the ground in the scuffle. I picked up a ruler, a pencil case with Wonder Woman on it, some books, and a spiral notebook so covered with scribbled drawings I couldn't tell where one ended and the other began. I walked four steps to where she was, holding out her things.

"Are..." I looked into her eyes. She looked terrified still. "Are you okay? Did they hurt you?"

She didn't answer, her lower lip quivering and her eyes filling with tears. She disregarded my extended hands and rushed at me, almost knocking me from my shaky feet. Her arms went around me, and she hugged me with what had to be all her strength.

"Thank you," she whispered. "Thank you so much. I thought you were going to leave me alone with them. Thank you for helping me. That was very brave."

I found my arms encircling her, and I returned her hug, patting her on the back with one of my hands. I realized she was the first girl I had ever hugged, other than relatives. My heart started to beat more quickly as I became nervous. Even the fight hadn't made me that tense. I gently pushed her shoulders away from me.

I couldn't seem to meet her eyes. Sure, she was an awkward, nerdy, outcast girl, but she was still a girl. I stared at the ground, the only safe place as far as I was concerned. "Are you okay? I asked again.

"I am now. Thank you." She tried to look into my eyes without being obvious she was looking into my eyes. I bent to pick her things up again. I had dropped them when she hugged me. "I'm Amy. Amy Selling."

She tracked my eyes as they flickered up to her and then away again and continued. "I know, it's a horrible name. Believe me, I've heard all the jokes."

"I think it's a beautiful name," I stammered. I felt heat travel up my neck to my face. "I mean, it's nice. I'm Daniel, Daniel Nickers." It was my turn to be embarrassed. "I have heard all the jokes, too."

She did that thing girls do, looking into my eyes and then looking away again while striking that pose I'm pretty sure they perfect when they're babies. You know, the one that makes the room hotter and leaves you unable to form a complete thought, one leg bent more than the other and the hip cocked just a little, hands in some kind of perfect configuration loosely in front of the waist. Even awkward girls can do it. It really wasn't fair.

"Well," I said, "I think you're safe now. We better go to where there are more people in case they come back. Which way are you going?" I saw disappointment in Amy's eyes. Or was that fear? "I'll walk you home, if that's okay. I could use the company right now, I think."

Her eyes darted up to meet mine. She looked relieved. Once I looked at them, I realized they were bright blue, reflecting the sunlight in a way that seemed to make them glow, only lessened a little by the thick glasses she wore. Her mouth twitched into tiny smile. "Thank you. I'm still a little shaken."

"Me too." We both laughed and began walking. I let her lead since she never answered my question as to which way she was going.

"Daniel," she said, looking at me sideways while taking her lower lip between her teeth. "What did you do to those boys? How did you chase them off like that?"

I had been wondering that myself. "I don't know."

She walked silently beside me, not looking at me, but not really avoiding looking at me either. She seemed content to allow me time to put my thoughts together. I appreciated it.

"At first, they threw me around like a rag doll," I said, touching the lump on my forehead and wincing. "Then, something changed. I can't really explain it, but time seemed to slow down. At least, it did for the others. When I moved, it seemed like it was normal speed, even though they looked like they were miming a fight scene in slow motion."

"I only caught a glimpse of what you did," Amy said, "but you moved faster than I've ever seen anyone move. Your hands were a blur when you grabbed that jerk's punch and then slapped him."

"Really?" I hadn't thought of it that way. It seemed like everyone else was slow, not like I was fast. "When I hit them, it felt weird. It was like I was pushing a paper doll. They didn't weigh anything. I didn't even push or slap hard."

I had gone two steps before I noticed Amy had stopped. I turned and looked at her. She had a look on her face as if she had figured out how to cure cancer but was afraid someone would steal the knowledge from her.

"Are you okay?" I asked.

She whispered, "Maybe you're a superhero."

"What?" I laughed. "Look at me, Amy. I am no superhero."

Her expression turned dangerous. She somehow looked down her nose at me even though she was inches shorter than me. "And what does a superhero look like? Who's to say they don't look just like you?"

"Come on, Amy. Don't tease me. You know what they look like. Superman, Spiderman, Batman, other *mans*. They're all huge with muscles on muscles and jaws you could crack a rock on."

"Maybe." Her expression softened, but she still looked as if she would scold me. "But what did they look like when they started? Maybe like you. Don't tell me you don't know about real superheroes. Not the ones in the comics, but the ones that have been popping up the last ten years or so."

"Yes, yes," I said, "I know." I ticked off the facts as if I was teaching a lesson. "The news always has tales these days of someone or another who suddenly developed powers. Flying, super strength, and other abilities beyond what normal people have are now reality for the lucky few. Sure, sure, I know all about it."

"If you know so much, then why would you doubt that you could be one of them?" she said, crossing her arms and tilting her chin for emphasis. As if she had made a valid point.

"That's ridiculous," I said, starting to feel uncomfortable. "I'm no superhero. I probably just got one of those weird adrenaline rushes. You know, the ones where a tiny woman lifts a car to save her child, things like that. I got an adrenaline rush, it saved my skin, and I'm satisfied with that. I don't want to make it into some big thing. Can we talk about something else?"

She sighed. "Okay. I'm sorry. Maybe I spend too much time reading and watching superhero shows."

"You too?" Now we were talking. "I love that stuff. Have you seen...?"

2

I walked Amy home, talking with her about superhero shows, comics, action movies, and a thousand other things. She was, by far, the coolest girl I'd ever talked to. Of course, I had so little experience in talking with girls that it could also be said without too much exaggeration that she was the *only* girl I had ever talked to. Still, our interests and senses of humor matched perfectly, and by the time I said goodbye to her at her doorstep, I knew we would be friends.

"We should hang out," she told me as she opened her door to go inside. She got my phone number, promptly texted me a smiley face, and went inside. I pictured the way her nose crinkled when she laughed, and a smile sprang onto my face as I started home. Maybe she wasn't so plain looking, after all.

While walking, I thought again about what she had said about what had happened. What had come over me? How did I do those things? Could she be right? Was I a superhero? I laughed out loud, causing an elderly woman walking past me on the sidewalk to move away from me, a concerned look on her face.

"Sorry," I said. "Just something funny I heard earlier." I felt my face flush as she nodded and hurried on.

By the time I got home, I had gone back and forth in my mind a dozen times. I went from believing I was the next Superman to worrying that those boys would find me and beat me up when they figured out what happened was a one-time thing. My stomach twisted into knots. They would not go easy on me if they caught me. I was sure I broke some bones in the biggest of them.

I went to the garage and dug out an old dumbbell wedged into the back corner. It weighed forty pounds. I picked it up with my right hand. Well, I tried to pick it up with my right hand. I put my left hand next to the right and strained. I lifted it, but not easily. That told me all I needed to know. Regardless of Amy's idea and my own dream, I was not a superhero. I almost crushed my foot when I dropped the weight. It wouldn't have been the only thing. My heart felt crushed already.

Lying on my bed a few minutes later, staring at the ceiling, it occurred to me that I shouldn't be feeling so sad. Even if it wasn't something permanent, I had saved a girl from having horrible things done to her that day. I had acted like a hero, and though it hurt—my head still throbbed—it was satisfying, too. And on top of that, I had a friend. She would probably get sick of me and decide not to hang out with me anymore, but for now, I had a friend.

Almost on cue, my phone beeped. It was a text from Amy. THANK YOU AGAIN FOR SAVING ME TODAY. YOU MAY NOT BE SUPER, BUT YOU ARE MY HERO.

I smiled at that. I'd never been called anyone's hero before. Maybe it hadn't been such a bad day after all.

I started hanging out with Amy after school, and even at lunch while at school. A month passed quickly in the midst of my new friendship and keeping up with my schoolwork. I didn't have any time to think about that day and the things I did. I was occasionally paranoid that I would be ambushed and beat up when I least expected it, but as time went on, I even forgot about that. Then, exactly thirty-four days from the fateful day, something else happened.

I was taking the trashcans from the house and emptying them into the larger waste bins outside before trash day, preparing to bring them to the curb. I wasn't thinking of anything in particular, just letting my mind wander while doing my assigned chores.

Something happened and my body seemed to act on its own. In one smooth motion, I set the empty wastebasket down, threw my other arm out behind me, and snatched something out of the air. When I opened my hand, I saw a water balloon in my palm. My brother Tim stood there, his mouth hanging open, eyes wide. I flicked my wrist and the balloon shot toward him, striking him in the chest, bursting, and soaking him instantly. He ran back toward the house.

Turning my attention back to the task at hand, I tugged on the large trash bin—one of the big, wheeled containers the city trash service provided—to roll it to the street, and I accidentally threw it ten feet in the air. I watched, slack-jawed, as it sailed up and then came down toward me. As if by reflex again, I caught it with one hand, holding it in my palm like a waiter with his tray. I set it hastily on the ground and looked around. There was no one else in sight, and my brother had missed the display, having already gone around the house.

I looked at my hands. I seemed to be getting into a habit of doing that. How did I know the balloon was coming? How did I catch it without looking? More importantly, how did I throw the heavy trash bin around like it weighed nothing?

Scanning my surroundings, I made sure no one else was around. When I was certain, I lifted the can up again with one hand. It did feel like it weighed nothing. I hurriedly emptied the smaller wastebaskets and then brought the cans out to the curb, even the green waste container, heavy with dozens of pounds of grass clippings. I lifted it one-handed with no problem.

I ran to my room and closed the door. Before it had shut all the way, I was calling Amy. Maybe she could make sense of what happened.

I met her in a park near her house before twenty minutes had passed. "I'm kind of freaking out here," I blurted before she even reached me. I told her about the balloon and the trashcans.

She scanned me with those hypnotic blue eyes, tapping her lip with her index finger. "Maybe I was right. Maybe you are a superhero."

"Come on, Amy," I said, "let's not go through this again."

"Just listen to me. No one really knows how the process works, how people develop powers. In the comics it usually involves someone getting dosed with radiation, but the real people with powers can't all have been exposed to radiation.

"What if it's something within us, something that takes a little time to reveal itself? Maybe certain types of stresses or situations make abilities come into the open? That day you met me, maybe that was enough to bring them out, and now that the cat's out of the bag, it won't ever go fully back in."

I looked at her with my mouth open. She looked back at me without batting an eyelash. She was serious.

"There has to be another explanation." I don't know why I tried to talk her out of it. I had always wanted powers, always wanted to be a superhero. Of course, that's when I thought it would never happen to me. I guess I was scared.

"Show me what you got," she said, a little smirk playing across her face. "There's no one around to see. Let's test you."

"Test me?" I said. "How?"

She looked around. Her eyes locked onto a tree a few feet away. It had a branch that curled away from the trunk, about fifteen feet from the ground, sticking out almost completely horizontal. "Jump up and grab that branch," she said, as if it was the most normal thing in the world.

"Are you insane? I can't jump that high."

"Try, Daniel. Just try once. Please." She did that thing girls do with their eyelashes and the shifting of their feet and their posture, and suddenly I wanted to try. Before I could even argue, I had made up my mind. I think all women have superpowers.

I squatted down, feeling like a fool. Looking around to make sure there was no one who could see, I pushed against the ground with both feet. I had never been much of an athlete, so I figured I'd go a few inches off the ground—awkwardly—and then land, embarrassed but vindicated. Instead, I found myself hurtling toward the branch at a speed I couldn't control.

I struck the branch with the front of my shoulder and somehow wrapped my body around it. All the air came out of my lungs as I struck. I was bent double looking straight down at Amy, fifteen feet below me. She was doing a little dance and smiling.

"I knew you could do it," she said.

Yeah, that makes one of us.

"Now," she continued, "I want you to grab the branch and hang."

I took a few deep breaths, trying to relax. The distance looked much greater looking down than it did when I was on the ground looking up. I put my hands on the rough bark of the branch and lowered my body until I hung there. "Okay," I said. "Can I come down now?"

"Not yet. I want you to do some pull-ups."

"I can't even do one pull-up. I fail that test every year in P.E."

"Daniel." Her voice was firm, like she was about to scold me. "Come on, just try."

I pulled myself up easily so that my head was above the branch. It didn't even feel like I had used any energy to do it. "Hey," I exclaimed, "I can do a pull-up." I did ten more with no trouble. I felt like I could do pull-ups all day.

"Now let go with one hand and do a pull-up with the other arm," she told me.

I didn't bother arguing that time. I dropped my left arm to my side and pulled myself up with my right hand. It was no effort to do another ten one-handed pull-ups. I giggled, feeling like I might be going insane.

"Okay, can I come down now?" I don't know why I needed permission, but it seemed I had better ask.

"Yes. Just drop."

"What? Are you crazy? That's got to be something like fifteen feet. I'll break both my legs!"

"No you won't. Daniel, trust me. As you hit the ground, bend your knees to absorb the impact. It'll be fine."

I looked around. There really wasn't another way to get down. I could go along the branch to the trunk, but there weren't any other branches I could use to climb down. The only other way would be to hug the tree and slide down. With how rough the bark was, it would scrape me up and probably tear my clothes. I guessed I'd just have to drop.

I looked down one final time. Big mistake. My palms started sweating, and my heart doubled its rate. Still, there was nothing else to do. I let go of the branch and plummeted toward the earth, trying to remember what Amy had told me about absorbing the force with my legs.

I didn't even feel a jolt when my feet touched the grass. I had forgotten to bend my knees, but it was all right. I looked back up at the branch and shivered.

"That was amazing," Amy said, coming up to me. "You didn't bend your knees like I told you, but I don't think you needed to. You're very strong, it seems."

I sighed. "I guess so. But what would have happened if I had lost the abilities like I did after that first day? If my strength blinks out when I need it, like on the way down from the branch, what then?"

"I guess we'll just have to figure things out." Amy smiled at me. "We'll take it slow, but we'll test you thoroughly and catalog everything. Isn't this exciting?"

I wasn't so sure. I nodded, and she took that as agreement, but I was uneasy. It would be great to have powers, but I could easily hurt myself—even kill myself—trying to test them. I would need to be careful and not let her push me into anything dangerous. *Sure*, I thought, as if I could tell her no. Not for the first time, I wished I had the power to withstand her smile.

3

"I looked some stuff up," Amy said to me the day after our little test of my powers. "This researcher, Dr. William Walters, has done a lot of work on the genetics of people who have special abilities. There are cases of people whose powers fluctuated like yours. Like I thought, he says the abilities are trying to *find themselves*, settling into something special that matches the person's metabolism and persona. There's not a lot of information yet, but I'll keep an eye out for any papers he publishes. It could help."

"Yeah," I said. "Anything that can help me understand or control this thing will be great."

Amy and I spent the next few weeks trying to figure out what abilities I had developed. Sounds simple, right? Well, it wasn't. First of all, because they were emerging, my powers weren't consistent. I was relieved to find they didn't blink out completely—that could have been a disaster—but their strength and even their nature changed.

During one test, I jumped nearly thirty feet straight up and, more importantly, landed safely from that height.

When we tried again a few days later, I left the ground and kept going, and going, and going, until the vision of the park where Amy was became obscured by clouds. I was actually flying. At least, it was flying on the way up. My ascent finally slowed and stopped. Coming down was more like controlled falling. I couldn't steer much, but I flew. Every attempt to do that again failed.

It seemed like my abilities were trying to figure out what they wanted to be. I pictured a big wheel in my head, like on the game show *Wheel of Fortune*. Every day I would spin it and whatever power it landed on, that's what I had. For that moment. To say it was frustrating would be an understatement. It was bad enough trying to figure out how to use whatever particular ability I possessed, but with them changing constantly, I was ready to rip my hair out. Which I could have done. Easily. Super strength seemed to always be present.

"Okay," Amy said, scribbling something in her notebook, "in every test we have run, you have tremendous strength. That never changes, though just how strong you are changes from test to test."

I'd easily lifted an old car down at the junk yard and pulled a forty-foot tree out by its roots in the middle of a nearby forest. We did a lot of our testing in that forest so we wouldn't be seen by anyone else.

"You are almost always very fast, too," she continued. "Whether it's running or punching or dodging things. More than half the time, you have that weird reflex thing that warns you of danger and makes your body react before you even know there is any danger to begin with."

That part was kind of creepy. At random times, Amy would throw something at me or activate something she had rigged to fall or shoot toward me. Nothing dangerous, things ranging from Nerf projectiles to water balloons to stuffed animals, but that protective mechanism would kick in about half the time. That would be useful, if it decided to protect me all the time. With it only on duty half the time, though, I couldn't rely on it.

"The good news is that the percentage of times it activates seems to be increasing. Maybe we just have to wait a little while and it will protect you all the time." She tapped her temple with the pencil and got a contemplative look on her face. "Or, maybe if it was truly something dangerous to you, it will work all the time. Maybe it knows that a teddy bear won't hurt you so it doesn't bother to kick in."

"Now you're making it sound like it's alive," I said, shivering despite myself. "You're kind of creeping me out. It's bad enough I'm going through what I am without you making it sound like there's an alien inhabiting my body."

"Oh, sorry." Her shoulders sagged, and she sighed. "I wish we could test your resilience better, though. It's hard to do without doing dangerous things."

That was true. I seemed to be tougher, more durable. It made sense. I had strength to punch through a brick wall, but without the toughness, I'd shatter every bone in my hand and probably in my forearm, too. I was opening a box with a utility knife one day and I slipped, slashing my hand with the sharp blade. It didn't leave a mark on me. A little experimentation revealed that unless I used more of my strength, I couldn't cut through my skin with that razor blade. But was it always like that, or did that come and go too?

There were just too many variables. Until my changes settled down, I wouldn't know what I was capable of.

"...and then there were those one-time things that happened." My attention returned to Amy. "The way you caused the earth to tremor by shifting your foot, that time you spit and your saliva burned a hole in the sidewalk, and the sneeze that made the closest tree explode, I don't even know what to think of those. God, I hope that sneeze thing isn't permanent. We'd need to send you away every time you got a cold for fear of you destroying the city."

I'd almost forgotten about those things. Scary. I had never thought about all these problems with superpowers. I guess that's the way it normally is. You wish for something, thinking only about the good, about the cool parts. When you finally get it, you find out that there are two sides to everything. Still—superpowers, am I right? I just had to figure out how to find and live within my limits. Isn't that what everyone did in their own lives anyway?

I immediately felt embarrassed by my thinking. It sounded like something a guidance counselor or my mother would say.

"Why are you blushing?" Amy asked, eyeing me carefully.

I told her my thoughts. She always understood me. Something about her—maybe her geeky way of analyzing everything—made it so I had no problem telling Amy anything. We had become even better friends during all this experimentation.

"Daniel," she said seriously, though her eyes shone with mischief, "I think that means you're growing up."

"Please," I said.

She laughed and threw a stuffed animal, a cow, at me. My body reacted and snatched it out of the air, threw it back at her. It hit her arm. I heaved a sigh of relief that my auto-defense power didn't use too much strength to throw it at her. I could have hurt her. She scratched something else in that book of hers, no doubt recording my reflexes activating.

She looked up at me again. "I was thinking about what you were going to do with your new-found powers. Do you have any ideas?"

I *had* thought about that. A lot. "Well, it's hard to figure out something when I don't really know what powers I'll have at any given moment. I think they need to be more stable before I can rely on them."

"Your strength is pretty consistent. At least, it's always there, though to a different degree."

"I know. I haven't come up with anything yet. I'll give it another week or two."

She nodded. "Okay, I was just wondering."

She wasn't the only one. I mean, here I was, just some dumb kid, with the opportunity to do something important. But what? I thought about my dream from when I was younger, the one about being a superhero, saving people and making everyone's lives better. I wasn't sure that was in the cards for me, though. I thought about it as I walked home.

Sure, I had some cool abilities, if erratic, but to go out and do something with them, that was frightening. Some people tried to do just that. They dressed up in some costume and patrolled the streets, looking for criminals. The news agencies loved those stories, following some of the successes the vigilantes had. It always ended the same way, though: with some thug putting a couple of bullets into the would-be hero's head. It could end that quickly. There would be no value at all in getting shot in the street.

I also thought about things in more practical terms. It was time to think about college, though my parents didn't really have the money for it. I hadn't applied anywhere, thinking that I might just take a year or so off to get a job and save up some money. The chances of me going back to school after that year would be less than if I continued after high school, but there didn't seem to be any other way. Maybe I should have applied for scholarships. Maybe it wasn't too late.

The idea struck me that I might be able to use my powers to make a little money. That wasn't unethical, right? My abilities were part of me. It wasn't like I took performance-enhancing drugs or did anything to gain more strength or speed. I would probably kill it in some sort of professional sport. Which one, though? I'd be laughed off the field if I tried football, stick-thin as I was. Baseball? How hard could that be with my new strength, speed, and reflexes? Soccer? Basketball? I could make a lot of money, and then I wouldn't have to worry about anything. I could even help my family out. The thoughts whirled through my mind, bouncing around, providing flashes of images that all seemed to run together into a movie-style montage of a great life.

I stopped myself. I had the privilege of gaining abilities far beyond normal people, and I was trying to make a buck. I sighed. I would work it out...eventually.

I turned the corner by a little strip mall a mile from my house and stopped cold. There was yellow tape surrounding the area and police cars everywhere. Some people milled around outside the tape, which enclosed a big section of the parking lot in front of a convenience store.

"What's going on?" I asked a kid I had seen at school a few times.

"Robbery. Some guys with ski masks came in, held the clerk up, and shot the place up. There are a couple of people hurt, but no one dead, I think."

A robbery? In broad daylight? I'd seen some news reports about crime getting worse in the city, but for some reason I always thought of it as more like stealing delivered packages off someone's doorstep or breaking into a house when the owner wasn't home. I never equated it with violent crime. Why would they shoot up the store even though they had already gotten the money? The world was going crazy.

Sueño, Arizona isn't a major metropolis or anything, but with over two hundred fifty thousand people, it's fairly large for my state. Though downtown had commercial buildings and traffic and all that, I lived in a suburb, with its quiet, peaceful streets and the trees that seemed like they should be out of place in a state known for desert and rocks and things like that. The crime rate had never been high, except in the center of the city. An armed robbery in my area was shocking.

There was no reason for me to stay there and watch for signs of blood like the vultures did, so I kept walking. The whole thing disgusted me. I often felt like I deserved something better, wanted to have more things or to do stuff I couldn't afford, but to steal to accomplish it? It just didn't make sense. Someone should really do something about it.

Yeah, someone should do something about it. I glanced back at the crime scene just in time to see the clerk on a gurney being lifted into an ambulance. His face was white from blood loss, and his eyes rolled dizzily as if trying to focus. I hoped he would be all right. He was just doing his job.

Doing his job.

I stopped walking and stared at all the people, at the cars, the yellow tape, the ambulances. What was my job? Did I have a responsibility since I had received the gift of wondrous abilities? I started off again, more quickly, trying to outrun something I knew I could never evade.

4

"You want to what?" Amy asked, her eyes wide and her mouth hanging open as we talked the next day.

"I just thought that, you know, maybe I got these powers for a reason. To help people. Don't you think I have a duty to—"

"Daniel," she interrupted me, "you have a duty not to go and get shot. You have a duty to be around to give your parents some grandchildren. You have a duty to your friends not to burden them with the memory of who you used to be. Are you out of your mind?"

I set my jaw and glared at her. "Amy, crime is getting worse here. You've seen it. The police can't handle it, and it won't get better on its own. Someone has to do something to help, so why not me? I am best suited for it."

"Best suited? You can hardly use the powers you have, when they bother to stick around. Okay, you're fast, and strong, and have great reflexes, and tough skin. Most of the time. But one gunshot and you die just like anyone else. Just one. It's too risky."

"It's risky walking down the street or going to the store." I crossed my arms and straightened my back without thinking about it. "Things are bad. How much worse do they have to get before anyone else does something about it? How can you think I should stand by watching people get hurt, watching as they get more and more fearful every day? How can you be so cold that you can refuse them the help they need?" I knew I had gone too far, but I was mad. Not at her, but at how powerless I felt, despite all my power.

Her words came out softly, almost a whisper. "I'm scared for you. You could die."

Embarrassment replaced my anger. I looked into her eyes, but it was difficult to maintain with the shame for how I felt. "I'm scared too," I said softly. "I just can't see sitting on the sidelines while people are afraid of leaving their houses. I think I can—I need to—do something to try to change that."

"I understand," she said, dropping her gaze first. "I'm torn between wanting you to help people and wanting you to be safe. It's hard to support either of those choices when it means ignoring the other."

I considered her a moment. She was my best friend, someone with whom I had been immediately comfortable, someone who shared my view on most things and understood everything I had ever tried to explain to her about my opinions or feelings on a subject. "What would you do if you had my powers?" I finally asked.

For almost a full minute, she said nothing, just looked at the ground and shifted her feet. I knew she heard me, but I was ready to repeat the question again. I opened my mouth to speak, but at the same time she looked up at me.

"I would do something about it, regardless of the risk." It came out as if forced. She sighed.

"Yeah," I said. "I thought so. Will you help me?"

Her eyes widened before narrowing almost to slits. "How can I...what...?" She took a deep breath. "Sure. What do you want me to do?"

And just like that, it was decided. I breathed out. Why did I feel so exhausted? It didn't matter. We had plans to make and crimes to stop. My heart beat a thousand times a minute. I wasn't sure if it was from anticipation or fear.

After discussing it over the course of a few days, we came up with a plan. She would listen to police calls and call me on my cell phone to tip me off, and I would go out and wander the streets and see if I saw any crime happening. That was it. It wasn't much of a plan but it was something, at least.

I had an old pair of gray—nearly black—sweatpants, a black long-sleeved t-shirt, and a hoodie that was a slightly lighter shade of gray than my pants. A ski mask finished the ensemble. I looked like a stereotypical movie thief. It would keep my identity secret, though, and allow me to move freely. The mask was uncomfortable and limited my vision, but it was the best I could do on short notice.

For three nights, I walked the streets in my makeshift costume. Amy monitored the police band, but nothing suitable came across—the calls we heard were either too far away from me or were things like domestic disturbances. She also found this cool service called Nixle that transmitted public announcements and warnings from our police department right to her cell phone. We thought we had a great system, just like we had both read about in the comics.

It became clear soon enough, though, that it wasn't a practical way to fight crime. I mean, if the police already knew about something and were on their way, why would I show up? Even if I could get there first, they would arrive soon after me and see me trying to do my thing. They'd think I was the criminal, and I would probably get shot...by the police, not the bad guy. But until we figured something else out, it was all we had.

I only stayed out a couple of hours each night, making some excuse or another to leave the house after dark so my parents wouldn't freak out if they found me gone. The first three days I patrolled on school nights, so I couldn't stay out past ten o'clock or so. I felt silly about that. Who ever heard of a superhero having to stop fighting crime because he had to go do school the next day?

One Saturday night, when I told my parents I had to pull an all-nighter to finish some school projects at a friend's house, I finally saw my first crime. At approximately 11:15 PM, while walking through a rough part of town, I found two guys tagging the wall of a grocery store. They were dressed almost like me, but without the mask. They could have been close to my age or maybe a few years older. They were busy with their spray paint and didn't see me.

I walked up to them and said—in as commanding a voice as I could manage—"That is private property. Put down the paint. You're under arrest."

They both started and then turned to look at me. Both of them leaned to the side to peer around me, as if looking for my backup. They smiled wickedly when they saw no one else. I mentally kicked myself. I should have just thumped them while they were busy.

With a quick look at each other, they came toward me.

"Are you lost, punk?" one of them said. "Why do you have a ski mask on? You getting ready to hit a convenience store or something?" His buddy laughed.

"Yeah," the other one said, "well, you picked the wrong

people to mess with. You already seen too much, so we're going to have to make you see that you need to keep your mouth shut."

They both sprang at me, one hitting me in the face with his fist, and the other driving his into my belly.

I panicked. It hadn't gone like this in my mind when I imagined it. I didn't know what to do, so I froze and allowed them to hit me several times each. It didn't hurt, like that punch to my stomach when I first met Amy. It was probably because of my extra tough skin, one of the few abilities that was constant. As far as I could tell, anyway.

I put a hand on each of them, one on the chest and one on the shoulder, and pushed. My self-preservation power, my reflexes, didn't work, but my strength was definitely there. They flew away from me, one grunting as he struck the wall he had been painting, and the other landing on his back on the ground several feet away. They were surprised, stunned even, but they got up fast.

Shaking their heads, trying to clear them, they looked at each other again and then back at me. Teeth clenched, they came back, one taking a knife from his pocket and unfolding it.

At that moment I realized something I had forgotten in my plans. I didn't know how to fight. I guess I had expected my powers to carry me through anything. Stupid! Well, I was in for it. What was I going to do? If I got stabbed, Amy would kill me. And she'd have to get in line behind my parents.

Using my keen mind and excellent planning abilities, I came up with a new strategy. I turned and ran away as fast as I could.

5

The taggers couldn't match my speed—thank you, powers, for not failing me completely—and I got away. I stopped running after a mile or so, sure they would have long since given up. I took the mask off and stuffed it into my hoodie's pocket.

How was I going to explain this to Amy? I had to, I knew that, but how? I felt like I might prefer to go back and fight the taggers. Shoulders slumping, I headed toward her house, texting her that I was finished for the night and was going to stop by. I had some explaining to do, another thing I'd never seen in the comics. The hero gig was tougher than it looked.

AMY OPENED the door as I walked up to it, her finger over her lips in a shushing gesture. "My parents are asleep. Let's go to the garage." She led me around the house into the garage, our normal meeting place. We were paranoid about talking about my powers in the house where someone could hear.

"I ran into some problems tonight," I said as soon as we sat down.

She handed me a bottle of water, but didn't say anything. That was one of the best things about Amy. She would sit patiently and wait for me to tell her whatever I was trying to say. Which was good. I often started a sentence and didn't know how to finish it, so I spoke haltingly, in starts and fits. I wish I had her patience.

"I found a couple of taggers and confronted them. They sort of jumped me, and I pushed them off me, but then they came at me with knives. Well, one of them had a knife." She let out a little gasp but didn't say anything. "I ran away."

She let out a loud breath and waited for a moment to see if I would continue. I met her eyes—I had been scanning the garage, probably because of my embarrassment—and she took it as a cue.

"I'm glad, Daniel." Her eyes widened a little, and she quickly added, "I mean, I'm glad you ran, not that you were attacked. Are you hurt at all?"

"Nope. Their punches didn't really do anything. Tough skin and all."

"Good. I think you did the right thing. Trying to take someone who has a knife, especially when he has a buddy to help him, is not a good decision."

I nodded. We sat there in silence. I drank from my water bottle, just to have something to do. She wore an introspective look on her face.

"What are you going to do?" she asked.

That was the question, wasn't it? "I don't know. I'm thinking I need to learn how to fight. Super-strength, speed, and durable skin are cool, but I guess I should learn how to use them. I hadn't thought of that before, for some reason."

"Yeah, me either. Sorry. Some sidekick I am, huh?"

I looked into her eyes, the first really good eye contact since I got there. "You're not a sidekick, Amy. You are my entire support network. Without you, I would still be trying to figure out what was happening to me. You have been the brains of the operation since the beginning."

Her cheeks flushed pink. "Well, some brains I am, not even thinking of fighting skills. It's pretty stupid, looking back. Of course you need to learn to use your powers for combat. The question is: How are you going to do it? Are you going to go to a boxing gym, learn some kind of MMA thing, or what?"

"I really don't know," I answered. "I don't have the money to take lessons, and even if I did I'm not sure I could train to fight with people without hurting someone on accident. I can't control my strength well enough to spar with someone without my strikes being super-powerful."

"Hmmmm," she said. "I see your point. Books, videos, something like that?"

"I don't even have the money for that right now. I guess I need to get a job. I think I can find stuff on YouTube, but just watching them won't help me. I'll need to hit things and practice not getting hit by things."

"I can help you," she said, excitement lighting up her face. "I've always wanted to learn to fight, too, so we can help each other."

"Amy, I don't want to hurt you accidentally. We can practice together, learn to shadowbox or something, but we can't spar."

She leveled a cool look at me. I gulped.

"Daniel, we can do things without actually fighting each other. I can hold targets or throw things at you, or try to hit you with a long stick or something. We'll come up with a way to do it. Quit being so silly about it."

"Okay, you're right. Maybe we can come up with something. Yeah, actually, I like that idea. You're the only one who knows my secrets, so it's logical. Are you sure it's not too much work or too much time? I don't want to take up all your spare time."

She laughed, making me hunch my shoulders and draw in on myself. "Oh, Daniel, you're so funny. I don't know. I'll have to check my appointment calendar. I'm so busy with all my social engagements that I'm not sure how I can fit you in, but I'll try." She glowered at me. "The only thing I have to do with my time is school. I like hanging out with you, and I believe in what we're doing. There's nothing else I'd like to do more than helping to prepare you for not dying when you go out and play superhero. It's settled. We're going to learn how to fight...together."

I smiled at her. "That sounds great. Thank you. Really."

We had a rough plan. A *new* rough plan. The superhero thing involved a lot of making and implementing plans, it seemed. If that was what it took, though, then that's what I'd do. I had a lot of research to do just to figure out how to design a training plan.

Over the next few days I was on the computer constantly looking up videos and websites on how to fight, how to train, and whatever else I could find that I thought would be useful. I was surprised both at the great information I was able to find as well as how much pure crap people put out there. Within a week, I had figured out what I'd do. What *we* would do. I was anxious to start.

Bringing my laptop out to a clearing in the woods, we practiced some simple punches and kicks. I was able to rip and copy some really good videos, and we followed them as closely as possible. We were awkward and slow. No, we were completely uncoordinated. Neither of us had ever been in any way athletic. My abilities helped me to pick up on it more quickly than Amy, but it still felt strange to move in ways I had never thought of before.

Within a few days, Amy said I looked like I knew what I was doing. It did feel more natural. I could shadowbox without looking like I was having a seizure. That was an improvement. After a week, Amy told me I moved like the guys in boxing or martial arts movies. She was just being kind, but I did feel more coordinated, more competent, more athletic. I felt dangerous. Apparently my powers extended to learning new things. How fortuitous for me. Amy decided it was time for me to step it up.

"I'm going to hit you with this stick," she told me, holding a broomstick out in front of her. "Your goal is to not get hit with the stick."

"Uh, okay." I was skeptical.

"Here, before we start, I want to try something. Just stand there. Don't move." I stood there. She swung the stick at me, slow and not very hard, but still right at me.

My reflexes kicked in, and my hand shot out with blinding speed, grabbing the stick, twisting it, and snatching it right out of her hands. Before I even knew I had moved, I had spun the stick and swung it toward her head. Thankfully, I—or my arm, or my power, or whatever it was —stopped it just before hitting her. She gulped and looked at the wooden pole, motionless an inch from her face.

I dropped it and stepped back. "God, I'm sorry Amy. That wasn't me. It was that crazy reflex thing."

She took a deep breath. "I know. It was just...a surprise. Can you repress that power? Can you force yourself not to react?"

"I'll try."

I stood there after she had picked up her broomstick again. I focused on my arms and pinned them to my sides. I told myself that I trusted her and there was no danger. She swung the stick at me, maybe a little harder and faster than before.

There was a loud thwack as the wood made contact with my shoulder. I felt a dull impact, like someone pushed me hard. It didn't even feel like I would have a bruise. I looked at her. "What was that about?"

She wore a pained look on her face. "I'm sorry. I just wanted to see what would happen if I hit you while we were training. Did that hurt?"

"Not a bit."

"Really?"

"Really."

She nodded. "Good. That means I can try to hit you with full force and speed, and even if I hit you, I won't hurt you. That'll make it easier. I'm not good enough to"— she looked at the stick and waggled it—"pull my punches, as it were."

She spent the rest of the day trying to hit me with the stick, and I'd try to evade, block, or take it. Sometimes my reflexes would kick in, and my body would do something I hadn't expected, but sometimes I actually did what I wanted, what I had thought about. She hit me with full force swings or jabs three times. Each time I felt that same dull ache.

"I'm done," she said, rubbing her shoulder. "I'm going to be sore tomorrow from doing this, you know."

"I'm sorry," I said. "I would like to say I'm going to be sore too, but I just don't think I will be. Thank you so much for this, Amy. I feel like I'm twice the fighter I was this morning."

She smiled at me, a satisfied grin that reminded me of someone who had just won an award. "I had a lot of fun. We'll have to step it up tomorrow. You learn things so quickly, it's hard to come up with ideas about what to do to challenge you."

6

We trained again the next day after school, the last day before we had a week off for spring break. A full week without school, and we had already decided we would use every bit of it to train and hang out together. Amy had started using two shorter sticks, one in each hand so that she could attack from two directions at once, and she had struck me several times, but I was learning and improving. I was looking forward to the next nine days.

I have to hand it to the girl. I had come up with the original training plan after scouring the internet for ideas. During the break from school, though, she took control of everything and came up with ideas I never would have dreamed up. Apparently, she was better at finding things on the internet or more creative than me. Probably both.

I had been doing odd jobs for people: mowing lawns, washing cars, walking dogs. I used the money to buy some striking pads so I could do more than just evade Amy's blows. We used these extensively, trying to emulate some of the boxing videos and tutorials we watched. It was tougher than it looked. I had no problem learning how to hit them with different kinds of punches, but Amy didn't have my enhanced speed and reflexes, so it took her a full day to figure out how to hold and move the targets, the focus mitts, even halfway effectively. That was okay, though, because she had many other things in her arsenal.

"Why do you have a gun in a holster at your side?" I asked, eyeing the weapon. "Is that real?"

"Of course not, silly," she said, drawing the gun in a smooth motion. She must have practiced that. When did she have time to do that? The gun, when I looked more closely at it, was made of plastic and had a bright orange tip on it. "Airsoft," she said. I nodded. "It's for when you're getting cocky because you can dodge strikes in the other things we do."

"So, if I start to feel confident, you're going to shoot me?"

"No, I..."she hesitated. "Well, yeah, I guess that's basically it. Don't get too full of yourself." She jiggled the gun in front of me as she said it.

I gulped. "I'll try not to."

She had a bag full of training items—which she made me carry because it was so full and heavy—and I was amazed as she kept bringing out more marvelous things. There were tennis balls with strings through them, light barbell plates that she tied ropes through, and sticks, rubber knives, and assorted other items meant specifically to work me and my abilities to the full. I whistled softly as she pulled each thing from the bag.

She directed me to tie the things attached to strings or ropes to branches hanging over the edge of the clearing we trained in. Those would be used as strike targets. The sticks, spring-loaded devices that shot projectiles, and several different types of Nerf items that could be thrown or shot were for my evasive abilities. Of course, I would have to evade or deflect the things coming at me *while* striking the targets she called out.

"How did you come up with all this stuff?" I asked her as we were getting ready to use it the first time.

"Some I read about," she said, "and some I invented. I'm sure they've been used before, but I haven't seen any reference to them. I just hope everything works well. I got hold of a paintball gun, too, for when you get too fast for me to use the Airsoft gun on you."

I moved through the hanging targets in a path that crossed in front of Amy. She would call out a number—each signifying a particular strike—and I would have to use that punch or kick on the closest hanging object. All the while, she would throw or shoot the Nerf projectiles, and I would have to catch, deflect, or evade them. Simple enough, right? Well, it wasn't.

We had spent a lot of time practicing individual movements, but putting them all together was much harder. When I focused on listening to the number she called out and trying to remember which strike I was supposed to use, it distracted my natural defensive abilities. I couldn't rely on my reflexes to make my body protect itself, so I had to consciously watch my surroundings while still hitting the targets.

That was difficult on its own, but as I relied more on my peripheral vision to see when something was coming, Amy started to mime throwing something, not really releasing it. Sometimes she would do a fake-out three or four times in a row. I did the same thing with my dog, acting like I was throwing a tennis ball for him to fetch, laughing when he started running after a ball that was still in my hand. It didn't feel so good from the receiving side. I vowed not to tease my canine friend like that anymore.

Even with her trickery, by the end of the first day, I had evaded all the things she threw at me and hit the targets with the correct strike most of the time. As we gathered everything together, I felt satisfied with what we had accomplished. She drew her Airsoft gun in one smooth motion and shot me in the neck.

"Ouch!" I said.

"Did that hurt? I'm sorry. I didn't think it would hurt with your tough skin."

I thought about it for a moment. "Well, no, it didn't really hurt. It just surprised me. Why did you shoot me?"

"You had a self-satisfied smirk on your face, like my cat wears when he gets into the milk in my cereal bowl. I wanted to let you know that we're a long way from done. I told you about getting cocky."

"Fair enough," I said. "Thank you for the reminder." I smiled a big, toothy smile at her. She raised the gun again, and I put my arms up. "Okay, I was just teasing you. Sheesh."

She chuckled as she holstered her gun.

"How did you learn to shoot like that, anyway?" I asked.

She flushed slightly. "Oh, I have cousins that like to play guns. They spent last summer out here with us, and we played shooting games all the time. I got to be pretty good. I have many talents that you don't know about."

"I'm finding that out. This training setup is amazing, Amy."

"Oh, Daniel," she patted my cheek. "You have no idea. Just wait. I'll make you a fighter yet."

The next day, she didn't bother with the Nerf projectiles. They were too slow to challenge me, she said. Instead, she brought out the plastic throwing knives and stars, some marbles, and a blowgun with blunt-tipped darts.

By the end of the week, Amy told me I looked as good as the guys in the bigger budget action movies. The quality movies, not the low-budget flicks. My confidence was high, no doubt partly because she pumped it up, but also because I could see for myself that I had gotten better.

Amy threw, shot, and otherwise launched things at me as I made my way through the different striking objects, hitting them and dodging or deflecting everything coming at me. When I stopped at the end of the gauntlet, I smiled widely and looked over to her. Just in time to see her shoot me on the side of the head.

"Ow!"

She giggled. "Sorry, did that really hurt?"

"Yeah, it actually stung a little. Why did you do that?"

"You stopped and rested, thinking you were done. If you're going to be a superhero, you can never let your guard down. At least, not when you're in costume. I guess you can when you're in your secret identity."

I eyed her warily, noticing that the gun was still in her hand, not in the holster. "Okay, you made your point. Put the gun away now."

Surprise leaped onto her face. She looked at the gun as if she didn't recognize it. Color rushed to her cheeks, and she holstered the weapon in one practiced motion. "Okay, okay. We're done." She raised her hands and smiled.

"So," I said as we gathered our training gear, "what now? Our break is over, and it's back to school tomorrow."

"Yeah, I was wondering that, too. What are you going to do, Daniel? It was fun training like this, but will you use it now? Are you going to try to patrol again, try to fight crime?"

My safe, comfortable feelings from the previous week all

came crashing down on me at that point. I had been so preoccupied with the act of training and trying to get better that I had forgotten why I did it to begin with. Would I go out and patrol again? That was the whole reason to practice, right?

"I...yeah, I guess so. I've had my vacation from all the bad things that are happening in the city. I suppose it's time to get back to work, to try to use some of what I've learned. It's time to do what needs to be done."

Amy looked at me, a blank look on her face.

I looked back at her, wearing a similar look on mine.

As if on cue, we both started laughing. Not chuckling, not politely humoring the other, but guffawing. The bending over and trying to get your breath kind of tear-invoking laughter. Neither of us could speak for several minutes.

Finally, Amy caught her breath. In a deep, movie narrator voice, she said, "It's time to do what needs to be done." She lost herself in another fit of laughter.

My laughter settled into chuckles as I watched her. "A little too dramatic?"

"Uh, yeah." She wiped the tears from her eyes. "It's good, though. It's what a superhero would say. Just don't say too many things like that. I don't think my body can handle that much laughter."

Impulsively, I reached out and hugged her. "Amy, this was the best week of my life. Thank you for helping me."

She stiffened at first but then wrapped her arms loosely around me and squeezed lightly. "It was fun for me, too." She released me and stepped back. "Maybe it'll keep you from getting killed."

"I hope so." Why did I feel so embarrassed? All that laughing seemed to have made me warm. I wiped my forehead, expecting sweat to be there, but it was dry. She looked at me quizzically. I did the only thing I could; I looked away and started picking the gear up again.

I walked her home, carrying all our makeshift training gear. Saying goodbye, I walked home feeling giddy. I'd become a trained fighting machine, or at least as close as I had ever been, and soon I would be helping out the people in my city, protecting them from crime, doing my little part. What was not to feel good about?

7

E ven though I spent most of the break training with Amy, I was all caught up on my homework, so the first week back was easier than normal. I used the opportunity to go out on patrol each night, but only until 10:00 PM. They were school nights, after all.

I lucked out on Tuesday night. At about 9:15 PM, I found three people trying to vandalize a flower shop. The store was set off from any other buildings, basically a little house with its own small parking lot. I heard a shatter like breaking glass or pottery as I passed by and went over to investigate.

The planters outside the shop contained meticulously cultivated flowers and plants, with river rocks placed to simulate a river going through one particularly beautiful area. I had always liked walking by and looking at the display. In the spring and summer, the different scents of the flowers reached out all the way to the street, and I'd close my eyes and enjoy the smell. But not tonight.

The three boys—I thought I recognized one who had graduated the year before—had found the planted area, and the river rocks, and were stomping around and breaking all the vegetation and some of the large terra cotta pots. One of them hefted a smooth stone half the size of his hand.

"Hey, Davey, check this out," he yell-whispered. The boy bounced the stone in his palm a few times, drew his arm back, and launched it toward the store's main window. The sound of crunching glass echoed in the night. The window didn't shatter, but the rock punched a fist-sized hole in it. I didn't hear an alarm. Maybe they had the kind that notifies the police without an audible siren.

"Nice," another of them said. "Toss me one of those. I bet I can make the whole window shatter." The third vandal stopped pulling a large flower bush up by its roots to watch with interest.

I had learned from my run-in with the taggers. I stayed in the shadows of a nearby hedge and surveyed the scene. There was no one else around but the three. The glint of the streetlight reflecting off glass caught my eye, and I saw a camera on the edge of the shop's eaves, pointing toward where the boys were. I searched the roofline and found another camera on the other side of the building, also facing toward where the damage was being done. A soft red glow emanated from the outer ring of the lenses. Probably night mode. Good. That would be useful. I hoped they were recording.

I was wearing my costume again, the sweats, dark shirt, and hoodie. I stalked closer to where the boys were, all three looking at the window that would soon be receiving another stone.

The vandal's arm cocked back, fingers gripping the projectile. The boy set his feet, sighted his target, and prepared to launch the stone. I took that opportunity to act.

Using my enhanced speed, I raced the ten feet from my

hiding place to where the stone-thrower was. I slapped down with my open hand on his arm, and the rock went flying off to the side. Without stopping, I whipped the same arm around and tapped him on the stomach. It was a tap for me, but for the boy, it was a full-force punch. He bent double with a grunt and was thrown back several feet.

Turning to one of the others, I slapped his face three times, alternating my hands. I didn't use much force, but again, the blows made his head snap back and forth until the last knocked him down. He fell to the ground, crying that I broke his jaw. I didn't. I would have felt it if it had broken, and I don't think he'd be able to whine like that with a broken jaw.

The last boy decided he didn't want anything to do with me and started to run. I kicked his legs out from under him, maybe too hard since I still wasn't completely in control of how much force I used, and he almost did a complete forward flip. His nose cracked when he landed on his face. I winced. That sounded—and looked—painful.

All three were on the ground and dazed. I took the long garden hose coiled at the faucet, bunched the vandals up, and wrapped and tied them with it. Rope would have been better, but the hose would hold them for ten or fifteen minutes, especially dazed as they were. For good measure, I tied them around an antique lamp pole in front of the shop.

Then I left.

I ran at my full power-enhanced speed to where I'd seen an old pay phone. I dropped in a few coins and called the police. I explained that there were three vandals at the flower shop, and they better get over there before the criminals escaped. I also mentioned that they'd have evidence if they looked at the security cameras. When they asked who I was, I repeated that they better get there soon, and then I hung up with "I'm just a concerned citizen." I had a secret identity to protect.

It was only 9:48. I texted Amy, and a few minutes later, thanks again to my super-speed—a guy could get used to this—I was in her garage explaining what happened.

After checking me over for injuries, she smiled at me and congratulated me on my first successful hero act. Well, the first since I had saved her that day. I had to get home, but we would talk about it the next day. Hopefully the police had picked the boys up.

At school, I ran up to Amy, all smiles. I had a feeling it would be a good day. Her expression told me maybe it wouldn't be that way after all.

"What's wrong?" I asked.

"Did you see the news or any crime reports online?"

"No, why?"

A disgusted look came onto her face. She looked around to see if anyone was listening, grabbed my arm, and pulled me onto the grass, farther away from everyone else. "The police didn't take the call seriously. The vandals got themselves free and left. The shop owner went to the shop at four that morning to prepare the flowers for the day and found the damage. The article said there was some video footage, but it wasn't clear enough to be able to identify the ones who caused the damage."

"Oh." I paused. What could I say about that? "Well, they shouldn't be hard to find. One has a broken nose, one probably has a swollen face, and the other one is at least bruised. Maybe that one even has a cracked rib or something."

"Yeah," Amy said, "that would be great. If they were looking. They're more concerned about the vigilante who's going around beating people up. Stupid cops."

"Oh." I was sick of hearing myself say that. "Well, I'll have to do better next time."

Amy looked me up and down as if I was some strange animal, but then she nodded. "Yes, I guess we will have to do better next time." A smile finally broke through her gloomy expression, and it made me feel a little better, as her smiles always did. The way the skin around those dazzling blue eyes of hers crinkled just a little bit when her mouth formed a smile was so fascinating. "I have some ideas. We'll talk later, okay?"

"Sounds great," I said. "See you at lunch."

I tried to hide it, but I was really disappointed. I had finally done something right, stopped a crime, and the police thought I was the problem? Why did I feel guilty? I hadn't done anything wrong. I was the good guy here. It bothered me, but I wouldn't let it ruin my day. I did a good deed, and even if no one else knew, I could feel good about it.

8

Over the next few weeks, luck seemed to be with me. On my patrols, I stopped three more minor crimes—vandalism, graffiti, and a pair of men trying to steal a statue from the front of the local library. After the first night, I carried a handful of zip ties with me to secure the perpetrators more efficiently than with a garden hose.

Happily, the police even started taking my calls seriously. I still called from a phone booth, not wanting to give away my cell phone number and thus my identity, but they responded to the calls and picked up the guys I tied up. The news still didn't report that anyone was helping to stop the crimes or arrest the criminals, but crimes were being stopped and the police were cooperating, so that was good.

Things seemed to be looking up. But like I read once, "There are moments when everything goes well; don't be frightened, it won't last."

One Saturday night I stayed out on patrol later than normal. Around midnight, I passed a strip mall. Only one store was still open, the same convenience store that had been robbed a few months before, the one I passed when all the police and ambulances were there. I watched as a car pulled up and four guys got out. One of them fiddled with something tucked into the back of the waist of his pants while looking around to see if anyone was near. It didn't look good.

I moved a little closer, staying to the shadows of the shoe store two doors down. I couldn't hear most of what they said, but I caught a "dawg" and "pop him" and "drop box."

They were about to rob the place. It was the biggest crime I'd seen so far. At least one of the guys had a gun. I wasn't sure I was up to the challenge. I stood there, indecision warring with my desire to stop what was going to be a violent crime. While I tried to decide what to do, all four men, as if on cue, put ski masks on and headed into the store.

I had hesitated too long.

Cursing myself, I moved quickly to the edge of the convenience store's windows and watched. The four went in and spread out, two circling around to make sure there was no one else in the aisles and two moving toward the clerk. Those last two had guns out and pointed at the young man at the register. I couldn't hear what they told him, but he raised his hands. His face was pale and he shivered, moving his mouth while facing the closest gun-wielder, pleading. When the gunman spoke again, the clerk slowly moved one hand to open the register drawer and then step back.

I still wasn't sure if I should intervene. Maybe they would just take the money and leave the clerk alone. I didn't want to put myself or the young man at risk if the robbers were only going to take some money.

As one of the men who had been scanning the aisles came forward to empty the cash register, he casually pistol-whipped the clerk in the face, striking him with the side of the gun as if it was a simple slap. It knocked the clerk down. "Get up!" the robber yelled, loud enough for me to hear clearly, and the victim staggered to his feet. Blood trickled from a gash on his cheek, and his mouth moved as if he was going to sick up. The robber I had seen readjusting his gun when he was outside came up to the clerk and put the gun barrel to the young man's head. I had a bad feeling that the gunman wasn't bluffing. If I was going to act, it had to be fast, or I was going to witness a murder.

I came through the door in a burst of speed, searching for something to use as a weapon. There were racks of candy bars and magazines to my left and an ice machine and soda fountain with empty cups to my right. None of those would help. I had to do something to distract the robbers or stop the guns from going off.

I still had a fraction of a second left before the gunmen could react when I found what I needed. Scooping up a water bottle in each hand—they were stacked in a convenient display a few steps into the store—I threw one with my right hand and one with my left. I'm right-handed, so the bottle from that arm went toward the man with the gun to the clerk's head. The one from the left was aimed at the robber standing next to him, still emptying the register.

My aim was true with my dominant hand. It hit the man in the face so hard that he flew back, his arms flailing. I had expected the gun to go off, but it didn't. The other bottle struck a glancing blow off the other gunman's shoulder, spinning him and making him squeal in pain. His gun did go off, and I heard the clerk moan as he twisted off onto the floor. I hoped he wasn't dead, but I didn't have time to think about it right then. Two more men swiveled guns toward me as I charged.

I dropped to my knees and slid the rest of the way toward them. Two gunshots sounded and I felt more than saw the deadly projectiles whizzing over my head, exactly where I was before I had dropped down. My sliding stopped when I ran into a mop bucket sitting on the floor.

My emergency reflexes caused me to snatch up the wet mop and swing it around. In slow motion, the two robbers in front of me aimed toward my new position. With blinding speed, I struck them both in rapid succession with the wet mop head before they could fire, knocking the gun completely out of the hand of one of the men and deflecting the gun held by the other. Reversing the direction, I swung the wet cotton with enough force that two unconscious attackers hit the floor.

I quickly rounded up the two I had hit with water bottles, disarming them both and zip-tying them before they could take a breath. Within seconds, all four were face down on the floor, hands secured behind their backs.

I checked the clerk. He had been shot in the shoulder and was bleeding heavily. I thanked whatever powers there were that the bullet didn't hit anything vital. After a quick call on the store phone to the police and some first aid I'd learned in school, he was stable enough that I didn't think he would bleed to death. I looked at his wide eyes, slightly glassy from shock, and told him he would be all right.

When I heard a siren, I turned to the clerk. "I have to go. I'm sorry you were injured." He started to speak, but I was already out the door, fleeing for my life.

I ran for a mile or so, ending up in a quiet part of town. I sat on a bench in the park, head in my hands. What was I thinking? I was almost responsible for someone losing their life. Never mind the danger I put myself in with confronting four armed men. If that bullet had been a few inches over, that clerk would be dead, and if my sliding maneuver hadn't worked, I would be, too. All because I wanted to be a hero.

I pulled the ski mask off my head and wadded it up in my fist. Someone's son, boyfriend, brother, he could have been dead because I didn't know what I was doing. I was playing like this was an adventure, but it was real. Very real. I looked down at my hands in the dim light of the street lamp. Blood. Blood covered my hands and clothes. Would it ever come off? Would I always see it there? I'm sure I would've if that young man had died.

I was done. I could not, would not, do this any longer. I was more of a hazard than a hero. If I hadn't acted, the worst the clerk would have gotten was that gash on his face. Maybe. Probably. Who was I kidding? I was no hero, just a stupid kid with delusions of grandeur, a menace to himself and others. No more. Leave it to someone better to be a hero. I wasn't cut out for this stuff.

I stayed in the park for another hour, thinking. I would go soak in the pond at a larger park I knew, try to get the blood out of my clothes and off my skin. Then I would go home and forget all about trying to be a hero. Done. My short-lived tenure as a superhero was done. Let the city rejoice.

9

Amy caught up to me at school just before the first bell rang.

"Daniel," she said, coming up to me slowly, looking for something in my eyes. "Are...are you all right?"

"I'm fine," I lied. "The bell is about to ring. I have to get to class." I turned to walk away from her.

Her hand on my arm stopped me. She was still scanning my eyes. Hers were liquid, pained. "Can we talk at lunch then?"

"Sure." I tried to smile but knew it was a sickly thing, almost a grimace. "We always do, right?"

Her hand dropped to her side. "Yeah. We always do." That last part came in a whisper.

Before I could react—and that was saying something because of my super-reflexes—she wrapped her arms around me and hugged me. As she hurried off to her own class, I saw tears in her eyes.

Great. That made it even worse. I was so busy feeling sorry for myself that I made my best friend sad, too. Maybe I could smooth that over at lunch. I hoped so.

I can't remember what the teachers talked about in my classes that morning. I was too preoccupied with what I would say at lunch. Amy would understand my decision. She always understood me. I understood her too, though, and I didn't think she would fully agree. That concerned me. I didn't want to argue; that was the last thing I needed. But I had to talk to her.

I rehearsed what I was going to say to explain things to her. I imagined her responses and what I would say to them. I had it all worked up in my mind as if I was watching a TV show. More, I had several different versions worked up. By the time the bell rang for lunch, I felt ready to present my case, to make things right with her, to ease the tension.

I was completely wrong.

Amy ran up to me where I stood by the tree under which we usually ate lunch. She rushed me and threw her arms around me, squeezing me until she grunted with the effort. "Oh, Daniel," she whispered into my ear as she hugged me. "Are you all right? I saw the news report about the robbery. Are you hurt in any way?"

All my planned speeches and responses flew right out of my head. I squeezed her back, glad to hold onto something, anything, but especially glad it was her. I found that I was crying, sobbing into her hair. The smell of some kind of berry shampoo wafted up, and I lost myself for a moment, enjoying the comfort and safety.

After what seemed like a long time, but was probably less than a minute, I opened my eyes and looked around. No one was close enough to hear us, but kids in other areas of the courtyard were looking at us, trying to figure out what was going on. It wasn't every day you saw two nerd kids trying to squeeze each other into diamonds. I hastily wiped my eyes and pulled back from her after one final, desperate hug.

"I'm fine," I said for the second time that day. It wasn't a lie. I was talking about being uninjured. Physically. "I didn't get hurt." The rush of her exhalation calmed me.

I held her out at arm's length and saw she was still crying. I wiped the tears from her cheek and repeated, "I'm fine, Amy. Are you okay?"

She sniffled, eyes downcast. She took a deep breath, and then her crystal blue eyes locked onto mine. "I was scared to death. You didn't text me to let me know you were done for the night, and I was afraid to text you because I thought it would give you away if you were hiding or stalking a criminal. I didn't sleep at all. When I heard the call about the robbery, I was afraid you were involved. When I saw the news report, I got even more scared. Why didn't you let me know you were safe?"

Her tone went from sad to hurt to angry as she spoke. I deserved the anger. "I'm sorry. I wasn't thinking straight. I was...kind of messed up. All I could think about was all the blood and how to get it off me and how I...I don't...there's no excuse. I'm sorry. Here, let's sit. I'll tell you all about it."

I told her everything that happened, every thought I had, every feeling. I gave her each little detail, all I remembered. I told her how I almost caused a man to lose his life, how I caused more damage than if I hadn't been there at all.

"No," she said. "They would have killed the clerk. The way you describe them, they would have at least injured him, if not killed him. You saved his life, I think."

"You don't understand," I pleaded. "I went in there and escalated the situation. What happens the next time? Will a child die because I want to play hero? Will *I* die? I can accept that fate for myself, but if I cause casualties that otherwise would not happen, what does that make me? Not a hero, I'll tell you that. As far as I'm concerned, that makes me pretty close to a villain myself."

"You are exaggerating your effect on the situation. You were trying to do good, trying to help."

I rounded on her, anger flashing up inside me, a fire suddenly stoked into an inferno. "Help? Trying to do good? It doesn't matter what I was *trying* to do. What I actually did was get an innocent person shot. I didn't have the courage to check the news report. Did the clerk even survive? Did he bleed to death?"

Amy sighed. "He's fine. The report said that the only reason he's still alive is that some Good Samaritan—wearing a ski mask, by the way—applied first aid and stabilized him until the ambulance came. Without that, the article said, he probably would have died from blood loss."

At least I did something right. "Did it also say I was the one who got him shot?"

"No," she said softly. "It said that the mysterious person helped and foiled the robbery. No one was sure if you had been shot yourself or not."

"It would have been better if I had been," I snapped. "I deserved that bullet that went into the clerk. Stupid. Stupid! What made me think I was cut out for this stuff? So what, I developed some abilities. So what, I can move faster and hit harder and do things better than normal people. There's more to being a hero than having super powers. I finally understand that. I...finally understand." I dropped my head in my hands. I felt tears coming on again, and I didn't want to allow them to show.

"Amy, I'm done. I won't have it on my conscience if someone dies because of my stupid actions or my incompetence. I'll try to figure out how to use my powers for something other than being a hero. I'm not cut out for that line of work. The heroing business is a tough gig, and I'm just not good enough to pull it off.

"I always thought that the goodness of someone's heart, the commitment to doing right, the ability to persist and sacrifice make someone a hero. That's not the case. Heroes are born, not made. I'm a nerdy high school kid, not anyone for people to look up to. Let someone better take the job. I can't."

Amy's eyes went wide, and her mouth parted as her chin dropped. She was speechless. For that moment, anyway.

"Do you really feel that way?" she asked. "Do you think you're not good enough, that you don't have what it takes? Daniel, you are the most heroic person I've ever met. I think you are wrong. Dead wrong. I think the powers are the least of what makes you super."

She took my hand and squeezed it. "I understand what you're feeling, the conflict you are facing. I can agree with your not going out to fight crime if you think that you're putting people at risk. I don't agree with you about not being a hero, though. You are. One day, you'll realize that. One day you'll see yourself as I see you. Until then, I'll help you in any way I can. I'm your friend, and I'll be right here if you need me."

That did not go even remotely as I had planned, but that was okay. I smiled at her, a sad smile but genuine. "Thank you. It means a lot to me that you didn't try to talk me out of it."

She patted my cheek and gave me a small smile of her

own. "You're welcome." She eyed me for another moment and then smirked. "But if you do decide to do something else, regardless of whether it's fighting crime or cleaning toilets, if you ever scare me like that again, all the super powers in the world will not save you from me. Just remember that."

10

As Amy had said, the clerk from the convenience store was fine. A week after the robbery, I found out when he'd be at work and went in to buy a pack of gum just so I could talk to him. I made small talk and casually mentioned the robbery, suggesting he must have been very frightened.

His name was Carson. He did admit some fear. "Sure, I was a little afraid, especially when one of them pistol-whipped me and the other one pointed his gun right at my face. I knew I was going to die. If it wasn't for that other guy who showed up, they would have killed me."

"Are you sure?" I asked. "The guy who showed up, the one who fought with them, he probably escalated things and caused them to start shooting. If he hadn't shown up, they probably would have just taken the money and then left."

Carson shook his head vigorously, wincing when it moved his body and aggravated his still-healing shoulder. "No. I'm telling you, I saw it in their eyes. At least two of them were not going to leave with me still alive. I was a dead man. As far as I'm concerned, they ought to make a statue of that guy and give him a medal. He saved my life. No question."

That took me by surprise. "If he's such a hero, then why didn't he stick around? Why did he run when the police were coming?"

Carson scrubbed the hand of his good arm through his hair, his eyes narrowing at me. "He did stick around. At least, he did long enough to stop my bleeding. I don't blame him for not wanting to talk to the cops. I would have done the same thing. They would have just hassled him for beating up people without a license or some other stupid thing. Listen, that guy is like a guardian angel. If you want to talk down on him, go somewhere else and find someone else to tell. Is that all you're buying?" He pointed to the pack of gum.

"Uh, yeah," I grunted. He rang it up, I paid for it, and I left. I didn't mean to start a fight with the man. He obviously felt strongly about what had happened. I didn't agree with him, but if he felt like that, well, he was entitled to his opinion. Maybe I hadn't screwed up quite as badly as I thought.

I walked down the street deep in thought, fiddling with the pack of gum in my hand. Only my heightened reflexes and peripheral vision kept me from bowling over Mrs. Sanderson, who was apparently out for a walk.

Mrs. Sanderson was my friend Craig Twyman's grandmother. He'd moved away after elementary school, but I saw her around town often and visited her occasionally to see if she needed anything. She was the sweetest old woman in the world.

"Good morning, Daniel," she said, a smile dominating

her wrinkled face. That smile always made me feel good, no matter my mood before I saw it.

"Good morning, Mrs. Sanderson," I replied. "Out for a walk?"

"Yes. It's a beautiful day, and I need my sunshine. Vitamin D, you know. And walking is God's own way of keeping us young. Too many old people don't walk enough." She shook her head. "What are you about this morning?"

I held the gum out. "I went by the store to get some gum. I just thought the walk would be nice. Too many young people don't walk enough." I winked at her.

"Will you walk with me?" she asked. "Talk to an old lady?"

"Absolutely." I put my arm out, and she hooked hers in mine. I had been raised to observe simple courtesies and, to be honest, I enjoyed the surprise and happiness it caused when I acted politely. We started walking back toward the store. I offered her some gum, and she took a piece.

"Did you hear about the robbery there," she pointed toward the convenience store, "about a week ago?"

"I did," I said. "I was just talking to the clerk about it."

"Oh. It was Carson, right? Nice young man, that Carson. He's always very polite to me, like you are. He must have been very scared."

I looked toward the store but caught a glimpse of her face as she said it. A turned down mouth and the shake of a head. It could have been fear, but it seemed like sadness. "Yes, he said he was."

"Things have been getting bad around here," the old woman said. "I remember, not too long ago, when we didn't even have to lock our doors and could leave the keys in our cars. At least there are some good people left, like that hero who saved Carson from those terrible men." Her face brightened as she said it.

"Don't you think that guy just made it worse?" I said. "I mean, maybe the robbers would have just taken the money and left. Instead, he almost got Carson killed."

"No, oh no. I don't think so, Daniel. Didn't you hear? They connected three of the four captured with two other robberies in other towns. In both of them, they killed the clerks, two at one and one at the other. The police identified them from the video cameras. That man saved Carson's life."

I stopped walking, almost causing Mrs. Sanderson to fall as she kept going.

"Daniel," she said. "Are you all right? Your mouth is gaping open like you just won the lottery."

I stared at her for a moment and then shook my head and closed my mouth. "I hadn't heard that. I guess it's a good thing that guy showed up." I started walking again.

"It is. He is some kind of guardian angel."

I realized my mouth had dropped open again. I consciously closed it with a click. That was exactly what Carson had said. If I didn't know better, I'd say everyone was conspiring to try to make me feel better about what happened. I'd have to talk to Amy about this.

"I hate to say I told you so," Amy said an hour later when I stopped by her house, "but I told you so."

After walking Mrs. Sanderson home, I wandered the streets for a while. It was a nice day, and I had a lot of thinking to do. I walked in a daze, my feet moving where they wanted. I realized I had stopped and looked up. I was in front of Amy's house. Well, it was as good a time as any to talk to her, so I knocked and we nestled safely in the garage, water bottles in hand.

"Okay, maybe," I conceded, "but it doesn't change

anything. Even if everyone felt the same way, I still think I caused more harm than good. Not to mention I really put myself at risk. I have extra tough skin, but I'm pretty sure I'm not bullet proof."

I waited for her to tell me how wrong I was, how it was obvious that what I did was heroic. I might have even wanted her to. She didn't.

"I understand. My mind hasn't changed, and I'm not going to try to talk you into anything. I'm happy that at least you heard from someone other than me that what you did was the right thing. We'll leave it at that for now."

We chatted for another two hours or so about anything that came to mind, both obviously trying to keep from talking about the whole superhero business. It was nice, almost like the first month I had known her, before I found out I had these powers. When I left, things seemed a bit brighter. I was far from being in a good mood, but I wasn't in a funk like I had been.

I watched over the next several weeks as crime continued to increase in the city. News reports of different acts being perpetrated seemingly multiplied every day. The police were hard-pressed to put even a dent in it. As I listened to the news and read reports or heard the word being spread around school, I tried to find a little bit of hope. I waited for news of some real superhero coming out of the shadows and taking up the sword for the common citizen, so to speak. There was not a whisper of it.

If it had been just thefts or even robberies, it probably wouldn't have been so bad, but it wasn't. Though all types of crime increased, from vandalism and graffiti all the way up to kidnapping and murder, the occurrence of violent crimes multiplied at a much higher rate than others. Rapes, muggings, and killings—things unheard of a year ago in our relatively small city—became almost commonplace. I, and everyone I knew, wondered what was going on, where it might end. There were only around two hundred fifty thousand people in Sueño, but we had the crime rate of one of the major cities.

I dreamed at night of some dystopian chaotic shell of a city where people hunted other people and no one was really safe, even in their own homes. Okay, maybe I had been watching too much TV and reading too many novels. Next I would be having nightmares about zombies or some such thing. Still, the dreams—and what I saw every day while awake—made me uneasy. I had the feeling I got when I was pulling a Jenga piece out of the stack toward the end of the game. Anticipation, anxiety, and more than a little fear. More could crash around me than a few wooden blocks, of course, but the tension was the same. Ratcheted up like a thousand times.

During this time, I started to feel guilty. I'd been granted powers other people didn't have. There had to be a reason for them, though I couldn't figure out exactly what. So, there I was sitting around with the ability to help my city, which crumbled around me, but not doing anything.

Once or twice, I almost regretted quitting. That's not true. I regretted it constantly, but once or twice, I almost decided to change my mind and jump back in. Then I thought of all that blood, of Carson being shot, of how close I came to dying, and how I nearly cost an innocent bystander his life. That made me keep my resolve to do as everyone else did: sit back, hope something could be done, and try to keep from becoming a victim myself. The only difference was that if someone did try to hurt me, I would make them sorry for it.

I considered going out and pretending to be a victim,

walking the dark streets to make an inviting target for the thugs. Then, when they attacked me, I could end their crime spree right then and there. No one else would be involved, and I could help out that way. I discarded the idea when I remembered I didn't really want to get shot and realized that other people in the area could be affected also. I'd heard about drive-by shootings where the only victim was some poor kid playing in his own living room, struck by a bullet that came in from the street. I would not be a bullet or the cause of one being fired. For at least a while, I'd sit back and watch, no matter that it made me feel like a total jerk.

Then I heard something that shook me to my core.

"I can't believe how bad things have been getting lately," my mom said as we were eating dinner one night. Meatloaf, my least favorite food in the entire world. Even worse than broccoli. In fact, I smothered the meat—was it really even meat?—with mashed potatoes and broccoli so I could get it down.

"I know," my dad agreed. "I don't understand why the police can't handle it all. The city council has cleared them to hire more officers, but things are getting worse."

"Oh, honey," my mom patted his hand, "it'll take a while to get new officers hired, trained, and working with the existing police. It'll get better. I know it will."

My brother Tim and I sat silently, pushing things around on our plates, wondering if we'd eaten enough to be able to leave the table.

"Robberies, break-ins, even murders," my father continued. "Murders! Here, in Sueño. Who would have ever thought it possible?"

"And that poor Mrs. Sanderson," Mom said. "I hope she'll be all right."

My ears pricked up. "What about Mrs. Sanderson, Mom? What happened?"

"You didn't hear? She was attacked yesterday evening. It wasn't even fully dark yet. They think it was a mugging, though she probably didn't even have any money on her. They beat her severely and left her there, lying in the street. Luckily a couple walking their dog found her fairly quickly. She's in the Presbyterian Hospital. As far as I know, she hasn't regained consciousness yet."

I stared at my mom, not able to say anything, aware of my dad and brother looking at me strangely. I was finally able to force some sounds from my mouth, but they didn't resemble speech.

"Honey, are you okay?" my mom asked.

I took in a breath and cleared my throat. "I...what...when did that happen?"

"Yesterday evening," my dad answered.

Yesterday. Mrs. Sanderson didn't have any relatives in the city. My friend Craig and his family had moved away several years ago, and she lived alone. The thought of her in the hospital with no one there to visit her made my stomach flip. Or maybe it was the meatloaf. Still...

"I have to—" I started. "Can I be excused?"

The look on my mom's face went from surprised to concerned in a heartbeat. "Are you okay, Daniel?"

"Yeah. I just...I need to go visit Mrs. Sanderson. She doesn't have anyone here, not since Craig and his family moved away. What if she wakes up? She'll be alone and afraid. She's my friend."

"Awww," my mother cooed as she came over to hug me. "You always were such a sweet boy. I didn't know you were that close to her. Here, I'll drive you there. It's not safe to walk in the evenings. Obviously."

I agreed to the ride, but I wished I could walk and that whoever attacked that sweet old lady would try me on for size. I felt like hurting someone. Felt like hurting them badly. It was probably better to get a ride. The fire building within me would probably cause me to kill someone.

At the hospital, I had trouble getting in to see Mrs. Sanderson. I wasn't family, and the rules said I wasn't allowed in.

"Please," I begged. I'm sure I made a pathetic sight. The hospital corridor and the nurse's station in front of me looked distorted, watery. I didn't want to cry like a child, but all the stress in my life lately and the thought of Mrs. Sanderson in her hospital room, waking up with no one around her, made it tough for me to fight. I blinked my eyes several times and sniffed, trying to regain control. "She doesn't have anyone. She needs to know someone is here for her, that someone cares. Can't you understand?"

The nurse's brown eyes met mine and then drifted away. The edges of her mouth turned outward and downward— not a frown, but something else, a sympathetic feeling. She took her bottom lip in her teeth and scanned the corridor. "She's in 423. Go on."

I smiled at her as one of the tears escaped my control and trickled down my cheek. "Thank you." I hurried down the hall before she changed her mind.

Mrs. Sanderson was in a room by herself. She lay there, motionless, with an IV and other tubes and wires attached to her. The monitor beeped with her heartbeat and had numbers for her other vital signs. I guessed they were normal. There was nothing red on the screen, and there were no alarms going off.

She was a mess of bruises. Her thin, wrinkled skin showed deep purple and brown spots so large they had to have been made by different blows, so close together they merged into one. It was painful to look at her like that. Her breathing seemed normal, but who knew what kind of damage she had inside. I was sure the doctors were taking care of all of that. She was safe and would be able to take the time to heal.

"Hi, Mrs. Sanderson," I whispered. "It's me, Daniel. I heard you ran into a little trouble and wanted to come visit you."

She didn't respond, of course. I wasn't sure if she was in a coma or if she was sedated or what else, but I didn't expect an answer.

"You really shouldn't have been outside after dark. It's getting dangerous out there." I shook my head. "Yeah, but I guess you knew that. We've talked about it enough. I just wish...I mean, there should...I—" I took a deep breath. It seemed to be getting hard to breathe in the room. It was stuffy and too close. The walls squeezed in on me.

I half fell into the chair by the side of the bed. "Someone should have been there to prevent it," I told her. "Someone should be doing something, sticking up for those who can't stick up for themselves. Someone needs to—" I realized I had been raising my voice and took another breath, purposely unclenched my hands which had somehow balled into fists. I looked at my friend, this sweet old woman who should never have been a target for crime. I reached over and pulled a strand of coarse gray hair out of her face.

"I should have been there, done something," I whispered, putting my head in my hands. "I'm so sorry. I have the power to help, but I don't. I'm too selfish and too afraid and find excuses for why I don't do what needs to be done. I'm sorry."

A hand on my shoulder made me jump. I'd been so fully

engaged in self-pity that even my self-defense power didn't activate. I turned and saw Amy's face intently gazing at my own.

I didn't think, didn't say anything. I just reached out and pulled her to me and hugged her. At least I had the presence of mind to keep from squeezing her as hard as I could, like I wanted to. It probably would have crushed her. Still, I held on as if she were the only thing keeping me from sliding into the abyss.

We held each other for a long time. When I felt my heartbeat slowing to normal and exhaustion try to take me, I released her and looked into her eyes. "Hi," I said. "Thanks. How did you get in here?"

She smiled mischievously at me. "Your mom told me which room and then distracted the nurse so I could sneak in."

Amy looked at Mrs. Sanderson for the first time. "Oh my God," she said, "she looks horrible."

"Yeah." I didn't trust myself for further words.

"I heard that last part as I came in," she said, eyeing me warily. "The part about it being your fault and all that."

I waited to see if she'd scold me or tell me I was wrong. She remained silent. I forced a sad smile onto my face.

"I've been stupid. I think I was so scared that I used any excuse to keep from having to put myself in danger. I'm a coward and a liar."

"No."

"I'm scared, Amy. I could be killed. That doesn't matter to a real hero. A real hero faces danger and death without blinking. Putting myself in danger scares me so much it makes me shake like a child watching a horror movie. I just want to cover my eyes and hide."

She took my hand and enfolded it in her own. "Is that

what you think? That heroes have no fear? Being fearless is very close to stupidity. The thing that makes someone a hero isn't that they don't have fear. It's that they are scared to death, but they act anyway. Without being afraid, you'd just be reckless and careless. That's not you, Daniel. Fear heightens your senses, revs up your metabolism, reminds you that you're doing something important. A hero is someone who sacrifices comfort and safety for the sake of others. That sounds an awful lot like you to me."

I was unable to speak. How did she sum up everything I had been searching for, everything I hadn't understood, in barely one breath? I realized I had been looking at her blankly for too long when she squeezed my hand and raised an eyebrow.

"What are you thinking?" she asked, nudging me with her shoulder.

"I'm thinking that I've been wasting time. I'm thinking I need to stop feeling sorry for myself and do something. It's bad out there, and it's obvious no one else is going to do anything about it. I'm thinking I need to. What about you?"

She squeezed my hand again, and her smile grew bigger. "I'm thinking that we have a lot of work to do."

We stayed for another hour, talking with each other and to Mrs. Sanderson. Before I left, I planted a gentle kiss on the old woman's forehead. "You just get better, Mrs. S. I'm going to give you some stuff to talk about when we next sit down to chat. Keep your eye on the news reports."

Amy was right. We had a lot of work to do. And right then, at that moment, I wouldn't have had it any other way.

11

I was at Amy's house, in the garage. I had started thinking of her garage as our secret hideout, my base of operations, as a second home.

It was Thursday, the day before I would officially go out and patrol once again. I was more nervous than if I was about to call Cindy Freeman, the most beautiful girl in my school, and ask her for a date. Okay, maybe not quite that nervous, but really close. What was the danger of death or injury compared to trying to talk popular girls? Not that I'd choose to go on a date with Cindy Freeman. Anyway, let's just leave it at me being nervous.

"Are you listening to me?" Amy asked. Her irritation made me think that maybe it wasn't the first time she had asked it. I put all thoughts of Cindy out of my head.

"Of course I am."

"Then what did I say?" She tapped her foot and crossed her arms in front of her. Uh-oh. Busted.

I sighed. "Okay, I was distracted. Sorry. What did you say?"

Somehow, the glare she had fixed me with got even

colder. I shivered. How did girls learn to do that? "I said I have something for you."

That caught my attention. "You have something for me?" I said. "What kind of something?"

She went to the back of the garage and pulled out a large box. It was wrapped in paper and had a big bow on it. I stared.

"It's something I thought might help. I hope you like it." She chewed her bottom lip, something she did when she was nervous or anxious.

"Oh, Amy," I said, "you didn't have to get me anything. It's not even my birthday."

"Yeah, well, I don't believe in waiting until someone's birthday to give them a gift. Besides, I didn't get it. I made it."

That made me even more interested. She handed the box to me—despite its size it was really light—and I put it down on the ground in front of my chair. With a look at her anxious face, I carefully unwrapped the gift. It was a plain white garment box, like the kind you get at Christmas, normally containing clothes. I lifted the lid to find some type of fabric that was a swirl of black, gray, and some almost-white highlights. I looked up at her expectantly. She motioned toward the cloth, but didn't say anything. I lifted an eyebrow, and she drew hers down.

I pulled it out of the box and stood so I could hold it up. My present expanded into what looked like a jumpsuit but with the zipper in the back. The zipper had an ingenious little lanyard attached to it, like wetsuits, to allow a person to zip it up themselves. Once zipped up, the leash could be secured out of the way on a little strip of Velcro sewn just to the side, on the upper part of the back.

The suit was dark, but the swirls made me think of clouds, as if I were looking into a thundercloud and seeing the black, gray, and small shards of light filtering through. It was beautiful. "Oh, Amy," I said again, "it's great. Is it my superhero costume?"

"Yes," she said. "Do you like it?"

"I love it!" I set it down and pulled her into a hug. "I hadn't even thought of doing anything like that. I just figured my sweats would work well enough."

"You can't be a superhero in sweats. What would the neighbors think?" She winked at me. "There's more."

I looked at the box and pulled out a long, dark piece of material, not quite black, and held it up. A cape. I swung it around me and realized it was large enough to pull around my whole body. With this, I could blend into any shadow. It looked like it might be useful for keeping warm, too. I always thought capes were lame, that they would get in the way in a fight, but I was willing to give it a try. If it didn't work out, I could always ditch it later.

"The clasping mechanism fits onto the suit, here," Amy said as she pointed it out. "That way if someone grabs it, you won't be strangled. In fact, I made it so that it is a breakaway type of accessory. Someone can't pull on your cape to throw you off a building or anything because the mechanism will unclasp first."

I looked from the clasp to Amy. "You're a genius," I said. "How do you think of all this stuff?"

"Because I'm a genius," she laughed. "And because I've read as many comics and books as you have. Every time I read one, I think to myself that it's easy enough to defeat that hero or villain. Pull on his cape and he'll just fall two hundred feet. It's common sense. There's still more, though."

I found a pair of snug-fitting gloves in the box also. They went halfway up my forearm and were made of soft leather with strips of rubberized material on the palms and fingers. They felt good when I tried them on. They fit, well, they fit like a glove, to go for the obvious joke.

The last thing I found in the box was a cowl that covered my head completely and had only a narrow slit for my eyes. Surprisingly, the slit allowed me to use my fully enhanced peripheral vision, which I had recently learned gave me at least two hundred seventy degrees of vision. It didn't affect my eyesight at all. How did she figure that one out?

"You'll probably have to get used to breathing through the cloth, but it's thin and shouldn't make it hard to pull air through, even when it's wet. It won't be the best thing when you have a cold or allergies, though. I couldn't think of anything to do about that. So, are you going to try it on or what?"

"Definitely. Turn around." When she did, I stripped to my underwear and then pulled the jumpsuit on. I pulled the zipper closed and quickly added the cowl, cape, and then the gloves.

"Okay, you can look now."

Amy turned around, and her eyes lit up. She gave a little hop and clapped her hands together. "Oh, it looks great," she said. "All the criminals are going to be shaking out of their shoes."

That reminded me. I had on a black pair of Chuck Taylors. I needed to get some appropriate footwear, some kind of boots or something. I'd have to do that later.

Amy rummaged around in the back of the garage and pulled out a mirror half as tall as I was. She propped it against a rack so I could see what I looked like. I turned this way and that, spun in a circle to see how the cape twirled, struck an action pose or two, and then nodded. Not bad, not bad at all.

The suit itself fit about as perfectly as anything I'd ever worn. It wasn't too tight—good thing, because I didn't have any muscle to show off—but it wasn't hanging off me like it was three sizes too big either. It was generally snug, but because of how awkward my body shape was, it was a little baggy in some areas, like the chest, legs, arms, and my behind. Yeah, just those areas. It almost looked like I had slept in it. When I pulled the cape forward to cover myself, Batman fantasies ran through my head. I laughed out loud.

"Do you like it?" she asked.

"Absolutely," I said, giving her my best smile. I realized a second later she couldn't see my smile, because of the cowl, but I'm sure she could see how the skin around my eyes crinkled. As I looked at my eyes in the mirror, I noticed something I had missed before. There was a faint, lighter gray line on the cowl, wrapping around my forehead, a couple of inches above my temples. It looked like I was wearing a silver band on my head.

"What is that?" I asked, pointing toward it.

Amy's smile disappeared, and she took her lower lip in her teeth again. "Um, it's a halo."

"A what?"

"A halo. I was thinking about what you said, about your talk with Carson and Mrs. Sanderson. They both mentioned guardian angels. I just figured, you know, it would be a good name for you. Your superhero name."

"What name?" I asked.

"Angel. It has a nice ring, right?" If she didn't stop biting on that lip, she was going to bleed. I put my finger on her mouth. She understood what it meant and released her lip.

"It does," I said, surprised that I was actually serious. "It totally does. Yeah, I should be a guardian angel, but I don't want to step on the toes of the crime-fighting group that started in New York. You know, the Guardian Angels, the people who ride in the subways to help make them safe? So yeah, Angel is perfect." I threw back my shoulders, put my hands on my hips, and stuck my chest out as far as I could. It was my best impression of a superhero pose. Amy clapped her hands again, and the smile came back with a vengeance. She really did have a very nice smile.

"Now all I need is some patrol time, some luck, and some hapless criminals," I said. "Oh, and better shoes."

12

I gathered up all the money I had earned from doing odd jobs and bought a pair of tactical boots from a military surplus store. They were black, mostly light-weight nylon, protected my ankles, had good tread on the bottom. I was ready to patrol.

The first night, alone in the dark with my costume and cape, I went back and forth between feeling silly and anxious. My last night out was still on my mind. The guns, the blood, the chance of not only myself but of innocent people getting hurt or killed bombarded my thoughts. I felt as if I'd lose my nerve. I called Amy.

"I'm feeling a little tense here," I told her as I hid in the woods in one of the parks. "Tell me again why I should be out here?"

"Mrs. Sanderson."

I felt my face heating. "Yeah. Mrs. Sanderson."

"Maybe if you move around, you won't think about it so much," Amy said. "Do you want to try to go straight to the bad part of town?"

An uncontrollable shiver racked my body like electricity

flowing through me. "Maybe a little later. I think I need to get used to being out here first."

"Okay, go ahead and move around, see what you can see. Why don't you practice moving around town without being detected?"

That seemed like a good idea. "Okay, that sounds good. Thanks."

"You're welcome. I'm tracking your phone with that app. You're not really alone, Daniel. I mean Angel."

I smiled as I hung up and tucked my phone into my belt pouch. Amy had sewn an ingenious belt and several pouches into the costume. They were lined up around my lower back so that the belt held the weight of anything in them. It didn't tug on the costume at all, and my cape hid anything I carried with me. She was a genius.

I jogged around for several hours that night and didn't see a thing. At least, I didn't see any crime. I did see two guys walking quickly down the street, and they saw me.

"Dressing up in Daddy's clothes," one of them said, laughing. "You better get off the street, boy. It's dangerous to be out at night."

They hurried on, looking anxious. I was doubly embarrassed. Once because they saw me to begin with, and the second time because of his comment about my costume. I did look kind of ridiculous. Not because of the costume itself, but because my body was so awkwardly shaped that nothing looked good on me. I definitely did not have the superhero body shape. I should probably do something about that.

The rest of the night, I didn't see anyone at all. No crime, no suspicious characters, nothing. I finally went home early in the morning, feeling like I'd wasted an entire night. I guess that was the way of things, though. Boredom punctuated with sheer terror. Funny, they never mentioned that in the comics.

The next day, I began looking up information about exercise and building muscle. I decided it would be good to develop my body so I looked better in my costume. If I was going to be a superhero, the least I could do was look more like one. How hard could it be? I had super powers. It should be easier for me than for others, right?

Not so much.

I enlisted Amy to help me design a workout program. "It's really simple," she told me. "You have to work out so that your muscles work harder than they are used to. The muscle fibers themselves tear and split, and when each part of the fiber heals, it becomes as big as the original, so then you have two fibers instead of one. You keep doing that and your muscle gets bigger overall, fiber by fiber. The key is to stress your body so that the little tears happen."

It did seem simple. There were other things to consider, of course, like which muscles to focus on and how to do that, eating so I had protein building blocks to help the muscles repair, and sleep to allow the body to do its repair work, but we'd get to that. We found some great basic exercises to start with. The internet was a wonderful thing.

"Bench press, squats, curls, military presses, push-ups, and pull-ups," Amy said. "That will cover most of the main muscle groups. We can expand the list as needed."

"That sounds easy enough." We had researched how to do each exercise effectively. I pulled an old bench press and some weights out of the storage shed and set them up in my garage. For a change, Amy came over to my house to supervise the training.

I started bench-pressing with the barbell bar without any weights on it so I could practice proper form for the exercise. When Amy approved my motions, we loaded the bar up.

"Are you sure you want to put all the weights on there?" she asked me. I had enough plates to make the total weight sitting on the bench supports a hundred fifty pounds. That was more than I weighed. Quite a bit more.

"I'm sure," I said. "I have super powers, remember?"

"Oh, yeah. Okay, well, be careful."

I slid onto the bench, looking up at the bar loaded with plates. "Here goes." I lowered the bar to my chest, using the form I had used with the empty barbell. It didn't feel much different. In fact, when I pushed it upward, I almost lost contact as the metal tried to leave my hand, shooting toward the ceiling.

I readjusted how much strength I used and pumped the barbell up and down a dozen times. I could do that all night and not get tired. I moved my left hand to the center of the bar and then released my right hand. I continued to move the bar up and down with just my left hand for another dozen repetitions. Nothing. I set the bar back on the supports.

"I don't think I have enough weight," I said, "or that I can even get any kind of burn from this." I stood up, grabbed the bar with my left hand again—I'm right-handed, so I figured my left would be the weaker of the two—and started to do curls with the weight. It wasn't even enough for that. I went through the other exercises and found none of them did the slightest thing for me.

"You don't have any other weight plates?" Amy asked me.

"Nope." I looked at the barbell. "Even if I did, I don't think I could put enough on that bar to get a good workout. I'll need to do something else."

I eyed my dad's car, parked on the other side of the

garage. "I have an idea." After looking around the car to make sure there wasn't anything lying there, I got on my back and slid underneath the vehicle.

"What are you doing?" Amy called out from where she was sitting on the weight bench. I didn't answer her.

When I raised the car up, bench-pressing it, I heard her gasp. I made sure to push on the frame supports so I didn't damage anything, but it was a dirty prospect. Little flakes of dirt and grit rained down in my eyes. Trying to blink away the particles didn't work, so I closed my eyelids tight, trying to prevent any more from getting in. I bench-pressed the car a couple dozen times and then settled it back onto the garage floor. "It's still not enough weight. I need something bigger."

Amy and I spent the whole day looking around town, mainly out in the woods and at the old, abandoned quarry, for things to lift. Even the massive boulders littering the area near the quarry didn't prove to be effective in fatiguing my muscles.

I frowned at the rock I had been lifting. "I think I need something like a cargo ship if I want to work my muscles enough to tear the fibers. Bodyweight exercises do me no good, and even these boulders don't tire me out until I've done nearly a hundred reps. Most people have trouble building muscle because they don't lift consistently. For me, it'll be because there's nothing heavy enough to lift."

Amy patted my shoulder. "We'll think of something. Maybe you just need to eat a lot and gain weight and it'll come on as muscle."

"Sure. Maybe." I figured I was stuck being a skinny kid with a costume that didn't fit right. There were worse things in the world.

"Hey, at least the criminals will underestimate you and your strength. That could be useful."

"Almost as useful as them laughing themselves to death when they see how my costume fits." It sounded whiny, but I didn't care. "Anyway, I guess my appearance isn't that important. I'm not trying to win a beauty contest. I'm trying to keep the bad guys from hurting innocent people. I suppose I should just focus on that."

"Come on," Amy said. "I'll treat you to a protein shake. We can talk about making your patrols more effective. I have some ideas."

13

I don't know what I would have done without Amy. She explained that she had compiled statistics of the different crimes being committed in the city. From that, she made a color-coded map, with different colors indicating the relative crime rate. She showed me the map on her laptop.

"I used the normal color scheme for such things. Red is the worst, orange a little less crime, yellow, all the way up to green, which is an area where there is hardly any crime."

"I don't see much green there," I said, noting that most of the city was yellow, with some concentrated orange areas and slightly fewer red spots.

"No," Amy answered. "We knew crime was getting bad in the city, but this map gives the proof. Anyway, we can use this to target areas where crime will probably be occurring. I suggest we start on the orange areas. We'll work up to the red areas soon enough."

I pondered the map for a moment. "Sounds good to me. Maybe with this, I won't waste as much time running around without seeing any crime."

"That's the idea. It's probably better not to hit the red areas just yet because you may end up getting caught in between two crimes or in the middle of some kind of gang war or something. We'll save that for later."

I swallowed, trying to make the lump in my throat go away. "Yeah, that sounds like fun. For later."

"We'll work up to it," she said cheerily.

It seemed to work. For the next two weeks, I seldom went more than two days without seeing some type of crime. Most of it was small stuff: vandalism, minor theft, tagging. I easily stopped them and left the perpetrators, and the evidence of their crimes, for the police to find. The little pouches Amy had sewn into the costume came in handy. I used some of my hard-earned money to buy a big box of zip ties and stuffed a couple pockets with them so I could bind up the hands of those I found committing crimes.

I hadn't seen much violent crime in my patrols yet, but I always expected it. I didn't want to become complacent. But night after night, I found only minor, nonviolent crimes. I felt a little pride that I was doing something about the overall crime rate in the city, but something inside told me I had to do more. Taggers and kleptomaniacs didn't put Mrs. Sanderson in the hospital. I had to step it up if I wanted to make the city safer.

"I'm going red tonight," I told Amy one weekend evening. It would be one of my late nights patrolling, and I wanted to go into a more dangerous area. I felt my face get hot as I heard myself say the movie-worthy line. I had no right to utter such a thing. King of beating up teenage minor thugs, that was me.

Amy's amused smile made me wish I had my cowl on. She schooled her expression so she wore a more neutral one. "Are you sure? It could be dangerous."

"I'm tired of stopping petty crimes," I said. "It's not doing anything for the city, really."

"It's making people take notice that there is someone trying to help. I hear people talking about it. It's a start."

"Yeah," I said, running my fingers through my hair. "I hear people talking, too. I guess that's good, but I feel like I'm not doing enough. If it was just these small crimes, there would be no need for me. I need to stop the violent crimes. I know that happens in the yellow areas, too, but it never seems to happen when I'm there. A red zone gives me a better chance of finding those types of activities."

"Okay," Amy agreed after a long pause to think. "Just be careful. Remember that you're actually out looking for danger. Don't underestimate the situation—"

"—or overestimate my abilities," I finished for her. "Right. Got it. I'll be careful."

So I sneaked into one of the rougher parts of town, made all the more dangerous because of the general escalation of criminal activities over the previous several months. It was early, so I slipped from shadow to shadow, scanning the darkened landscape, but not expecting to find anything yet.

Footsteps echoed from somewhere off to my right. Several sets of feet pounded the pavement hard. Voices drifted on the wind, following closely behind the other sounds. I couldn't make out the words yet, but it sounded like whooping and laughing. Whoever was making the noises, they were coming toward me.

Suddenly, a figure hurtled out of the shadows between a grocery store and a second-hand clothing store. It resolved into a man, running for all he was worth, stumbling, and barely keeping upright. He wasn't speaking, but I could hear his panting breaths as he tried to suck more air into his lungs. He was older, maybe in his mid-thirties, and a little overweight.

Right behind him, three other figures closed the gap between them at a rapid pace. Eyes intent on the first man, the three didn't see me, probably didn't see anything else around them. They were all younger and fitter looking than their prey. They would catch him any second.

"Get him," the tallest of the hunters told his companions. "Give him an extra beating for running."

One of the other chasers threw a leg out and kicked the lead man's rear leg. It flew to the side, unbalancing him and making his other leg crumple. He struck the street hard, rolled and skipped across the ground, and ended in a heap a dozen feet away. I winced. He lost a lot of skin on that maneuver.

The three younger men stopped and surrounded him. They were all breathing hard from the run, but nowhere near as hard as the man still curled up on the ground in front of them.

"You could...have...just given...us the wallet," one of the thugs said to him. "And...we wouldn't have...beaten you too...badly." Giving up on speaking, he took a deep breath and kicked the grounded man in the ribs.

I had seen enough. If I didn't take action, they may very well kill the man. As one of the other attackers brought his leg back to kick, I rushed into action.

I ran toward the kicker. With my speed, I was easily able to reach him before he was able to land a blow. I simply pushed the attacker out of the way, not even using that much strength. He left his feet, flew six feet, and slammed against the wall of the clothing store with a sickening crunch. I hoped I hadn't killed the man.

His two friends turned toward me and I saw their eyes

narrow in the dim light cast by the lamp over the back door of the grocery store. They looked at each other, turned, and lunged at me, one of them pulling a knife from somewhere.

In my speed-enhanced vision, I had all the time in the world to react to their attacks. The unarmed man reached me just before the knife-wielder did. I slipped to the side, putting him between me and the knife.

I casually slapped aside the slow-motion punch coming at me, causing my two attackers to run into each other and tangle up. The guy with the knife almost cut his friend on accident.

Instead of waiting around for them to coordinate their attacks, I swung out with my left hand and slapped the unarmed attacker, striking him on the shoulder blade. His body shot forward, almost causing him to do a flip. He rocketed past the knife-wielder and landed face-first on the alley floor, sliding several feet before stopping. He groaned and rolled, trying to get back to his feet. I wouldn't have to worry about him for the time being.

The man with the knife seemed to be more talented than the other two, though it was hard to tell because it hadn't been much of a fight up to that point. He struck out with his blade like a viper, trying to find an opening to hit a vital target. Of course, even a viper wasn't too fast for me. I evaded the lunges and stabs, though some just barely. Even having time to react, trying to figure out what to do when deadly sharp steel came at you wasn't easy.

I shot my hand out to grab him and almost got a slash to my arm for my trouble. If it wasn't for my super-reflexes, I would have been bleeding all over the alley. I wondered if my skin could withstand a slash from a razor sharp knife wielded by a skilled fighter. I didn't want to find out. I really needed to practice actual fighting techniques.

The knife darted toward me, faster than before. So fast it surprised me, and I thrust my hand out to intercept the blade. As I did, something shot out of my fingers, spraying at the man's eyes and face. It was something white, a cream of some kind. His eyes widened just before they were covered in the stuff, and I knew my eyes reflected that surprise. I had no idea what was going on either.

I took advantage of the distraction and punched the forearm of the knife hand. The sound of bones breaking was much too loud in the confined space between buildings. The knife clattered to the concrete. I finished up by slapping the side of my foe's head, causing his head to whip to the side, spattering the white stuff everywhere. The attacker went down, looking to be unconscious already.

I scanned the alley. The victim was still curled in a ball near my feet, too scared to move. Two of the men were not moving, and the third was still getting to his feet shakily. Some of the white stuff that came from my fingers still stuck to my hand. I raised it to my nose and sniffed it. Then I licked it. Yep, whipped cream. Not the prepackaged, Cool Whip type of whipped cream, but the good stuff, the hand made sweet that you sometimes get on coffee from one of those little coffee shops. What the hell was going on? Well, I could think about that later. I had some cleanup to do.

Walking casually to the conscious assailant, I pulled his hands behind his back and zip-tied him with one of the restraints I took out of my pouch. I checked the other two, and they were both breathing though they didn't appear conscious. I soon had them tied up as well, and all three next to each other on the floor of the alley.

That done, I checked on the victim. He was just peeking out of his curled-up position, looking around for danger.

"You're safe now," I told him. "You can get up."

He looked at me, cringed, and curled up into a tighter ball.

I tried again. "I'm one of the good guys. I'm not going to hurt you. Are you all right? Are you injured badly?"

"You just beat all three of them up, in like two seconds," he said, through his voice was muffled with his head tucked into his chest.

"Yeah."

"Why?" he asked, uncurling himself halfway.

"You were in trouble. Did they try to rob you?"

"Yes, but I ran." He unfolded his arms and legs and got into a seated position on the ground. "Maybe that wasn't the best thing to do. I thought they were going to kill me."

"Well," I said, "they're not going to be able to hurt you now. I need you to call the police to come pick them up. Do you have a phone?"

He patted his pockets, front and then back, and pulled out a cell phone. "I do."

"Good. Call the cops, tell them what these men did, file charges." When I saw the look on his face, I knew he didn't want to do it, didn't want to make enemies of these three men. "Do it," I said in my firmest voice, thanking God that it didn't crack, as it sometimes did.

I watched him as he dialed and then reported the crime to the emergency operator. I could hear the operator asking questions. When he hung the phone up, I decided it was a good time to go. Even if he fled, he had given them his name so they would be able to get a statement out of him eventually.

"I'm going to leave now. Tell the police every detail about how they tried to rob and beat you."

He looked at me, seeming to notice the costume for the

first time. "Why? Why don't you stay and talk to them. Who are you anyway?"

"I'd rather not be noticed," I said. "I'm...you can call me Angel. Be safe."

While the last word still hung in the air, I put on a burst of speed and tore out of the alley and down the street. I wasn't quite fast enough to keep him from tracking me—I wasn't the Flash or anything—but all he'd be able to do was tell the police into which general direction I'd headed. I would double back later and go another way.

A few minutes later, I was walking toward Amy's house. I licked the last bit of whipped cream off my finger and thought about that particular talent. I had seen some abilities pop up in training that didn't remain permanently, but this one had to be the strangest.

I threw my hand out and willed stuff to come out of it.

Nothing.

I tried again, really focusing and thrusting it out more emphatically.

Still nothing.

I needed to talk to Amy about this. I texted her as I walked, warning her I was on my way. And then I ran.

14

"What's up?" Amy said through a yawn as I met her in front of the door to her garage. "How did it go tonight? Anything exciting happen?"

"Kind of, yeah."

She opened the door and motioned for me to enter our secret hideout. "Tell me."

I settled into the chair as she took two bottles of water out of the old refrigerator sitting along one wall. She threw one to me. I snatched it out of the air and nodded. "Thanks."

She narrowed her eyes at me and then scanned my clothing, probably looking for blood or some sign of how the night had gone for me. "Are you okay? You look a little frazzled. Or confused. I can't decide which."

"Both." I gave her a blow-by-blow account of my evening, watching her lean toward me while her eyebrows rose when I told her about the whipped cream part.

"Wow," she said. "Whipped cream, huh? Do it for me now."

"I don't think I can."

"Try."

I did. Try, that is. Nothing happened. "I tried to duplicate it afterwards, but I couldn't do it then, either."

"Aww," she said, "that's too bad. A little whipped cream would be nice right now." She laughed.

"Come on, Amy," I said. "It's serious. It kind of has me concerned, you know?"

"Serious? Serious." She put on a stern face for just a moment before a smile cracked through and she laughed again. "Daniel, it's whipped cream. Whipped. Cream. How serious can that be?"

I suppose I was glaring at her because she became serious. "Okay, I understand. I was just trying to cheer you up. What we need to do is keep track of when you have this power and any other ones you get. You had some random powers when we were training, but I thought that was just because you were getting used to your new abilities. It's been a little while."

She pulled out one of her notebooks and a pen. "Tell me exactly how you felt before and during your whipped cream power episode."

"I don't know," I said honestly. "I did feel something different, but I can't explain it."

"Have you felt that particular feeling before, maybe when the other random powers manifested when we were training?"

"No. I'd never felt it before. Thinking back, I can't remember if I felt anything when I had unexplained temporary powers way back then. Too many other things were going on for me to pay attention to that."

She tapped the pen on her lip and then used it to push her glasses up on her nose. "You'll have to pay attention from now on. If you get any other abilities, make sure you analyze exactly how it feels, and you tell me as soon as possible so I can write it all down. We'll get to the bottom of this."

"Thanks, Amy. You're the best." I looked at her, really looked at her, sitting there in her oversized clothes with her huge glasses and her dark hair a mess. "I couldn't have done any of this without you. I think your superpower is the ability to dream up cool things and to tell me what I need to do. We'll have to come up with a superhero name for you, too."

She met my eyes for a moment but then dropped hers. Her cheeks colored, and she busied herself with scratching something into her book. Something that looked an awful lot like a doodle and not words. With her writing, though, it was hard to tell. Honestly, her writing was worse than mine.

A sudden smile lit up her face. "What would you call me if I was a superhero?" she said.

Uh-oh. I meant it when I said she was like a superhero, but I hadn't expected that question. "I don't really know. Let's see. Brainiac?" I saw her wince. "No, that's already taken. Plus, it's lame."

She was looking at me excitedly. I didn't want to mess this up. I could easily insult her if I wasn't careful.

"I was thinking of something related to Angel, like the Harp, or Wings, or something like that but those seem too much like nicknames and besides, you're no sidekick. Your superpowers can stand on their own, without anyone else."

She nodded enthusiastically. Okay, that part made her happy. I racked my brain.

"You control every part of what we do, so Puppet Master might work," I said, and saw the edges of her mouth start to turn downward. I continued before she said anything. "But that sounds like a villain's name, and it sounds like you're a control freak, which you're not." I saw from the way her mouth relaxed that she was satisfied with that.

"The Goddess? The Nymph? The Boss?" I couldn't seem to think. "No. None of those work. Can't you help me out?"

"The question I asked," she said, "was what *you* would call me. I'll let you flounder around before I suggest anything." She paused. "Besides, I can't really think of anything, either. I'm no superhero."

"You are," I said and was half-surprised that I really meant it. I couldn't leave until I came up with something that fit her. And it wouldn't hurt if it was something that flattered her and made her happy.

"I'm just thinking out loud here, brainstorming," I said, "so don't be insulted with any lame name I come up with."

She nodded, put her pen down, put her elbows on her knees, and rested her chin in her hands, looking at me. Those bright blue orbs were filled with excitement and anticipation. I swallowed the lump in my throat. I was in the hot seat.

"The Temptress?" Wow, that one actually made electricity run up and down my spine for some reason. "The Analyst. The Protector. Too bad Wonder Woman is already taken. Amazing Girl. The Enforcer. Argh! This is really hard."

Amy didn't move, barely blinked. She sat there, chin propped up and eyes looking into mine. "Keep going. You're doing fine."

I started to think about the time we had spent together, the training, all the ways she was solely responsible for any success I had up until then. Why was the perfect name so hard to find? I felt that my command of the English language wasn't good enough to find a label that embodied her. I thought of times we had spent together just chatting and enjoying the sunshine. Sometimes we watched the animals in the woods, especially the birds. She loved birds.

"The Robin. No, Batman's sidekick already took that one. Bluejay. Shrike. Hawk." There was something there. "I think I'm getting close, but even though a bird of prey would fit—not because you're mean or anything, but because you're so competent, so good at things—it's not good enough because those birds aren't colorful or beautiful enough for you." I thought of what I had said after the words already came out.

"I mean...the birds...they're—"

"So you think I'm beautiful?" She fluttered her eyelashes in almost a comical fashion. She was joking. But she also wasn't.

"No. I mean, yes. I mean, well, you know what I mean." I stammered.

"I don't. Explain it to me." Her expression was neutral, but I thought I saw a teasing glint in her eyes. I opened my mouth to speak, and she cut me off. "I'm just poking at you, Daniel. I know what you mean. Give me some more names."

She had let me off the hook. For that, more than anything else she had done that night, I wanted to hug her until she couldn't breathe. She truly was the best.

"Kestrel!" I said and knew it was perfect as the word came out. It had just popped into my head.

"Kestrel?" she asked. "Hmm, Kestrel."

"Yeah, kestrels are awesome, like you." I swept my hand out toward her as if announcing her to an audience. "They are amazing hunters, can hover—most birds can't—are very cool looking..." I watched her face as it reacted to each thing I said. She seemed to be getting more excited. "True, they aren't that colorful, but I have seen pictures of them with nice reddish feathers, prettier than the normal hawks we see around here. But that fits you, too, because you wear clothes that are meant to hide you from attention, but that camouflage can't hide all the magnificence. Kestrels are graceful and powerful and clever hunters. Yeah, Kestrel. Your superhero name should be Kestrel. What do you think?"

Amy looked at me for a full half minute, not saying anything. I began to think maybe I had made a mistake. But no, I hadn't. That was the name for her. I was sure. It surprised me when she threw her arms around me and hugged me. When she loosened her hold, she kissed me on the cheek. "I think it's perfect. I would love to be a superhero named Kestrel."

"You are," I said, my face flushed and on fire. "You totally are."

15

I still kept up with my homework. There was only a week until summer vacation, and then one school year until I graduated from high school, so I figured I could survive spending a lot of time with my new superhero hobby. About all I did was go to school, do homework, fight crime, and hang out with Amy to try to become better at what I did. You know, just a normal high school schedule. Things changed when the school year finished, though.

I seemed to develop a knack for finding crimes. Most of my patrols resulted in one type of illegal activity or another being foiled and more lawbreakers being left for the police to pick up. Sure, it could have been because I concentrated on the worst parts of town, but it could also have had something to do with the fact that the crime rate was actually rising, despite my best efforts.

About one in every four confrontations surprised me with a new power that manifested itself and then disappeared without a trace. It was frustrating, more than a little nerve-racking, and maybe a bit exciting because I never knew what would happen next. Amy thought it was fascinating.

I had displayed quite a list of intermittent powers, some useful if I could ever rely on them to be there when I needed them. I had to think quickly on my feet when they activated. That was maybe the scariest part. It concerned me that my safety depended on my ability to think on my feet.

There was the whipped cream thing—which actually happened twice, the only power to make a repeat appearance—and the time when my whole body was suddenly covered in hair. That was a weird one. I shot out some kind of ray from my eyes once, burning anything flammable in its path, but not even causing a color change to things that don't burn easily. One time in a fight, the lower half of my body turned to the consistency of rubber. I flew once, on accident. That was kind of cool, except for the fear that it would disappear while I was in mid-air. Once, I started sinking into the ground, parts of my body passing through whatever I tried to touch. Luckily I only sank into the sewer and then solidified before I went into the earth's crust. I still shudder to think what would have happened if I had solidified while encased in rock. Oh, and I had about half an hour when I could see in the dark like it was daylight. Strange.

Amy filled her notebooks with details on my powers, the crimes I stopped, the people I left for the police, and every other thing that anyone could think of. I asked why she didn't do it all on the computer, and she said she liked writing things down the old-fashioned way. I had a feeling she did enter it all into the computer, too, but I never asked.

"I want to try to shock you," Amy said as if she was saying that it was Wednesday.

"Stop doing your homework," I deadpanned. "That will shock me."

"No, I mean shock. You know, with electricity."

I stared at her, wondering when she had gone insane. "What? Why do you want to try to electrocute me?"

"Oh, don't be such a wuss. I'm not going to electrocute you, just shock you a little."

"A little."

"Yeah," she said. "Regular household current. I think maybe I can stimulate your powers that way."

I still couldn't believe what she was suggesting. "Why would you think that?"

"Well," she said, "a lot of the body's signals are electrical in nature. A strong jolt may activate something. Plus, your self-defense powers may see it as a threat and give you some ability that I can observe. I've noticed that a lot of the times your intermittent powers manifest in a high-stress situation, a big fight. It only happened once when you were not in danger." Her mouth quirked into a mischievous smile.

I didn't want to think about that one time. It was embarrassing. How was I to know that the girl I saved only wanted to kiss me on the cheek to thank me?

"I don't know," I said, shaking my head. "I don't want to get shocked."

"How are we ever going to find out more about your powers if we don't experiment a little?"

"Oh, that's easy for you to say. You're not going to have electricity running through your body. Kestrels don't use electricity. Why don't you just sing to me?"

Her flat look told me all I needed to know about the chances of her serenading me. "Come on, stand over here."

She always did that to me. She would discuss things, but when it came down to taking some kind of action, she acted like we had agreed to do it her way. What kind of superhero was bullied by his sidekick like that? The kind of superhero I was.

I went and stood where she told me. I grumbled.

"Stop being a baby," she said. "It won't hurt. Much."

I opened my mouth to say I wasn't being a baby and she jabbed my arm with two exposed wires. I felt the bite as the current raced through me. It wasn't as bad as the time I accidentally shocked myself with the loose plug on an old lamp, but it wasn't pleasant, either.

Something gushed out of the center of my forehead and splashed over Amy. I couldn't tell what it was as it came out, but when I shifted my focus to her, I saw her standing there, covered in some kind of goo. It was nearly black and fat droplets fell off the layer of the stuff that coated her. She sputtered and spit some out of her mouth.

"Are you okay?" I asked. "Are you hurt?"

She wiped her mouth with her hand, which was also covered in the goo. She tried to scoop it out of her eyes, but didn't have much luck. It was too thick and seemed to resist being cleaned. "I'm not hurt."

I burst out laughing. I didn't have a drop of the stuff on myself. It was all on her. In fact, other than the drops that fell on the floor, it had not gotten on anything else in the garage. Just her.

"It's not funny," she growled.

"Yes, oh yes, it is," I answered. "You were so keen on shocking me. I guess neither of us thought maybe you could have been injured. I don't know if my self-defense powers know you're my friend. It was really pretty stupid to put yourself at risk like that. The least I can do is laugh at you."

"Whatever." She walked over to a cabinet that had the towels her dad used when he washed the cars and started to wipe the goo away. It was resistant, seeming to want to stick to her.

"It seems to like you," I said, chuckling still. "It wants to hug you. That's sweet."

She threw the towel at me. I snatched it out of the air without getting a drop of the goo on myself. "Turn around," she said.

"What?" I said. "Why?"

"Because I need to change out of these clothes, and I don't want you staring at me when I do it."

"Whoa, wait a minute. You're not going to change here, even if my back is turned. What happens if someone walks in? How are we going to explain that? Besides, it will make me uncomfortable."

That level look came back. Somehow she pulled it off, even covered in black goo. "I'll lock the door. I can't go back in the house like this to change. I'll get caught for sure. It has to be here. And don't even think you're going to go outside and wait. With my luck, my parents will see you hanging around outside and wonder what's going on. Stop being a whiny little baby and turn around."

I tried to come up with an argument, but I couldn't have told someone my name at that point. I blamed it on the fact that a girl was getting ready to strip her clothes off a few feet away from me, whether I was facing her or not. I was too nervous. I turned my back to her and stared at the wall of the garage.

Fabric rustled behind me, and the room grew hotter. I actually started to sweat, a small trickle of perspiration sliding down the side of my face and my neck. I closed my eyes, but the sounds of what she was doing—she was actually taking her clothes off!—made me open them again to distract myself.

"Relax, Daniel," she said. "I'll be done in a minute." Her speech was muffled. It could only be because she had been pulling her top over her head at that moment. I took a deep breath and thought of how stupid it was that I could face down armed men but lost my mind because my best friend was changing her clothes behind me.

"Almost done," she said, as if giving me progress reports would make me feel better.

I tried to occupy myself by looking around the part of the garage in front of me. There was a cabinet there, no doubt with Amy's dad's tools and such. The little refrigerator with the bottles of water we always drank when spending time here was off to the left. Three bikes hung almost directly in front of me, dangling from rubberized hooks screwed into the ceiling.

As I swung my head to the right, I saw a flash of movement. When I looked more carefully, I caught sight of an old mirror, the one we had used so I could see my new costume when Amy had given it to me. In the mirror, Amy, wearing only her bra and panties, stepped into another pair of baggy jeans. My blood froze in my veins. Still, I couldn't quite force myself to take my eyes away.

My breath caught, and I made a small gasping sound. She had an athlete's body. I mean, I had seen some of the girls at school flaunting their bodies when we had swimming in P.E., but none of them compared. How did she hide the fact that she was so fit underneath all those baggy clothes? *Why* did she hide it underneath those baggy clothes?

I stared for a moment longer, burning the picture of her into my mind, and then I looked away. She hadn't seen me looking at her in the mirror. I closed my eyes, but all I saw was the memory of her. Instead, I opened my eyes, looked at the ceiling, and started to count the spokes on one of the bikes in front of me.

"Okay, you can turn around now," she said cheerfully.

I did but couldn't meet her eyes. She took it to mean that I was still embarrassed. That mischievous smile crept across her face.

"Thank you for not peeking. Kestrels have been known to kill things for peeking. You know, things like Angels and such."

"I...wouldn't want to upset you like that," I stammered. "I wouldn't want to see your awesome body and fall in love with you or anything." I hoped it sounded like I was joking.

She didn't miss a beat. "True. I'd never be able to get rid of you then." She laughed, which loosened up the nerves in me just a little bit.

"Hey," I said, "I have to go. Thanks for helping me, for... umm...shocking me with live electrical current."

"No problem. Any time you want to experience my electric personality, come see me. No charge." She winked. I suddenly didn't know what to do with my hands.

"I will. Well, goodnight. I'll talk to you tomorrow, okay?"

"You bet." She came toward me to hug me, something we did more often than not when we said goodbye, but I turned to the door and left before she could actually grab hold of me. I practically ran from the garage into the night. The disappointed look on her face drove a spike into my heart, but I couldn't let her hug me. She would have felt me trembling and would have asked what the problem was. Much better that I escape quickly.

I went over it in my mind as I headed home. I really liked Amy. In fact, I felt closer and closer to her as time went on. I had little dreams and fantasies of being with her, being her boyfriend. Because of my anti-social nerdy life, I didn't even know how that stuff worked. Still, I had thought maybe we could figure it out. I even thought occasionally that maybe she liked me, too, but wasn't sure how to tell me.

In that moment, though, I could see that wasn't going to happen. I already thought she was beautiful, with her oversized glasses, messy hair, and her clothes that looked like they had belonged to her older brother. I still figured maybe I had a chance because, for some reason, others didn't see her like that. They only saw a social outcast, a strange girl. But with a body like that, guys at school would be climbing over each other to get to her. She was way out of my league.

I stopped at a park on the way home and sat down on one of the benches. I was starting to feel happy, finding my place in the world. I had a friend that meant more than anything to me, and I had thought we were developing a relationship beyond just being friends. Why would the universe dangle something in front of me and then yank it back out of the way when I tried to grab it?

My shoulders slumped, and I sighed. I guess I'd just have to accept things the way they were. I still had her as a friend, even if she was out of reach as a girlfriend. I didn't know how I'd feel when she got a boyfriend, though. How would that affect our relationship? What would it mean to the superhero team of Angel and Kestrel? Would she tell my secret to her guy?

I stopped myself from going any further. I'd drive myself crazy like that. I would have to talk to her and make sure she would never reveal my secret to anyone. I could trust her. She was my best friend. That hadn't changed. I lumbered to my feet and slogged the rest of the way home.

16

"Police are reporting that there is a new crime boss in Sueño, responsible for much of the increasing local crime, one who has been consolidating many smaller criminal groups and gangs," the news announcer's voice said from the television speaker. "He apparently has some sort of enhanced abilities, though details are not available at this time."

I watched the news report with interest. Unless I missed the point completely, the newscaster had just stated that there was a supervillain in the city. That would explain why, despite my best efforts, crime increased.

My phone rang. It was Amy. I seriously considered not answering it, but my conscience would have pummeled me all day if I hadn't. It had only been a half a day since I fled her garage, but we rarely went that long without talking or texting.

"Hey, Amy," I said, trying to muster a cheerful tone but only accomplishing something neutral. She picked up on it, if the pause was any indication.

"Daniel." She didn't say "good morning." She always said

that to me when we talked for the first time in a day. It felt like there was a lump of clay sitting in my stomach. "Are you watching the news?"

"Yeah, I just saw it. The part about the supervillain?"

"Yes. We should probably talk about this. What are your plans for today?"

My mind raced. How could I avoid her? It was too soon after what had happened last night. I still hadn't figured things out, and I would be uncomfortable. "I... uh...there's—"

"Are you trying to avoid me?" she asked. "What's going on? You need to talk to me, Daniel. Either on the phone or in person. Don't think you can dodge me. If I have to go to your house and drag you out of your room, I'll do it. Now, are you going to come talk to me or not?"

I was trapped. I couldn't hurt her feelings because I felt self-conscious. Best friend, remember? I had to talk to her. "I can go over there."

"Okay, good. Come over in an hour or two. We need to figure out what to do about this villain." She paused. "And Daniel?"

"Yeah, I'm still here."

"You know you can talk to me about anything, right? We're best friends, aren't we?"

I smiled a sad smile. "Yes, Amy. We are."

"Good." There was a short silence and then she sighed. "Good. I'll see you in a little while. We'll talk."

"Sounds good," I said, lying as if my heart was at stake. It was. "See you soon."

Why did time go so much more slowly when you had to do something you didn't want to do? I think Albert Einstein explained it in one of his theories, but I don't understand it. The hour and a half I waited until I left my house to walk over to Amy's was the longest day I had ever spent. I took a shower, ate some breakfast, paced in my room, and still had plenty of time to sit and do nothing. I wondered if my clock had run out of power or something.

Finally, I headed out, walking at a normal pace. The sun was shining, the temperature was perfect, and the birds seemed extra loud. Summer break had just started, and it felt like the world was trying to put me in a good mood. It failed.

I didn't know what I would do if Amy asked me what was wrong, if she used those special powers she had to look into my gut and see what was actually going on with me. My palms sweated, and my feet felt like they weighed a thousand pounds each. Actually, with my powers—make that ten thousand pounds each.

But still I trudged on. I would face this like a hero, even if I felt like a small child.

Amy was sitting out in front of the garage when I came up. She smiled at me, and I felt a pang of sadness rip through me. I smiled back, or at least tried. Hers slipped a little at that, but she recovered well.

"Hey there!" she said with a cheeriness that seemed forced after the concern.

"Hi." I tried to sound cheerful, too, but couldn't quite manage it. All I could think of was who she would pick as her boyfriend once people started realizing how awesome she was.

"So, we need to talk." She grabbed my hand and hauled me toward the garage.

I resisted for a moment, until I saw the stricken look on her face. I tried to play it off like I was stumbling, and when I regained my balance, I followed her willingly. The look she had disappeared. Mostly.

Once inside, she grabbed a couple of bottles of water from the refrigerator and tossed me one. As I reached out to catch it, I caught a glimpse of the mirror and almost dropped it, juggling it from hand to hand to keep it from falling. I sat down and fiddled with the bottle's top.

"So," she said, sitting down next to me, her leg brushing mine. "I looked up all the reports I could find on this new criminal mastermind." She paused, her eyes narrowing as she looked into mine. "Daniel, are you okay?"

"I...uh...sure. Why?"

"You just seem a little off. Is something bothering you? Are you sick or something?"

That was it. That was the excuse I was looking for. "I'm not feeling all that well. Maybe I am getting sick. You should probably not get too close so you don't catch it."

She eyed me suspiciously. "Okay, no problem." She moved a little farther away. I could still feel the warmth on the spot where our legs had touched. It was all I could do not to sigh.

"Anyway," she said, "there's not much information yet. Apparently, he calls himself The Crusher. No one knows where he came from. For all we know, he may have always lived here and started developing powers like you did. He's young, maybe in his early or mid-twenties. Still, he seems to be gathering a lot of the smaller gangs and groups of criminals beneath himself. I think he's going to be a big threat."

I took a drink of water. "But what am I supposed to do about him? I have my hands full just trying to find petty criminals and stop them. I can't go attacking a guy who not only has superpowers but probably has guards around him all the time."

"Well, I've been thinking about that," Amy said, leaning

toward me and putting her elbows on her knees. I had the urge to back away because the closer she came, the less I was able to think, but if I did, she would want an explanation. "I think we should start planning our attacks better."

"Planning our...we? What do you mean?"

"Up until now, you've just been trying to chance upon crimes as they happen. That has worked, a little. You have found people doing bad, and you stopped them. I think we've reached the point, though, where we need to actually strike at known criminals before they commit crimes."

"Wait." I was confused. "If they haven't committed a crime, I can't go and just beat them up and tie them down for the police to take them. There would be nothing for them to be arrested over."

"True, but I'm not talking about arresting them for small crimes. I'm talking about systematically targeting and taking down criminals that the police already know are bad guys. You know, ones they're looking for but haven't been able to get. Or ones who they know are doing things that they can't find the evidence for."

"And just how do you suggest we do this? I know you have thought about it. You and your Kestrel superpowers have already planned the next fifteen steps." She smiled at that, and before I could think, I smiled back. A kind of warm, squishy feeling spread in my chest. I shook my head to clear my thoughts.

"I have," she said. "We can start with the public service announcements the police put on their website and through Nixle. There are people who they are looking for, some with rewards for information leading to their arrest. If you can catch them in the act, or just find out where they are, we can move down the list and eliminate some of the really bad players in the city."

"Hmm." I had to hand it to her; she had thought this out. "That may work. I suppose you already have a few in mind for me to go after?"

That beaming smile lit up the garage again. "As a matter of fact, yes, I do. We can gradually work up to Crusher this way. Would you like to hear about it?"

I tilted my head sideways and squinted at her. Despite the underlying sadness I had about inevitably losing her to some jock, I felt happy just to be working with her, just to be here talking with her. "You know, you are amazing. I could never have done anything without you, Kestrel. Yes, tell me about it. I'm all ears." The excitement on her face was contagious, and it made my heart race.

"Okay, the first thing we need to do is…"

17

Following Amy's plan, I began to search out individual criminals. It turned out to be easier than I expected. The first one I took down was Adrian Webster, also known as the Fifth Street Clown. Honest. Of all the gang names to have, why would Adrian—what is a guy named Adrian doing being a criminal anyway?—choose that name?

Amy had given me the address of the place I needed to go. Apparently, Adrian ran a small-time car theft ring, centered in an auto body shop owned by his cousin. My simple task was to go in, find stolen cars, and leave the evidence and the Clown himself for the police.

I curled myself up in my cape and waited in the shadows outside the shop. Within an hour, three men came out, getting into a car. They carried small duffel bags they hefted as if they were heavy. I figured they had tools in them. A prepared criminal was a successful criminal, I supposed.

I didn't have any trouble following the car. With my super-speed, I tracked them easily for the five miles until they pulled up to a street consisting of a few bars and clubs, a gas station, and a convenience store. Two of the men got out and split up. I watched both of them from the roof of the building where I had perched. I didn't have to wait long.

Both of the men selected cars in dimly lit parking lots along the street. It didn't take them long to break into the cars and disable the alarms. They were very good. Once each had started the cars and driven away, I rushed back to the shop.

Taking shortcuts over roofs and through alleys, I actually got back to the auto body shop before they did and waited in the shadows as they pulled both cars in through the large door. No sooner had one of the men looked up and down the street and closed the door than I heard the whine of pneumatic wrenches loosening the tires. The clatter of other tools sounded dully through the building's walls. Time to get to work.

I made my way to the roof and then down through one of the windows at the top of the building. I slipped in and watched them from the ceiling beams for a few minutes. There were the three I had already seen and another man who had come out of the small office. He had two teardrops tattooed on the left side of his face and a clown tattooed on his neck. It wasn't too much of a stretch to think that was Adrian.

I had to do something. Grabbing hold of the beam I had been sitting on, I lowered myself so I hung about fifteen feet from the ground and dropped. My super-strong legs absorbed the shock, and I landed quietly. At least, I didn't make any sound that could be heard above the sounds of the men working.

I pulled the first car thief off his feet before he even saw me. I had his hands behind his back and zip-tied before he could react. I dragged him to a utility closet, threw him in, and closed the door. One down.

The other three had noticed me by that time. One of them grabbed a tire iron as the other one grabbed a pole with a heavy magnet head on it. The Clown reached behind his back and pulled out a gun.

The gun was the top priority. With a burst of speed, I closed the twenty feet to the man. A bullet came out of the barrel just as I reached the hand holding the gun and moved it to the side. I saw out of the corner of my eye that the projectile struck the wall to the office. A sharp twist of my wrist and the gun came out of the Clown's hand and into mine. I'm pretty sure his trigger finger broke as it got caught in the guard. An open-handed slap to his face and the ringleader slammed into the wall behind him and slid down.

My self-defense mechanism activated, and I ducked without thinking, narrowly avoiding the magnet pole. I threw my leg out and casually kicked the wielder, sending him rocketing off to stop abruptly when he hit the car he had been working on. That was three. Only one left.

The thief with the tire iron was only a half step away from the thug I had just dispatched. He swung the long metal bar like he wanted to crush my skull. I didn't do anything fancy. I merely put my arm up to block it. His eyes lit up when he realized that the iron would strike my arm, obviously figuring that the bone would break. When it struck me and bent partway around my arm, the vibration was so severe that he yelped and lost hold of his weapon. I pushed him hard with the hand I had just blocked with, and he flew through the air to collide with another car.

It was a simple matter to tie the others up. I zip-tied their hands and feet and used a pneumatic hose to tie them to each other, back-to-back. That would hold them for a little while. I used the phone in the office to call the police, told them they would be interested in the cars and the four thieves themselves, opened the large door, and left.

And just like that, I had bagged my first minor crime boss.

Amy was all smiles when I met her in our garage hideout that night. I congratulated her on her plan, and she congratulated me on my successful capture of the criminals.

"You know," she said, "people are starting to take notice of what you're doing. I hear some of the kids talk about you, wondering who you are and what your powers are. If you're not careful, you'll have a fan club before too long."

"Yeah, right," I said. "I'll be a real celebrity."

"I'm serious, Daniel. What you're doing is making a difference, and people are taking note. It's a good thing. All that stuff about having fans aside, it calls attention to the fact that there is at least one person who is trying to do the right thing, trying to help others. Maybe it will make them want to help, too."

I thought about that for a moment. Maybe she was right. If others followed my example—not in going out and actually fighting crime, but in helping others—it could make a big difference. I hoped it did, anyway.

I continued, with Amy's help, to search out some of the other minor crime bosses and deliver them to the police. Things seemed to be going well, which concerned me. It felt like something bad would happen soon. I wasn't disappointed.

18

I n one of our normal pre-patrol meetings, Amy presented me with the news. She had found our next target.

"Forget about regular patrol tonight," she said. "You have to work on this one. He just hit the police department website's top ten criminals." She handed me what looked like a wanted poster.

I looked at the mug shot of the man on the poster. He had a shaved head, tattoos everywhere, and a frightening, thousand-yard stare. The ink covered his head, parts of his face, and his neck. Any skin that peeked out of his clothing had tattoos. He looked like a rough one.

"Angel Gonzalez," Amy said. "He's the leader of a small but vicious gang called the Demons. I guess he thought the irony was funny. They're involved in a lot of stuff, but mostly guns and drugs. He's wanted for murdering two people, but the police haven't been able to get him yet. They think they know where he's at, but his headquarters is fortified so well that they will need SWAT and some help from other agencies. If you get him first, though..."

"This guy looks really tough," I said, handing the paper back to her. "If the police haven't been able to crack into his hideout, it sounds like it's probably beyond me. I'll need to work up to it."

"I think you can handle it. The police have to get warrants and all that stuff. You can just break in, take him down, and be done with it."

I looked at her incredulously. "Amy, we're talking about breaking into a heavily fortified building filled with gun runners. I'm not bullet proof."

"Not that you know of," she said. "With your powers, you could prevent a loss of life. If SWAT goes in, people are going to die. Maybe innocent people, maybe cops."

"I don't know," I said. "This is a big jump from what I've been doing. It sounds pretty dangerous. Pretty risky."

"I saw a posting on a discussion board that one of Angel's henchmen was bragging how he beat up some old lady who tried to talk back to him as he was robbing her."

I stared at her. "Are you just making that up to force me to do this? If you are, that's not very funny and not very nice."

"Nope, I'm serious. I don't know if it was Mrs. Sanderson, but it very well could have been. I've been trying to find information about who attacked her. This sounds as likely as any other information I got."

Mrs. Sanderson was doing better. At least, she was conscious. I went and visited her a couple of times. She didn't remember much about her attackers, just that one of them had a dragon and flames tattooed on his neck. Thinking of taking vengeance on whoever hurt her was not the right thing to do, but I was still angry that she had been assaulted.

I looked carefully into Amy's eyes. She wouldn't lie to

me, but everything fit much too conveniently in support of her argument. She gazed back at me as if she didn't have anything to hide.

"Fine," I said. "I have to tackle bigger fish eventually, so it might as well be now. What's your plan? I know you have one."

Less than a week later, after scouting for several nights to get the information I needed, I was outside a normal looking house, albeit a large one. It was in a typical middle-class area, mostly cookie-cutter tract houses with a few custom homes sprinkled in. It had a fair-sized yard for the area, probably just less than half an acre. It was fenced all the way around. I picked out cameras set at strategic locations all around the fence line. I wondered if they were monitored or if they were just recording.

Angel's car had rolled through the gate an hour before, so I was fairly sure the criminal was home. I only saw one person in the hour I watched the house, a man who came outside to smoke. There was no way to know how many others were actually in the building. I didn't like all the unknowns. Not for the first time, I wondered what I was doing there, why I thought I could handle this. I was just a kid. I could die that night.

Before I lost my nerve, I forced myself into motion. I had already picked out an area that was darker than the others. I chose that location to go over the eight-foot fence surrounding the property. Pulling my cloak around me, I jumped up and over the obstruction into the yard. Jumping straight up more than eight feet was easy for me with my enhanced strength.

As I landed, I rolled—I'd been practicing that particular maneuver—coming back up to my feet and continuing to a patch of shadow near the corner of the house. Even if the cameras were being monitored, it would have been difficult to spot me, I thought.

I clung to the darkness and slunk around the house to the back door. Light spilled out from the windows, but I didn't see any people. Slipping up to where the camera covering the back door was mounted, I jumped up to the eave and tore it down in one smooth motion. Anyone monitoring the cameras would see it go dead, but it was the best I could do.

The back door was unlocked, for a wonder. I would have bet that wasn't supposed to be the case, but good help was so hard to find. I smiled at my own joke. Angel Gonzalez would not be happy with whoever had left it unlocked like that. I opened it silently and entered the house. It was time to take care of business.

The door led into the kitchen, where I found the same man who had come out to smoke earlier. A burst of speed and I had him in a chokehold, trying to regulate the pressure so I didn't crush his neck and his head. His feet drummed on the floor and his hands scrabbled at my arm, but he may as well have been a child for all the good it did against my strength. I held onto him for a fast five-count after he stopped moving to make sure he wasn't trying to fake being unconscious, and then I lowered him to the ground. I gagged him with a dish towel lying on the counter and some thin rope I brought out of one of the pouches in my suit. I zip-tied his hands behind him and moved on.

As I tried to look around the doorframe bordering the kitchen and other parts of the house, I heard muttering about cameras breaking down. I pulled back, kneeling low and waiting.

It was a surprise to the man when he came through the door and saw me an instant before I clocked him on the side of his head with enough force to knock him out, but hopefully not enough to do serious damage. It was a tricky thing trying to render someone unconscious without breaking their head. I think I had gotten fairly good at it, but it always made me nervous. I didn't want anyone to die.

I secured the second man like I had the first. I had to search for another dish towel to gag that man, too. I didn't want him waking up and sounding an alarm. That task done, I scanned the dining room and, seeing no one about, went through it to another part of the house. My goal was to find Angel himself, though it was a crapshoot as to where he would be.

Luckily, the house was all one level so I could work my way through it methodically and try to find the criminal. I wasn't great at moving silently, so a two-story would have been tough once I got to the second floor. Even on the single floor, I winced as I tried to make my way around without making too much noise.

I guess I shouldn't have bothered, though. As I approached the family room, I heard several voices, plus loud explosions and gunfire. I peeked around the corner of a hallway and saw three men in the room, two of them with game controllers in their hands, the third sitting nearby. All of them were intent on the big screen TV as they played some kind of first-person shooter game. The speakers were so loud I could probably have spoken in a normal voice and walked into the room, and they wouldn't have heard me.

I could leave them there, hoping they'd continue to play their game and not notice anything else, but I doubted that would work. They would probably come up on me from behind as I moved through the house. I didn't want to be surprised like that. I needed to make sure they were safely out of the way.

I walked slowly and carefully toward the men. They were all on one couch, all facing the same way, so if I came at them from directly behind, they shouldn't see me in their peripheral vision. I was two steps from them before the one not playing the game looked over his shoulder and saw me. His eyes went wide, and he reached down on the couch next to him. When his hand started coming up again, it was wrapped around a gun.

I lunged, grabbing the gun hand and squeezing. Bones cracked in my grip, and the gun fell back to the couch, bouncing off to rest on the carpet. Before it hit the floor, I had bludgeoned the back of his neck, right where the skull met it, and he sagged as if he was a puppet and his strings had been cut.

The other two started to look around at the motion, and I punched both of them in the back of the head, one with each hand. One of them spilled off the couch to the floor, unconscious, but the other one cursed, rubbed the back of his head, and reached for a gun on the side table. I hit the side of his head with my palm and then he, too, acted as if his energy source was disconnected, knocking the bowl of chips next to the gun off the table onto the floor as he fell.

I spared a moment to make sure they were all breathing and pinched them hard to be sure they were unconscious before I continued on. I wondered how many minions were in the house.

I had checked each of the men I had taken care of so far to see if they had the tattoos that would identify them as Angel. None of them were the crime boss. None of them had the dragon and flames mentioned by Mrs. Sanderson, either.

I methodically went through the house, finding four more of Angel's minions, but not the man himself. I began to second-guess whether I'd seen him coming back home but then remembered the large garage. It looked big enough for ten cars. Maybe it was more than a garage.

I heard people talking as I came upon the door from the house to the garage. I listened at the door for a moment, but couldn't make out anything they said. I would have to go in blind and hope I didn't get myself killed.

I kneeled down and turned the knob, pushing the door open just enough to look inside. There were three men discussing something heatedly.

One of them was Angel.

Another of the men saw the door open out of the corner of his eye. In a blink, he had a gun out and pointed at me. It would only be a second until he actually saw me. Angel stopped talking and looked toward the door as the first man's eyes dropped down to meet mine. A loud bang echoed through the building as I let the door close and saw a hole appear, ejecting splinters out of my side of it.

Great. What was I going to do? There were three of them, with guns. My mind raced. I ran through the hall, took a left into the kitchen—the two I had tied up were still there, one unconscious and the other just coming to, wiggling in his bonds—and sprinted out the door outside.

I headed around the garage, keeping an eye on the window on the opposite side of the building from where the kitchen was. Before I could do anything else, the main garage door started to open. I heard an engine start. Wonderful. He was going to make a run for it. Just perfect.

The two men who were with Angel burst out of the doors on foot, guns in hand. They scanned the area looking for me. A whirring like a dog-sized hummingbird assailed my ears. The main gate to the property started to open. So, that's how it would be, huh? The two would run interference while their boss fled.

It still irritated me that they hadn't chased me through the house. Why would they choose these tactics? Maybe they had recognized me, knew that I had been taking out the lesser criminals in the city. They knew who I was and adjusted their strategy accordingly. A part of my brain thought that was interesting. Criminals never figured that kind of stuff out in the comics. Chalk it up as another lesson in real life.

I had to take out the gunmen. I looked around for some kind of weapon to use. There was a garden hose nearby, but I couldn't figure out how to use that for anything. A planter was a few feet away, roses with bark chips covering the ground at their roots. Another planter, to my right, had some kind of ornamental flowering plants, smooth river stones arranged at their bases. That would have to do.

I slunk to the river stones and gathered up a handful. I couldn't wait long. The front gate was almost open, and I heard the engine being revved up within the garage. If I didn't take out these gunmen soon, I'd lose my chance and Angel would escape.

About twenty feet from me, one of the gun-wielders poked his upper body out of the garage to look around. I put the small pile of stones in my left hand and chose one out with my right. I hefted it. It was about a quarter of the size of my palm and barely weighed anything at all to my super-strength. I knew it had some mass to it, though, even if I couldn't feel it.

Squinting my eyes, I judged the distance, drew my arm back, and tossed more than threw the stone.

The window of one of the cars parked near the man exploded when the rock went through it. The point of impact was a good two feet from my target. I silently cursed my horrible aim.

The second rock was closer, bouncing off the garage wall right next to the gunman. He looked toward me and raised his gun. Just as he did, the third rock struck him below the ear with such force that he slammed against the wall and slid down it. I hoped I hadn't killed him.

It took four more rocks—four!—to finally hit the other gunman, the final one striking him in the forehead before he could figure out where to aim his gun. He dropped, too.

All the rock throwing only took a few seconds, but during those seconds, the gate opened completely and the black SUV shot out of the garage as if it were a bullet from a gun. I saw Angel in the driver's seat through the open window waving his middle finger at me. Rude!

He traveled fast, but not faster than I could run. I thought. I began running after him, chasing him out of the garage and through the gate. Once he hit the street, he started accelerating.

I wasn't sure how fast I could actually run. There was no good way to clock myself without calling attention to a guy running faster than humanly possible, but I was pretty sure that I couldn't run a hundred miles an hour. If I didn't catch him in the next few seconds, he'd be gone.

Porch lights winked on all along the street, probably because of the gunshots, and people walked out of their houses. I was concerned that someone might be hurt—high speed chases were notoriously dangerous—but if I could just get to the car before he got too much speed...

As I ran to intercept the car, I saw there was no way I'd catch it. Angel had started accelerating even before finishing the turn from the driveway onto the street. He was only thirty feet or so ahead of me as I went through the gate, but he was pulling away. I was so close, but just a little too late.

A strange feeling shot through my body, not unlike something I had felt before, but not exactly the same either. It felt like a bottle brush made of fine glass fibers was being pulled through all my nerves at the same time. The feeling had in common the invasive energy tingle I felt when one of my strange random powers took hold, but each random power seemed to have its own unique *taste* of the same feeling. I didn't recognize it as anything that had manifested before, not exactly, and I wondered if it would help me or hurt me in this situation.

I didn't have much choice, though. I could run my hardest and watch the car speed away from me, or I could try to use whatever ability was quickening within me and hope it was something that helped or at least didn't make things worse by affecting all the bystanders that gathered to see what the commotion was. With a mental shrug, I let my body do what it wanted and allowed the power to take control.

My arms came up in front of me as I took a few more steps and then stopped running. I was already several houses away from Angel's, in the middle of the suburban street. I planted my legs—though I'm not sure if I did that on purpose or if my body did it without my participation—as if to brace myself.

It was a good thing, because I felt like someone had both my arms and was pulling me inexorably toward him. I braced harder, planting my boots against the edge of the sidewalk and flexing my legs. Some kind of force pulsed from my hands. I couldn't see it, but I sure felt it.

It took a moment to realize that Angel's SUV was slowing. Then it stopped. To my surprise, the stress on my legs lessened when it halted its motion. I was even more surprised when I felt—not saw, but felt—it coming back toward me. It was like I could sense the distance shrinking in that strange force coming from my hands. As the vehicle passed a manhole in the street, the heavy lid wobbled as if it, too, wanted to come to me, but it settled back down after the vehicle passed. Ahh, magnetism.

I pulled the vehicle back toward me, despite the tires spinning and filling the air with the acrid smell of burning rubber. There was hope after all. I hunkered down and pulled harder, somehow using my newest power, though not exactly sure how I did so.

By the time the SUV had come back to within ten feet of me, the tires stopped spinning and the door opened up. Angel had apparently figured out that he wasn't going anywhere, so I figured he would either give up or try to kill me.

The barrel of an assault rifle poked out of the door. It was aimed right at me. Okay, he wouldn't be giving up.

I jerked my arms back, allowing my magnetic power to shake the vehicle violently. I saw the gun wobble, sending a few random shots up and away from where Angel had been aiming. I hoped those projectiles had not struck any of the people milling about.

I had to end it soon or someone could be shot and killed. Maybe even me. Especially me.

I shifted my body weight forward and sprang toward the SUV. Landing right in front of the open door, I grabbed the gun barrel, hardly registering that it was hot—my extra tough skin apparently kept me from getting burned—and yanked the weapon out of Angel's hands. Grabbing an arm, I pulled on that also, throwing him from the car. He did not land gracefully.

The minor crime boss landed hard on his shoulder and slid five feet on the asphalt. I spared a moment to look inside the vehicle, confirmed there were no passengers to waylay me, and then swung my head around to face Angel.

He grunted as he tried to get to his feet, pulling another gun from his waistband as he did so. He had it up and aimed at me faster than I would have thought possible in his condition.

I was only ten or fifteen feet from him. His hand tensed and his finger squeezed the trigger. I wasn't sure I would survive the night. I jumped to the side and felt a tug on my costume at my left shoulder. I dodged to the left and saw—actually saw—a bullet pass by and narrowly miss my right side.

Another quick jump, to the left again so I wouldn't be predictable, a roll under a shot aimed directly at my face, and I was in front of the gun. With a speed probably nearly invisible to the onlookers, I snatched the gun from Angel's hand, breaking two or three of his fingers in the process. But he wasn't done.

I hadn't noticed before, but he had pulled a knife from somewhere with his left hand. As I took the gun from him, he plunged the knife toward my belly. Even with my speed, he was too close and the movement too far into its path for me to evade it. With no other alternative, I threw my forearm into the path of the weapon. I felt a sensation on my arm not unlike someone using a backscratcher with too much force.

I growled under my breath and gritted my teeth. I'd had about enough of this. I simultaneously raised my injured forearm under his elbow and slammed down on his wrist with the hand holding the gun. With minimal effort on my part, the arm made a loud crack, like the sound of splintering wood, and the limb contorted into a position nature never intended. A light front kick to the chest knocked Angel back several feet, and he landed hard in a heap, unable to lift himself up with his damaged extremities.

I looked around again for other enemies and then walked calmly to the crime boss. I didn't really see a need to zip-tie his damaged arm and hand, so I tied his legs instead.

"You," I said to a man standing ten feet away, his mouth still open in astonishment, "call 911 and tell them there is a mess to clean up here. Make sure there's an ambulance. He nodded dumbly and took out his phone to make the call.

"Was anyone hit by those bullets?" I asked to no one in particular. No less than fifteen people had gathered around us, neighbors who had come out when they first heard the gunshots and the car screeching a few minutes before.

"Yes," a man's voice said. My stomach dropped to my feet.

"I was hit...in the calf," he continued. I noticed as he spoke again that there was a strain in his voice. I walked over to where he sat. In the dim light, it was hard to tell, but he seemed to be pale.

I pulled up his pant leg and looked at the injury. It was bleeding, but the bullet seemed to have passed right through the muscle. I tore a section from my cape and wrapped it around as a makeshift bandage, just to slow the bleeding.

"An ambulance should be here soon. Keep pressure on it, here." I showed him where to hold.

No one else was injured, so I took some of the precious time remaining to look through the SUV. On the floorboards in the front passenger seat, there was a duffel bag with some packages that looked like the drugs I'd seen in news reports, a few more handguns, and some cash. A lot of cash. I zipped the bag up and left it where it was.

I looked around and chose a man and a woman. I asked their names.

"Sally Sorenson," the woman said, just before the man said, "Frank Dyson."

"Sally, Frank, I need you to make sure no one goes near this vehicle until the police get here." I could hear sirens getting closer as I spoke. The two nodded and planted their feet as if to guard the SUV.

"Thank you," I said as I turned to leave.

A voice from the crowd sounded out. "Who are you?" the man asked.

"You can call me The Angel," I said, and ran in the opposite way from where the sirens and lights were coming down the street. The police didn't see me, probably a mixture of my black costume and the distraction of all the people gathered around.

I figured my next stop needed to be Amy's house. I might have been injured, and I would have needed a costume repair. Not for the first time, I wondered why I never read about superheroes having these kinds of problems. How many costumes did the average superhero have so that there were enough spares?

19

"Well, you're famous," Amy said to me the next day in her garage. She and I had spent two hours going over what had happened the night before, every little action and nuance, especially regarding my new power, which of course faded away within minutes of helping me stop the car.

"Famous?" I yawned until my jaw cracked. I'd been too amped up from my adventure to sleep much the night before. And a little stressed out. It had been the first time there were bystanders while I was wearing my costume. "What, did someone in the crowd of neighbors start gossiping about what they saw last night?"

"Oh, it's much worse than that."

Uh-oh. "What do you mean, worse?"

Amy swung her laptop around so I could see it. She clicked and I watched in horror as I ran down an SUV, pulled it back toward me, dodged more quickly than bullets could find me, and then proceeded to calmly—that's what it looked like anyway—smack the stuffing out of a hardened criminal with a gun and a knife. Then I commanded people in the crowd to do things like I was some kind of army general. And they did them! It showed me using my paltry first aid skills, too. The video ended right after the onscreen me said, "You can call me the Angel" and flashing lights filled the screen. The title of the video was "Angel Vs. Angel." Cute.

"Oh," was all I could get out.

"Did you notice the view count?" Amy pointed to the screen. Over three hundred thousand views in less than a half a day. I slumped in my chair.

After a moment, I ran my fingers through my hair and spoke. "So, what does that mean?"

"It means it was viewed over three hundred thousand times," Amy deadpanned.

I frowned at her. "I know that. I mean, what does it mean that there's a video up on the internet and more people than I'll ever meet in my lifetime have watched it?"

"It means you're famous. It means you're not going to be able to keep your activities quiet anymore. It means there will probably be criminals targeting you now."

I fidgeted in my chair. This might be a good thing or a bad one. Well, being targeted by criminals was bad. But the other stuff? I wasn't sure.

"There's more," Amy said. "Social media is lighting up with comments about you. People are talking about making a fan club for you. Locals, and people all over the world."

"That's insane," I said. "They see me one time in a video, and they want to make a fan club? They're just talking. No one is going to make a fan club for me."

"Wanna bet?"

"Yeah. I don't have much, but I'll bet you five bucks there's no fan club."

"You're on," she said, reaching her hand out to shake mine. We'll give it a week and see. Does that sound fair?"

"You can have two weeks. It's not gonna happen."

The light in her eyes told me she wanted to laugh out loud instead of the muffled chuckle she actually made. "Okay, two weeks from today. If there is a fan page or group for the Angel, you pay up. If not, then my whole view of the world and of social media is wrong, and I'll pay you."

Less than a week later, I handed Amy five dollars. "People are crazy," I said.

"People are people," she responded, stuffing the money into her pocket. "They're not happy with their lives so they want to hear about other peoples' lives. Other people are glamorous and mysterious, powerful or beautiful, different."

"I never understood people obsessing over celebrities. I think the world started to end when reality shows became popular."

"Here," Amy said, pulling her laptop out, "let me show you something."

She clicked on the keys, moved the pointer around for a minute, and then swiveled the screen toward me. "What do you think of this?"

It was a website, splashed with color and links, a blog scrolling down the left side and video panes on the right side. The color offset the dark and grainy pictures, and images scattered across the screen. It wasn't well designed. My jaw dropped when I read the larger text in some fancy cursive-type font at the top. AngelIsHot.com was displayed proudly across the top of the site.

"You've got to be kidding me," I said.

"Nope."

"These people are insane," I whined.

"Look at the blog, at the comments." Amy could hardly keep from giggling.

I read some of them. There were a few guys who braved crushing their stereotypes to comment, but the vast majority was from girls. Declarations of undying love, proposals of marriage from older women, and requests to go to this prom or that dance from the younger. The world had gone completely mad.

"There's another one, for the guys. It's called TheAngelIsABadass.com. Do you want to see that one?"

"No," I said. "I've seen enough. Okay, Amy, I'll ask you this again. What does this mean? How is it going to affect things?"

Amy closed the lid on her laptop. "I really don't know, Daniel. I guess we'll have to wait and see. It could be good that the community is behind you, but extra notoriety may also mean someone trying to make a name for themselves will try to take you down. I just don't know."

As it turned out, one of the two thugs I took out with the stones had a dragon tattoo on his neck. Mrs. Sanderson confirmed that he was the guy who attacked her. That was good, since most of Angel's minions that I had left for the police were released right away. At least, the ones who didn't have drugs in their pockets were released. With no crime to tie to them and no victim, the police simply couldn't hold them. That was fine with me, though. Angel was the one I was after, and the guns, drugs, and money were enough to keep him behind bars for a while, not to mention shooting an assault rifle and injuring a bystander.

I kept up my patrols, still trying to target the minor crime bosses that Amy sent me after, but I constantly looked over my shoulder, both for criminals trying to kill me and my increasingly vocal fans. Every time I stopped a crime or took down another small organization, the numbers of people following a blog or joining a social media group grew, and the louder they became.

I began to dread the crimes I stopped that involved other people, such as muggings or other assaults. Three times after I had dispatched the bad guys, the victim pulled out something for me to autograph. I always declined in case someone could use my writing to figure out my identity. Amy nodded and told me she was proud of me for realizing that. I just thought I was using common sense, the only time I had seen that applied in weeks. I was sure something in the city water supply was making everyone crazy.

The worst part was when the t-shirts and other paraphernalia started to appear. I saw a woman—she was probably twenty years old and looked like a super model—wearing a very tight t-shirt with a picture of me on it and the caption "He can take me to heaven any time." I tripped and almost fell on my face as I was walking. Amy, right next to me, grabbed my arm to steady me. Her mouth was a thin, tight line. No one else much noticed my gaffe, though, because every guy within sight was staring at the t-shirt. Well, staring at the girl wearing the shirt.

That occurrence made me think about the problem I had been worrying over a few weeks before, the problem that Amy was out of my league. All the commotion with the video and the fan club and the merchandising on top of it had distracted me so that I was just running on auto-pilot.

It all came crashing home when I saw that look on her face and when she started to draw away from me and become more aloof in the days after. With zero experience, I was usually pretty bad about detecting these kinds of things, but even I noticed.

"The fan club," I told her one day as we went over

information from my patrol the night before, "it's for someone nobody knows. It's not for me."

Amy's head jerked up. "What do you mean?"

"People are crazy, as we've talked about. All these people, these fans, especially the girls—"

"Groupies."

"Yeah," I continued. "Groupies. They're all chasing after something they don't know anything about, just because it's mysterious. They don't know me. They don't like me."

"Okay," she said, her expression becoming as close to neutral as it had all morning, an improvement over the tight expression that had been on her face before.

"So, I just want to tell you how much I appreciate you, Amy. You're my best friend and my favorite person, and I know that you like me for me, not because I saved you from those boys that time or because I fight crime at night. I want you to know that means a lot to me. It means everything to me. Okay?"

A slow half smile crept onto her face. "Okay." She swept me into a hug, squeezing me hard. "Thank you. I forget, sometimes."

I wasn't sure what she forgot, but I wasn't going to question her. For the first time in weeks, I felt as comfortable with her as I used to, before I saw her undressing.

20

"Do we know anything else about Crusher?" I asked Amy. "I'm nervous about running into him and not knowing what his powers are."

"Nothing else," Amy said. "He keeps to himself, directing his growing crime organization through his underlings, not even usually having contact with the minor crime bosses he's gobbling up to bring into his group. I'm always looking, but there's been nothing so far."

That concerned me. The whole purpose for taking out the lesser criminals was to move my way up to him. As long as he was in the city, things would be bad. I succeeded in stopping the increase in crime, but I hadn't decreased it. For every crime I stopped, there were still a dozen others. It was time I stepped things up.

I felt pretty good about myself, though. I was helping people. I had a large group of adoring fans and a best friend who was smart, competent, and seemed to be getting more beautiful every day. Things seemed to be going my way. Of course, at other times, such as when I was still treated like an outcast by kids I knew from school, things didn't look so rosy, but I couldn't really complain much. The fact that I was still invisible to most girls and beneath contempt for most of the coolest kids kept me grounded. It made me remember that people loved the Angel, not me. That made all the difference.

As the Angel, I was becoming more proficient. I was learning how to use my abilities—the permanent ones— more efficiently, how to deal with different weapon attacks, and how to knock people out without hurting them permanently, something I'd never thought a lot about as I was growing up and watching TV shows and movies. In those, the hero just slammed something hard into the back of someone's head and they went unconscious. It worked every time, no problem. Not so easy in real life. It was actually fairly difficult to knock someone out without doing serious damage, other than a good, old fashioned punch to the jaw. If you struck too hard, you could kill someone, cause permanent brain damage, or give them a concussion. There were times when I had to hit someone three or four times before they went under. Better that than hitting too hard one time, however.

I seemed to be moving more fluidly, too. Amy and I trained at least one day a week so I got some practice in with whatever current method she had concocted, but being out there fighting the criminals was training. You can't fight night after night without getting better. And I did. Get better, that is.

"I think I'm ready to step it up a little," I told Amy. "I want to take down some of the other crime bosses, ones a little bigger than those we've already been targeting."

"Are you sure?" she asked. "The ones higher on the police's wanted list have a lot more guys and better weapons. They're more organized, too."

"I think I'm ready," I said. "I don't think I'm doing enough with the small fry I've been nabbing. I'm not happy with the overall crime rate staying where it is. I want it to decrease. That will never happen if I keep nipping at the heels of Crusher's organization. I need to make them hurt, make them bleed."

Any studied me. "Have you been watching rogue cop movies again?"

My expression was the perfect picture of offended indignation. "No. I just think I'm ready to move up to the big boys." I could tell I hadn't fooled her.

"Okay, if you think you're ready, we can move to the next ones up the list. Tremaine Jackson, aka Big Dog, runs a nice little protection racket over on the west side of town. He extorts money from some of the local businesses there, mom-and-pop shops. It's just like a bad 80's movie. You wanna try him?"

"Sure," I said, "that sounds fun."

She looked at me again with that blank expression. "Daniel, don't get cocky. One bullet can end everything. You have to take this seriously."

"I know," I said. "I was just joking with you. I do take it seriously."

So I headed out the next weekend, armed with the information and plan given to me by Amy, to try to stop Big Dog from squeezing money out of poor small business owners. I couldn't help but to feel like I was stepping into the big leagues. The Big Dog had been known to do horrible things to those who crossed him. He was even more dangerous than Angel and his gun dealers. There were countless movies made about precisely the thing I was doing. I only needed a girl to rescue and an evil villain kingpin to fight after going through his minions, and I'd have a blockbuster movie.

It didn't really turn out that way.

The plan was to hang around some of the businesses his henchmen frequented. They still collected the money the old-fashioned way, going from business to business and demanding cash. It had been going on so long it was almost amiable, unless the Big Dog felt disrespected, but that rarely happened anymore. Three or four guys would walk in, the shop owner would give them cash, and they would leave. No commotion, no violence, no damage to anything.

It was late evening in July, barely dark because of the time of year, when I climbed up on the roof of a building in the heart of the shopping area of this part of the city. Small shops spread out as far as I could see. If I waited long enough, I'd find the Big Dog's puppies.

Soon enough, four rough-looking men strutted through the area, stopping at each shop for a few minutes and then moving on. I hardly thought they were shopping. I watched them for a half an hour, moving to a different roof three times, before they stopped going into shops and headed back the way they had come. They were going to leave.

I was faced with a dilemma. It was still too early, with too many people out and about, to confront them on the street. On the other hand, if they got into their car, I'd never be able to chase them down without attracting even more notice. I wished a lot of things then. I wished I had some cool tracking device. I wished I could fly. I wished there was some way to figure out which car was theirs so I could disable it. What I wouldn't have given for some random power. Something I could use. Like heat vision or something. Thinking of things I didn't have did me no good, though. I had to change my thinking. And fast.

I flashed back to the conversation Amy and I had before I went out looking for the Big Dog's goons.

"Just do it," Amy had said.

"There's no reason. It'll just be a hassle and cause me to have to deal with something I don't need to deal with."

"Daniel," she had said firmly, "Do it. I'm not kidding. You better do it. You'll be sorry if you don't."

"Fine," I grumped. "After tonight is done, I'll be telling you 'I told you so.'"

"Wanna bet?" she said.

"Yeah, I do. Five bucks?" I pulled out my wallet.

"Sure."

So there I was, racking my brain to try to figure out how to deal with the four men possibly getting away from me because I didn't have a vehicle and couldn't use super speed in public.

They were still moving down the street, getting closer to their car, which had to be in one of the parking areas within the next two blocks. I finally had to admit I wasn't able to come up with anything to do. I leaped an alley to another roof and retrieved what Amy had told me to stash there. I pulled my backpack out of a little space between an air conditioning unit and the roof's parapet. Cursing my lack of ideas, I changed into my street clothes. Another five dollars of my hard-earned money would be going to Amy when that night was done.

I wondered if she insisted I bring my street clothes because she thought further ahead and considered all the possibilities, ones I hadn't considered, or if it was just a guess. Smiling a little at my competent friend, and losing the smile when I thought about her being five bucks richer at my expense, I made my way to a drainage pipe to get down to street level.

I caught up to the men by running as fast as a particularly gifted runner my age, or just a little slower. If I ran too fast, I'd draw too much attention. I stayed a half a block behind them and slowed to a normal walk. I wasn't even breathing hard. Super powers were the best.

Another block and a half and they all got into a vehicle. Another black SUV, with a Raiders Nation sticker on it. Yeah, like that was unexpected. As they pulled out on to the street, I started walking more quickly.

For the next several minutes as we went through the city, I played a cat-and-mouse game. I chased them, sometimes running at a speed a normal person could maintain, sometimes just walking quickly or walking at a leisurely pace, all depending upon traffic conditions. Because of all the shops, traffic was heavy, and there were stoplights at every intersection. I didn't have any trouble keeping up with them. My backpack with my costume in it bounced on my back, but I tightened down the waist strap and it remained in place fairly well.

When they got to a less congested area of town, I looked around to see how many people were out and tried to map a path to keep the SUV in sight without them seeing me racing up behind them. My luck was in, though. We didn't have far to go.

Between stoplights and turns, I kept the men in sight until they pulled up into what looked like a small warehouse from the outside, faded red brick with few spots where graffiti had been sprayed over.

After they went inside, I found a dark area in a nearby alley and slipped into my costume. I left the backpack with my street clothes behind a dumpster. Checking to make sure my cowl was secured and that the uniform was all there, I headed into the Big Dog's lair.

The door I tried was unlocked, there were no guards, and none of the four goons there or Big Dog gave me any trouble. I almost felt sorry for them as I tied their unconscious forms up in a nice package for the police. I dragged them outside and piled them atop the duffel bag full of money they had collected. Pinned to Tremaine, the Big Dog himself, was a note we had printed out from Amy's computer earlier: "If you don't have any evidence of the Big Dog's extortion racket, talk to the shops on Fifth Street." That should do it.

To be honest, it was kind of a disappointment. In the comics, there was always a grand battle, some helpless individual to save, some long speech by the villain about his plans or the way society had caused him to be a lawbreaker. I guess sometimes important things happen without a lot of fanfare. Maybe Big Dog should have been lower on the list than Angel, despite his more violent tendencies. They could probably discuss that in jail.

There was a nice item on the news the next day about the Angel cleaning up a protection ring. The fan club went wild.

21

The second of the bigger-fish crime bosses I tried was Eduardo Peña. This guy was a real piece of work.

"He does what?" I asked Amy, incredulous.

"Child labor, teen prostitution, basically anything he can do to exploit children," she answered.

"And he's still walking free why?" I asked. "How come the police haven't hauled him off to jail long ago?"

Amy's lip curled even talking about it. She was as disgusted by it as I was. "They've tried, but they can't seem to tie anything to him. It's another one of those cases where they know he's the leader, but they can't get to him."

"And I'm supposed to? How is that?"

"I have some ideas," she said. She hesitated, biting her lower lip. Then she licked both of them. If she felt uncomfortable about this idea, I was willing to bet I definitely would.

"I'll pretend to be homeless," she finally said. "That's who he preys on mainly. I'll let him capture me and—"

"No!" I said. "Are you out of your mind? This isn't some

movie. You will be helpless. There's no way of telling if I'll be able to track you or get to you before something happens. No. Absolutely not."

"Daniel, he's doing that to all those kids. Someone needs to stop him."

"Not by sacrificing yourself. No, Amy. Not gonna happen. Come up with another brilliant idea. We are not doing this. *You* are not doing this. Promise me."

She glared at me for a moment. "I want to do my part. You always take the risks. It's time I took some, too."

"Amy, you are the heart of what we do. You do much more than me to get these criminals off the street. Sure, I take physical risks, but that's my part of it. I have powers that make the chance much smaller I'll get hurt. Promise me."

Amy crossed her arms in front of her chest. The way it pushed up her baggy sweater distracted me.

"Amy."

"Oh, fine," she hissed. "I promise I won't go out and do anything without discussing it with you."

"Amy."

She sighed. "And getting your agreement. There, are you happy now?"

I smiled at her and went over to hug her. "Yes. Thank you. I don't know what I'd do if you got hurt trying something like that. Thank you."

She hugged me back, somehow managing to be indignant and warm at the same time. When we let go of each other, the room seemed hotter. It was probably just that we were arguing. We sat down and tried to figure out how we could do what the police had not been able to do.

For a week, we racked our brains to come up with a plan to find out where Eduardo Peña had his hideout and base of operations. We came up with some wild ones, but nothing that would in any way work for us. We began to get frustrated.

"Let's target another of the crime bosses on the list and go after Peña when we figure something out or get more information," Amy finally said. "We're just wasting time here. I can't remember anything I've ever dealt with that was this tough to figure out."

"It's probably just because you have a mental block because you're too attached to your other plan." I slouched in my chair and sighed. "I think you're right, though. We need to do something else, come back to this after a short break."

I ONCE SAW a television program about gangs and how they work. It explained that a lot of the taggers aren't just going around and putting graffiti on things to ruin others' property or even to have their street names visible for all to see. A lot of it was gang-related, things like marking territory, challenging other gangs, or indicating that someone was marked to be killed. The show was interesting enough, but seeing it might well have saved my life.

I didn't usually pay attention to graffiti, any more than most people do. I see it, get angry that someone has defaced someone else's property, and don't think any more about it. One night while on a regular patrol, the smell of fresh paint lured me to a wall already thick with spray paint. There, a silver halo was crossed out with a big letter K right next to it. According to that program, it meant I was marked for death. When I realized it, I stood staring at the image in the dim light of the nearby streetlight. Then I looked nervously around to see if anyone was pointing a gun at me.

As I continued with my normal activities for the next

several days, I paid closer attention to graffiti around town. That image wasn't the only one. I counted four more spread throughout the city. There was no doubt. The city's criminals were fed up with my interference. They were going to take things into their own hands and eliminate me. Permanently. It wasn't only one gang's territory, so it appeared they were *ganging* up on me.

I know it sounds weird, but I was honestly confused by my feelings. On the one hand, I should have been scared to death, and I was. I guess. On a more analytical level, a hit out on me might be helpful in cleaning up some of the worst scum in the city, the ones who would stoop to killing for money. The one overriding question, though, was if I should say anything to Amy. I wasn't sure how she'd take it, but I didn't want her to worry.

I was still mulling it over when the first attempt came.

A mugger that had been in the middle of beating an older man, who apparently didn't have as much money in his wallet as the thief wanted, lay at my feet, unconscious. I bent over to offer the victim a hand up when my foot slipped in a puddle in the alley. I caught myself with my hands, ending up in a kind of push-up position.

There was a sharp crack like a large branch breaking and a loud smack of something striking the wall beside me, followed by a pinging ricochet. I dove for cover behind a dumpster. Someone had tried to shoot me. There was a sniper, and the only reason I was still alive was that my foot had slipped. Was it luck or was it my powers trying to protect me?

I'd wonder about that another time. Right then, I was pinned down with a sniper somewhere out there trying to get a bead on me.

I took a deep breath, closed my eyes, and thought. From

the source of the original sound, I estimated where the shooter had to be. He might still have been up there, or he might have fled. I needed to find out. The mugging victim had scrabbled to the edge of the alley and was huddled behind a trashcan. He'd be fine. The sniper wanted me, not him.

With a burst of speed, I charged out from behind my cover and raced down the alley. Another shot sounded. It didn't seem that loud. I wondered if the gunner was so far that the sound was muted or muffled somehow. I didn't know if you could put a silencer on a sniper rifle. I really didn't know anything about guns. I should probably learn. If I survived the night, I had a feeling I'd have an intimate relationship with them from now on. Not from the handle side, sadly.

I zigzagged through the alley, varying my speed so I was more difficult to track. The shots stopped when I turned the corner at the mouth of the alley. That information, too, helped me estimate where the bullets came from.

I sped up the street, feet a blur, until I came to the building I was heading for. I jumped ten feet into the air onto the fire escape. Pulling myself to the platform, I raced up the stairs. Once I got to the top, I jumped straight up and grabbed the edge of the roof parapet.

I pulled myself up until I could just see onto the roof. A man was heading through a door into the building. I only caught a glimpse of his back as he disappeared. He must have heard me going up the fire escape. I mentally kicked myself for rushing rather than climbing silently. Well, no use beating myself up for it; I'd have plenty of time to do that later. I hoped.

I was afraid if I waited for him to come down, I'd lose him, so I had to chase him, even though my common sense didn't agree with running into a dark stairwell after a guy with a gun. Still, I pulled myself up over the parapet and headed through the door.

As I came through the door, I heard frantic footsteps rushing downward. That was good, at least. If he stopped, I would hear and then know he was trying to ambush me. I jumped over the rail and landed on the stairs a floor below, trying to do so as softly as I could. If he didn't know I was following him, I didn't want to tip him off.

I paused, listened to the footsteps, jumped to the level below, and listened again. Each floor I bypassed brought me closer to those footsteps. The building was only seven stories tall, so I needed to finish this chase soon.

I heard the sound of the footfalls just below me slow to a walk. The sniper must be preparing to head out onto the street, wary of being seen running. It was my chance.

I leaped the stair rail, letting my legs absorb the force of the jump so I could land as silently as possible. The man ten feet in front of me heard, though, and spun to aim his rifle at me.

I hadn't even finished landing when he began to spin. I let my right leg collapse and threw my right shoulder toward the ground, turning the momentum from my jump into a forward roll. As the man got the gun all the way around and was ready to fire, I came out of the roll directly in front of him.

This guy had tried to kill me. Worse, he had tried to kill me from the shadows, without facing me at all. That seemed worse somehow. Because of this, I might have used too much force. Just a little.

The barrel swung around toward me. Before I was even standing up straight from the roll, I grabbed it with one hand and pushed it up and away from me. It kicked in my hand, and then heat spread along the metal. Despite that heat, I squeezed and twisted my wrist, crushing the metal and bending it into a U shape. As I yanked it out of the sniper's hand to throw it down, I heard his finger break as it got caught in the trigger guard. I snatched his other arm, the one that had been steadying the rifle, pulled it toward me, and then slammed my other hand up on his elbow. It also broke like dry kindling. The man screamed in pain.

Before he could do anything else, I kicked at one of his knees. It bent backwards with another sharp snap, followed by a louder scream. I grabbed his hair with my left hand, lifting him almost off his feet, and drew back my right arm to punch through his skull.

As my fist was traveling toward his face, it occurred to me what I was doing. If that punch connected, there would be nothing left of the man's head. Nothing. No brain, no face, no skull. It would kill him.

Frantically, I tried to stop. The distance was too small for me to change the trajectory to either side of his head for a glancing blow. Besides, with my strength, even that would kill him. Instead, I had to stop the punch cold.

I did two things in the fraction of a second I had to try to keep from becoming a killer. I let go of his hair, and I pulled back on my fist as hard as I could. The result was...unexpected.

The good news was that I was able to stop my punch about a hair's breadth from actually touching the man's face. The bad news was that there were still some effects.

I remember seeing some old Kung Fu movies where a monk punched at candle flames, not hitting them, but pulling the punch short. When he did that, the wind generated from his strike put out the flame. As the monk trained and became a master, he could put a torch out at twenty feet just by punching at it and creating the wind. I always liked seeing it, but it was obviously fantasy, not reality. I'm here to tell you that I now believe things like that are possible.

The shockwave generated by the punch I pulled struck the man's face like a thick wooden board. I think I actually heard a small sonic boom. I saw his face deform like in the slow-motion scenes of boxing movies I'd seen, but I couldn't see what hit him. I heard his nose crack and watched helplessly as he flew backward as if I had really landed that strike. His back slammed into the wall five feet or so away, and he grunted as the air rushed out of his lungs.

When I checked him, I found him a mess, but still alive. He bled from his nose, and his lip, and underneath one of his eyes, but he was alive. I released my own breath. I stood there, watching him for a moment to see what he would do. He slumped down, regained his breath, the air whistling wetly through his nose as he tried to breathe through it and his mouth both. His eyes were dilated more than the light would account for, which wasn't a good sign, but he was moving them, trying to focus on me.

The gunshot had brought people from out of the many doors in the hallway. I guessed that the building was an apartment building or condominiums or something like that.

"You," I said, pointing to the man closest to me, phone in hand. "Call 911 and tell them that a sniper has just been caught. They need to send the police, but they also need to send an ambulance. The sniper has several broken bones and probably a pretty severe concussion." He punched the number in and put the phone to his ear.

"Thank you," I said.

I looked at the people starting to gather. "Sorry for the noise, folks," I said and turned to leave.

"Are you the Angel?" a little voice said. I located its source in a young girl, maybe nine or ten years old, hiding behind a woman that was obviously her mother. They both shared fine black hair, fair skin, and large green eyes, not a common combination.

"I am," I responded. "What's your name?"

"I'm Tabitha."

"Well, Tabitha, I'm sorry if I interrupted your sleep. I had to chase the bad man down from the roof and here is where I caught him."

She nodded solemnly as if it was the most reasonable and most normal thing in the world. Her mother tried to shoo her back into the apartment they stood in front of. "Can I have your autograph?"

"I'm sorry, but I don't do autographs," I said. "I'm not really famous." The pouty look on her face almost broke my heart.

I had to think fast. Something occurred to me, and I reached around to one of the pouches along the back of my costume. I pulled something out and walked over to her. "Hold out your hand," I said. She did. I put an object in it and watched her little face light up.

"Oh, thank you, thank you," she said.

"You can show that to your friends and tell them how you saw me make too much noise and beat up a bad guy in front of your house, okay?"

"I will." She rushed up and hugged my leg. "I wanted to join your fan club, but my mommy wouldn't let me. But this is even better. Thank you."

I smiled at her and left.

The object I had given her was something Amy had

been working on. She made a logo for my superhero name, consisting of a glowing halo with a stylized "A" going through it. She tried several different designs before settling on the one we'd use. It was tough. We didn't want people to confuse it with the logo for the baseball team in California.

She had made some small disks, about as big as a half dollar, out of plastic. I'm not sure how she made them, actually. She had produced a handful and said I ought to use them to leave with criminals I caught for the police. She said it would make sure I got credit for the capture. I had never used any of them. I didn't care about getting credit. Stopping the crime was good enough for me. Let some other poor sap get the credit...or the blame. I kept one in my pouch as a souvenir, and that's the one I gave Tabitha. I thought I might have to start carrying more of them.

22

The interaction with little Tabitha had me on a high for the next few days. It was one thing to have adults or kids my age in a fan club; it was another to have a child look up at you like a hero. With the club, I figured a lot of the people were just interested in someone who was in the public eye. It could have been anyone: an actor, sports star, singer, whatever. But to Tabitha, I was a hero, plain and simple. That made me warm all over.

Amy teased me about it, calling Tabitha my little girlfriend, but she made more of the disks. I could tell she was proud of me. She looked at me sometimes as if reminiscing, smiling slightly while her eyes seem focused on nothing.

"What are you thinking about?" I asked when she had that faraway look in her eyes one time.

"I was thinking about when I was little," she said, smiling at the thought. "I saw some old reruns of He-Man episodes. Have you ever seen it?"

"Yeah, one or two of them. It's an old show."

"I became obsessed with She-Ra. She was beautiful, powerful, and a hero in her own right. I wanted to be She-Ra, a tough, cool warrior woman that could beat up the bad guys. I used to daydream about it all the time."

I felt a huge smile start to take over my face as I looked at my friend. She looked something like a child at that moment. The beautiful innocence of her face, the excitement painted there. I got a shiver. I narrowed my eyes more carefully at her, studying her. She noticed and her smile slipped a little.

"What?" she asked hunching her shoulders and crossing her arms in front of her like she was cold. Or like she was hiding.

"I just realized how beautiful you are," I said before I could stop myself. I pictured myself in my mind reaching out to snatch the words back before they reached her. It was too late, though. Her eyes grew wide, and she withdrew into herself even more. She wrapped her arms around her elbows and drew her shoulders in together like she was going to try to curl into a ball.

"I...uh...I mean." I stopped talking to take a breath. "You looked so happy and peaceful and child-like. I just thought...I'm sorry."

"You're sorry you said I was beautiful?" Those eyes of her drilled into me, making me feel like I was in trouble. "Or are you sorry that I look like a child?"

Uh-oh. This wasn't going well. "No, Amy. I'm sorry if I insulted you, or made you feel uncomfortable."

She flashed a quick smile at me. "I'm just teasing you, Daniel. Do you really think I'm beautiful?" She ran her fingers through her messy hair.

I was looking down, not quite able to meet her eyes again. "I do. I don't understand why the boys aren't all over you. Sometimes I can't stop looking at you." Damn. I hadn't meant to say that either. I decided I needed a new strategy. I would keep my mouth shut and leave. I flicked my eyes up to her. Her eyes were fixed on my face.

"Thank you." She was blushing. "I think you're very cute, too."

My heart was going to explode if I kept this up. "Oh, I have to go. I'll talk to you later, okay?" I didn't quite run out the door, but I walked as fast as I could without making it seem like I was trying to escape.

She giggled as I left. "Okay, Angel, I'll talk to you later." I don't know why, but when she said it, Angel seemed more a term of endearment than my superhero moniker. I kind of liked that.

I continued my patrols, and Amy continued to try to find information on Eduardo Peña's location. She also tried to find out anything she could about the people out there hunting me or how much the contract paid. She didn't have any good contacts, either with the police or on the streets, so there wasn't much she could do. We carried on the best we could, wishing for a lucky break.

"Be careful what you wish for; you might get it," the old saying went. I always thought it was stupid, but I learned that there was wisdom in it.

It was just a normal evening patrol. It had been slow so far, and I wondered if I'd see any action at all. Two hours in and not a peep from anyone. No crime, no activity, not even any new graffiti. I perched on the roof of a three-story building looking around for any signs of trouble. Not only was there none of that, there didn't even seem to be any people at all out. That was unusual.

My eye caught some motion off to the left, deeper into the

alley between buildings. I looked, but couldn't see anything. I watched the spot where I was sure the motion came from for a moment but wasn't able to spot anything. I turned my head to check out another part of the alley, and I saw the movement again, in the edge of my vision. When I turned my head to look directly at the spot, there was nothing there. I started to get frustrated. Maybe I was just tired and my eyes were playing tricks on me. I had to make sure, though.

I averted my eyes to another part of the alley, but tried to look at the spot in question in my peripheral vision. A few seconds later, I saw something shuffling along the wall of the building, but I couldn't quite pick out what it was.

Another few minutes and several shuffles later, the moving thing entered the globe of light given off by the lamp over one of the doors on the building. It was a person —of course it was, what did I think, that it was a monster?— and it moved slowly, like it was injured.

I scanned the alley and found no other movement and nothing else that would be a concern. I had to go down and investigate. If the person was hurt, I needed to help him or her out.

Carefully arranging my cloak so it covered and camouflaged me, I made my way down a drainage pipe as silently as possible. Soon, I was standing on the alley floor looking towards the shambling shape. I approached it.

As I went nearer the person, I hugged the shadows and moved with careful steps. I didn't think I had been detected yet. When I was within a few steps, the head of the shape snapped up. Light reflected off two orbs. It shook like it was convulsing, head whipping back and forth, looking for escape.

"I'm not going to hurt you," I said. "Are you okay? Are

you injured? How can I help?" The shape, seeing that it couldn't escape, huddled in on itself but remained silent.

"I'm called Angel. Do you need help?"

The head lifted marginally and tilted to the side. "Angel?" a tiny, trembling voice said. "Are you *the* Angel, the superhero?"

"I'm *the* Angel, I guess," I said. "I fight bad guys."

I heard a sobbing noise as the shape rose and turned toward me. The light finally caught it and allowed me to see what I was looking at more clearly. It was a girl, a young girl, in tattered clothes, bruises showing darkly in the pale lamplight.

"Help me," she said and then fell toward me.

I caught her and easily picked her up. Even without my super strength, she would have been easy to pick up. She weighed almost nothing. Shock jolted me as I got a good look at her face. "Tabitha?" I asked, unable to believe it. It was impossible.

She stopped her sobbing long enough to say "Michelle." She burrowed her face into my chest and added, "My family calls me Shelly."

It wasn't Tabitha, but it could have been. They looked similar and were about the same age. No, maybe Shelly was just a little older. Anger and sorrow suffused my body as if I were a sponge in a rainstorm. I clutched her tighter to me, whispered "You'll be all right now," and ran toward the nearest hospital.

"Wait," Shelly said. "I have to tell you something. I need to show you where the bad men are that did this to me."

"Bad men?" I said. "What are you talking about, Shelly?"

"The bad men that beat me up. They told me you needed to know where they were, that I had to tell you or they would hurt my friend Cindy and the others worse than me. They're waiting for you."

Great. So this was a trap, and Michelle was the bait. A ball of fire started in my belly, radiated up through my limbs, and seemed to come out of my eyes. I would hurt these men. Badly. "Okay," I said. "You can show me where they are, but then I'm taking you to the hospital so you can be looked at by a doctor and fixed up. Okay?"

She hung her little head and squeaked, "Okay." Then she added. "I don't want you to be hurt. You're nice to me."

I gave her a sad smile. Hopefully she was too young to see it for what it was, a thinly masked attempt to keep from screaming. "I'll do my best to not get hurt. And to try to rescue Cindy and the other kids."

That seemed to help her mood. She lifted her head to look at me. "That would be nice, to have the other kids rescued. I don't want any of them hurt either."

She guided me to where she had come from. It wasn't far. She was so injured she hadn't gone for more than a short distance before I found her. Lucky for both of us, I guess.

It was a simple building, not distinguishable from any of the others around it, in an industrial park, not too shabby but not too new either. In a word, it was unextraordinary, if that was even a real word.

"That's it?" I asked her. "That's the place you were hurt?"

"Yes. That's where the other kids are. The bad men said if you tell the police, they'll kill some of the other kids. You have to go alone."

"Okay," I said. "I know where it is now. Now we're going to get you fixed up."

A group of kids kept captive, men beating them. This had to be Peña's work. We had been looking for him for weeks, and suddenly he had sent me an engraved invitation.

Engraved with the blood of children. Or at least the bruises. I ran toward the hospital again, carrying Michelle, and with her my hope that I'd survive the night to see how she was in the morning.

I burst through the double doors of the hospital ER. "I need help for this little girl, right now."

The nurse on duty looked at me like I was from another planet. I began to get angry and then realized I still had my costume on. She probably thought I was some crackpot. I tried again.

"This little girl was beaten and tortured by Eduardo Peña's men. Are you going to help her, or do I need to find someone on a higher level?"

That seemed to get her attention. I don't know if she recognized the gangster's name or if it finally clicked that the little girl was hurt badly. She came around the desk as she called for another nurse. I stepped back to let them talk to Shelly.

When the other nurse came to help with the girl, the first nurse turned to me.

"Is that costume the real thing? Are *you* the real thing?"

I didn't have time for this. Instead of answering, I lifted a crash cart sitting nearby. With one hand. Then I spun it on my finger like a basketball.

"Okay, okay," she said. "I was just asking. Some people are wearing homemade costumes like that. There was one in here earlier. Gunshot wound. Apparently some bad people are not happy with you and want you hurt."

I looked at her. I wasn't sure if my glare came through or not because of the cowl, but I didn't care. "Tell me about it. Somebody did this to her and left her for me as bait so I'd go into their trap."

"Are you going to?" she asked. "Go, I mean? Are you going to step into their trap?"

I sighed and went to run my fingers through my hair and stopped with my hand halfway to the cowl covering it. "Yes. I have to. They'll kill some kids they have there if I don't, and they'll kill some if I involve the police."

She gave me a level look, searching my eyes. "You're real. I mean, you're an authentic hero, huh?"

"I'm just a guy doing what he has to because no one else has the tools. Listen, will you call the police and tell them about Michelle here? Tell them what I told you about Peña's men and that I'm trying to take care of it. If I am able to pull it off, they'll be the first ones to know. If not, well, I'm sure the criminals will mount my body somewhere that everyone can see it."

"I will," she said. "Are you going to tell me where?"

"No. I can't involve the police. Tell them to stand by."

I turned to leave.

"Hey, I'm Sharon Richardson. It's an honor to meet you. You're the first real hero I've ever met." She put her hand out to shake mine. "And I don't mean because you have superpowers. I deal with a lot of great people: doctors, firefighters, cops. But I don't know any who would go willingly into something they thought they wouldn't survive to save someone else's life."

I shook her hand. "I'm glad to meet you, Sharon. Thank you. I think, though, that maybe you aren't giving some of those folks enough credit. I think most people would sacrifice themselves for someone else."

"Maybe," she said. "Hopefully I'm wrong. But I'm not wrong about you. Thank you. Really. I have a daughter about Michelle's age. I can't imagine her being in that situation. I would hope I would have the courage to do what you're doing, but I just don't think I do. I hope to see you again."

I laughed. "If I'm successful, you may actually see me soon. I'm sure I'll be wounded. Maybe you can help fix me up."

She didn't return my smile—she couldn't see it through the cowl anyway—or laugh herself. "I'm required to report all gunshot wounds, but if you came in with one, or God forbid, more than one, I might just forget that rule, if you understand me."

"Thank you. I may take you up on that. I better get going. There are children in danger."

I said goodbye to Michelle, gave her a hug, and left before I had a chance to change my mind. I didn't look back. I didn't think I could bear the look on her face.

23

I really wanted to go and talk to Amy first, but I was afraid that if I took too long, Peña and his goons would start killing the kids. I compromised and called her. It was after 11:00 PM, but she had a habit of staying up late on nights I patrolled. Probably worrying about me.

"Hey Daniel," she said when she answered the phone.

"Hey, Aim. Listen, I don't have much time, but I wanted to tell you about this." She listened silently as I told her what had happened earlier. I didn't leave anything out. I also didn't try to sugar-coat any of it.

"You're not going, Daniel," she said when I finished.

"Amy," I said, "you know I have to. If I don't, they'll kill the kids. They beat up Michelle pretty bad. They're not bluffing. They know I can't abandon kids like that."

"I know, but that's why you can't go. They'll be prepared for you. They'll kill you, Daniel. You're not Superman."

I sighed. "I know, Amy, but I have no choice. You would do the same thing. You were willing to risk your life just to find the place."

The line went silent. I looked at my phone to make sure

we were still connected. I thought maybe she had hung up. Finally, she spoke. "What can I do to help?"

Relief washed through me. I had been afraid she would keep arguing. "There's nothing you *can* do. At least, not to help me. What I do need you to do is to note the address that I'm about to tell you. Give me three hours and then find a way to give it to the police, maybe through their anonymous tip line. If I don't make it, they'll need to raid the place. Those kids need to be rescued. Can you do that for me?"

"I can," she said. "I just wish there was something else I could do to help you, to give you the edge."

"I know, Aim," I said. "Send good vibes to me and cross your fingers. It may make a difference. Who knows?"

"I will. Call me when you've wiped the floor with those bastards, okay?"

I laughed. "I will." I needed to get going, to save the kids if I could. "Amy, I just want you to know how much you mean to me. You know, how much I like you and how important you are to me. In case I don't talk to you again... for a while. Or whatever. Thank you for everything you have done for me, and thank you for being my best friend. I can't imagine a happy life without you."

"I feel exactly the same way, Daniel. Be careful. I don't want to do without you either. Come back to me, okay?"

"I'll do my best. I better get going. I don't want any more kids hurt tonight."

"Okay," Amy's voice sounded rough, almost hoarse. "I'll talk to you later."

"Definitely." I tried to smile, hoping it would come through in my voice, but instead it betrayed me, and my voice cracked. "Bye."

We hung up. I stared at my phone for a moment, looking

at the picture I used as a background, one I had memorized a long time ago. It was Amy and me, sitting on a bench under a big tree in the park we often used for training. We had taken it one day during a rest break. I touched Amy's face with my finger, tracing her hair and her smile. I took a deep breath, stowed my phone in the pocket she had made in my uniform specifically for it, and made my way to the greatest challenge of my life. Hopefully I would live to face other tests.

The building and everything around it were quiet. I had been watching it for a few minutes, after I did a complete circuit of it to figure out how to get inside.

There was a main entry portal, right next to a large bay-type door. Other business space was on either side, so that only left the other side of the building, on which there were some high windows and another normal-sized steel door.

Breaking through the doors was not an option. It would make a lot of noise and would basically be a suicide mission. The windows on both sides of the building, however, would also be watched. They would expect me to try to get in that way. In fact, one of the windows was open halfway. I was hesitant to use the convenient way, though.

I wondered if there was a basement or lower level. I could really use Amy's help, but I couldn't contact her again. I already felt my resolve weakening just thinking about it. No, I'd have to figure things out on my own.

I decided to check out the roof, so I climbed up the window ledges on the building across the alley from the hideout. The building I climbed was taller than the roof I needed to get to. It was an easy matter with my enhanced strength to run and jump from the taller building onto the lower. I landed softly and rolled to expend the energy from my leap. I hoped it hadn't made too much noise, but I didn't figure it mattered much. They knew I was coming.

It was a standard roof, flat with a parapet and that roof material, the tar stuff covered with sand, across the whole thing. There were some air conditioning units and some big chimney things and pipes coming up through the roof, but not much else. I finally located a trap door or hatch. It was closed. I pulled up on it gently to see if it would open. Nope, locked.

I sat down and thought about my options. I could easily get in the window that had been conveniently left open for me. I could break down a door. I could probably tear the trap door from its hinges, but it would be loud. None of these options seemed good. Time ticked by. I had to do something soon.

I decided to use the trap door, for no other reason than because it was in front of me. There was probably a ladder going down from it, but as soon as I tore the door off, there would be bullets coming toward me. I'd have to take my chances, though.

Squatting down, I grabbed the edges of the metal door and prepared to tear it off in one motion. Just as I tensed up to straighten my legs, I saw something I had missed because it had been on the other side of an air conditioning unit when I looked earlier. About fifteen feet ahead of me was a skylight, the plastic cover bubbling up into the night.

I went over to it and peered through the clouded, sun-damaged plastic. I could see the floor twenty feet below. It must have been a mezzanine or something because the building was much taller than that. There were machines of some kind strewn about. It was hard to tell, but they could have been sewing machines or something similar. I guessed that was where Peña forced some of the kids to do labor.

The clouded plastic obscured my view, but I made out several people stationed in different areas, looking around and waiting. They must have heard me land on the roof. With the way they fidgeted and their heads swiveled back and forth, they seemed to be on high alert. I doubt they had been in those positions all night. Still, this seemed like my best option.

I inspected the skylight cover. It had a metal frame and many little bolts along the sides of it, securing it. The plastic bubble was all one piece and pretty thick. I could smash through it, but it would take a few blows to make a hole big enough for me to get through. I'd have to tear the entire thing off the frame, tearing loose the bolts. It was going to make some noise, but the men down there seemed to be looking toward the trap door, the obvious entry point. The element of surprise might just be enough for me to get into the building before all the gunfire started.

I ran my fingers along the edges of the skylight, trying to find the best place to grab and pull. As I did so, a strange feeling prickled along my nerves. I recognized it as another power making its appearance, a new one. Maybe it would help me. I could have used all the aid I could get at that point.

I waited as the power built. The unpredictable abilities could be useful or could cause problems, and I never knew which until they manifested fully. It quickened in me. It seemed to be moving toward my head, concentrating there. My brain started to feel hot. It wasn't uncomfortable, exactly, but I thought it would become so if it kept going like it was.

The heat grew and then suddenly exploded out of my eyes. I was looking around the roof, so the beam coming from me—it seemed like a laser from some science fiction movie—strafed the area. It mostly missed any objects, but the beam passed through a pipe coming up through the roof and a small air conditioning unit, cutting both cleanly in half. It seemed that I had heat vision like Superman, at least temporarily.

I closed my eyes and felt the stream cut off. I was half afraid it would burn right through my eyelids. When I opened them, the heat vision shot out from me again, but this time, I tried to focus my eyes and control it. I was able to narrow the beam—shooting straight up into the sky at this point so I wouldn't destroy anything—and slow it to a trickle by narrowing my eyes, finally succeeding in shutting it off completely even though my eyes were still open. Yes, this would definitely be useful.

The heat beam throbbed behind my eyelids like it wanted to come out, just waiting for an opportunity. If I relaxed, it would explode out and vaporize anything in front of me. I kept it under control, though. With this, I could quietly cut away the skylight and maybe surprise the goons waiting below.

I looked at the frame of the skylight and prepared to cut a hole. I released the power, controlling it to a fine beam. It immediately burned a hole where I was looking. All I had to do was sweep my eyes over the area I wanted cut and I'd have my entrance.

Then it fizzled and stopped.

I opened my eyes wider to let more of the beam out. Nothing. I forced them to go larger, straining to push the heat vision out instead of just letting it come out on its own. Nothing. I cursed silently. I had wasted time playing around with it, and it had passed. The strange feeling faded. I had missed the opportunity.

I looked at the small hole I had cut. It cooled from the deep red to a pale orange as I watched. It wouldn't do me any good. I'd still have to rip the top off the skylight off and go in as fast as I could. Well, it had been worth a try. At least I'd recognize the power and be able to control it if I ever got it again. It could be useful.

If I survived the next hour or so.

There was nothing left but to go ahead with my only option. I waited until the area around the hole I burned was cool to the touch and then took both sides of the skylight in my hands. I squatted down, took a breath, and tore up with my arms while straightening my legs. There was a screeching, tearing sound and the entire skylight, frame and all, came loose in my hands. I threw it aside and jumping into the hole, feet first.

24

The floor of the mezzanine, twenty feet below, came up to meet me. I landed in a stable stance, letting my legs absorb the energy from my fall. Even as I landed, I heard gunshots. I needed to find cover right away.

I ran to a large cabinet. It looked like it was some kind of machine or electrical center, but it was large and the metal looked thick enough, so I'd use it. As I reached it and ducked behind, a sharp pain hit my left shoulder. I stumbled, but was still able to make it out of sight.

I looked at my shoulder. It was bleeding. I rolled it around and felt more pain, but I could still use my arm. That's more than I could have hoped for, jumping into the middle of an army of criminals wielding guns like that. I tried to picture what I had seen through the skylight, where the men were positioned. I needed to take them out one at a time, while staying out of sight of the others, if possible. It was time to get to work.

There were no more gunshots or any other sound in the place, at first. A footstep sounded to my right, the shadow of someone coming around the edge of my cabinet shield. I waited.

The long barrel of the gun appeared first, followed by its holder as he swung around quickly to surprise me.

He didn't.

With my speed-geared vision, I spotted him before he could shoot. I ducked, shuttled toward him, grabbed the barrel to swing it out of the way, and kicked him in the chest. He flew backward from the force of the kick, his hands tearing from the rifle butt as he did so. I was left with a gun in my hand—I think it was some kind of assault rifle—and one less enemy to worry about. He slammed into a work table, flipped over it, and landed hard on his belly.

I hoped I didn't kill him with that kick. I always tried to control how much force I used when I struck others, but I had a feeling I'd be hurting people more than I wanted to tonight. There would be so much going on, I might hit a little too hard. Shrugging—it pulled on my shoulder and pain shot through my arm—I resolved to do my best not to kill anyone and left it at that.

I was still out of sight of most of the gunmen but assumed they were maneuvering around to catch me in a crossfire. I needed to start moving. I wished I had a plan. I also wished Amy was there to help me. While I was at it, I might as well wish I was invincible and could fly. But I had to make do with what I had. Looking down at the gun, I considered using it, but I had never shot a gun and probably couldn't hit anything anyway. I'd hold onto it for the time being.

Delaying would only let Peña's minions surround me and trap me. I had to keep moving, taking out as many of them as I could in ones or twos. I took three fast breaths and psyched myself up.

I swung around the cabinet and headed toward the wall off to my left. There were carts with bolts of cloth on them and a couple of bins that held some type of finished clothing. Before I'd even taken two steps, the gunfire started again.

I made it behind the bins before anyone could hit me, probably because they couldn't have predicted how quickly I could move. Two men waited there, guns aimed at me. Their fingers tensed to pull the triggers.

Still moving forward, I dropped to the ground and slid. One of the gunmen started firing his handgun at me, but the bullets passed over me. I slid into him, feet first, and knocked his legs out from under him. As he toppled to the floor, he let go of his gun to try to break his fall. I hit him in the head with the butt of the rifle I was holding, trying to do so as gently as I could. Still, the thud was sickening. I hoped I hadn't broken his skull.

The other man swung the barrel of his own assault rifle toward me to shoot me. I was just getting to my feet and didn't have time to dodge. Instead, I threw my gun at him. He flinched but the weapon struck him hard in the chest, knocking him back. He kept his grip on his own gun, though, so I wasn't done yet. I took advantage of the distraction and zipped over to him, slapping the side of his head so hard I heard his teeth clack together. He fell backward and stopped moving. So far, so good. I picked up the handgun the first man had dropped.

A bullet ricocheted next to my head. I looked up quickly enough to see the source duck behind a piece of machinery. It was some sort of industrial sewing machine, large with a flat bed at least five feet long with a housing surrounding it. I was partially exposed to him, but couldn't move to be completely covered without opening myself to some of the other guns around. As I ran, I had spotted at least three others, and I had no doubt that more were coming up from the lower levels since they knew the action was on the mezzanine.

I watched for the gunman to show himself again. When he did, I threw the handgun at him. It bounced off the side of the machine but didn't hit him. I'd run out of ammunition in a hurry this way, and there was no way I'd be able to hit him if I shot at him. There was only one thing I could think of.

When he next poked his head out to shoot, his eyes went wide as he tried to figure out if what he saw was real. The bin full of clothing flew through the air, struck the side of his hiding place, and delivered a glancing blow that sent him careening off to the side to strike a wall. The bin continued its spin toward him and knocked him down. Hard. He wouldn't be playing hide 'n' seek with me again anytime soon.

Just as I was congratulating myself, I saw movement from both sides. Two of the remaining gunmen jumped out from cover to catch me in a crossfire. I dove out of the way just as they fired, doing some sort of back flip thing. Not realizing I could move that fast, the men had already begun to fire. Right into each other. They had both fired bursts, so each was struck with several bullets each. Dead or not, two more were out of the battle.

There should be only one enemy left on the upper level. I looked around but couldn't find him. It made me a little nervous that there might be someone to come up behind me, but I had to move on. There was the whole downstairs section to clear out.

I went to the rail on the mezzanine and looked over. More thugs scurried around, trying to get to a better location to ambush me. They seemed to be covering the stairs leading to the upper level to ambush me as I came down. I chose the more direct route.

Leaping over the rail on the mezzanine, I dropped another twenty feet to the concrete of the main floor. I moved fast enough that most of the gunmen didn't see me. Unfortunately for the one who did see me, I saw him watching as I launched myself downward and went straight for him.

I fixed my vision on the man as I descended, watching his eyes go wide when he thought I'd land on him. The shock of seeing a person with a costume and a cape dropping quickly toward him made him freeze. A lucky thing for me.

As I moved, he finally snapped out of it and swung his gun toward me. He was too late. I was already in front of him, blocking his movement with my arm. I smiled as I picked him up and threw him over my shoulder toward the group of men aiming their guns at the stairs. They had seen me when I landed anyway, so I wasn't giving anything away. The man flew over two racks and landed right in the middle of the group. My aim was good, and I mentally patted myself on the back for it.

Until those left standing started to shoot. No one appreciates a job well done anymore. I ran toward the opposite wall, zigzagging through racks and bins. Luckily, the human projectile kept the group from organizing. They would get organized, though, and I needed to be ready.

Most of the lower floor was comprised of workstations set up in orderly rows, each consisting of a small table, a chair, and a sewing machine. The aisles between the stations were maybe four feet wide. I ran down one, my eyes straight ahead but my peripheral vision registering movement all around me. As I passed, I tore two of the bolted-down sewing machines off their stands.

Movement flickered to my left, and I launched one of the machines. It hit the man who had jumped out into the aisle to shoot me, taking his legs out from under him. The machine was probably fifty pounds or more, and I was sure it had broken both of his legs. Or worse. In any case, he wouldn't be shooting at me anytime soon.

A few more machines torn from their mounts and thrown, and I felt a little better about my situation. So far, between my speed, my strength, and my enhanced peripheral vision, no one had been able to shoot me more than that once. Not yet.

Then I came around some racks and a large piece of machinery, and I ran into the corner of the building. Uh-oh.

The remaining gunmen had me trapped in the corner of the warehouse. They closed in, coordinating their efforts. They had watched what I was doing and were working to catch me in a crossfire. I wasn't quite sure how I'd get out of it. I had thrown my last sewing machine, expecting to find more on the other side of whatever the large piece of equipment was I went around.

Frantically, I looked for something that could help me. I didn't see anything, but I knew there must be something that could save my skin. No one else was going to do it for me. *Think, think!* I told myself.

I looked more carefully at the machine in front of me. There was a square part, like a big metal box, but what dominated the space was a rounded tank thing. It looked like one of the propane tanks my uncle had at his house in the country, and it was hot. From several feet away, I could feel heat radiating from it. The dials on the square part showed temperature and pressure. I finally figured it out: it was a boiler.

Any second guns were going to appear around the edges of the boiler I hid behind. They didn't even need to see me, though. If they shot toward the concrete wall, the ricochet would probably kill me.

Just as a crazy idea occurred to me, the first person poked his head around the boiler enough to see me. He fired several rounds in my direction. I barely hit the ground in time to allow the bullets to pass over me and ricochet off the wall, going through several of the folded cloth items on the racks.

I rolled almost directly under the boiler, preparing to get up and make my last stand when I heard the noise.

It was faint at first but then grew louder. As it did, I recognized it. It was police sirens. Amy had notified the cops, and they were on their way. Had it already been three hours? I hoped it didn't result in the death of any of the kids, but it was a welcome sound. I might survive after all. Or at least there would be someone there to retrieve my body.

The sound of the sirens caused the men in view to look at each other and then out toward the street. They looked uneasy and confused. I had to act.

I reached down and grabbed one of the steam lines coming out of the boiler. My skin sizzled, but I paid it no attention. I'd deal with the burns later. I had the children's lives to save, not to mention my own. I pulled up on the pipe until it broke. Steam shot out of the end toward the unfortunate gunmen who happened to be in front of me. They screamed as the super-heated water sprayed them.

I swung the pipe back and forth, burning any I could. It wouldn't last long, and I needed to get as much benefit as I could from it while it lasted. Sure enough, after less than a minute, the safety systems activated and the steam fizzled, then trickled out, and stopped completely. I let go of the pipe, leaving a good amount of skin on it. I might have been in shock because I couldn't feel anything more than an uncomfortable warmth.

The entire area was misty like a fog had rolled in, and I took advantage of it. I swept through the steam like some sort of monster, breaking arms, delivering blows to the head, or using chokeholds to cause some to pass out. I began to think I could end up winning, especially if the police were right outside.

Then one of the men took charge.

"Kill him," he shouted. "Don't hesitate. Shoot into the steam. Keep shooting until he's dead."

Uh-oh again.

There was no more warning than that. Bullets started flying from every direction. I didn't know how they kept from killing all their friends, but though I heard a few grunts, it didn't seem like most of the bullets struck the other gunmen. I wasn't so lucky.

In the first minute, I was hit by at least three bullets: one in the leg, one in the side, and one in the shoulder, close to where the first one had struck. I didn't make a noise, but I wanted to scream. If I kept this up, I'd be dead before the police got inside. As always, I was on my own.

I ducked as low as I could—not easy with the pain in my right leg where a bullet had either entered my flesh or as least grazed it—and moved toward one of the racks. It was time to see what I was really capable of.

I grabbed two of the supports on one of the racks, which was probably ten feet high, four feet deep, and at least twenty feet long. Trying to ignore the pain in all my limbs—including the new pain from the gunshot wound to my other leg—I heaved upward. There was a ripping, grating sound as the rack twisted and items fell to both sides, some of them on top of me. But I was committed and had to finish.

I hurled the rack forward with a mighty effort. I heard grunts and screams from those in its path. I hoped I hadn't killed anyone, but at that point, it was either me or them, and I wasn't ready to die.

When the rack and all the twisted metal that had been in its way stopped moving and making noise, there was only the soft sounds of movement mixed in with grunts and groans. The steam dissipated and visibility returned.

The warehouse floor looked like a battlefield. Wreckage from the racks, the machinery in the way, and the men who had surrounded me were strewn about. There was blood, too, but not a lot of it. That, at least, was good.

I picked up the man nearest me. He was crawling away, dragging one of his legs with the bottom at an awkward angle to the top. He cringed as I lifted him. All the fight was gone from him. His courage was probably connected to his gun, wherever that was.

"Where are the children?" I asked.

"I don't know," he said.

I slapped his broken leg. It wasn't a hard slap, but he screamed in pain, shutting his eyes as if to block it out by not looking at it. "Think hard," I said. "I'm not in the best of moods right now, and there are lots of other guys here I could ask. Don't make me kill you as an example to them."

He opened his eyes to look at me. When he saw the look in mine, they kept opening wider and wider. "I really don't know. I've never seen any children. I just got hired on as an extra gun. You have to believe me."

I did, unfortunately.

"Is there a basement, some other part of the building besides the mezzanine and this main floor?" When he didn't respond right away, I shook him, causing him to clench his jaw to keep from screaming out again. "Quickly."

"I...I think there's a lower floor. There's a door near the office, over there," he pointed to a small office complex tucked into the corner of the building. "I heard some guys talking about going down. That's all I know."

I dropped him, causing him to cry out in pain once again. My path was clear. If I didn't find the children in the lower level, I would have risked my life for nothing. The thought made me growl. The man I had dropped glanced at me and crawled away as fast as he could. I didn't suppose I looked very friendly at that moment, even with only my eyes visible through the cowl.

I picked up a twisted piece of metal, probably one of the support poles for the rack I had thrown. It wasn't much to look at, but it would make a serviceable weapon in a pinch. Looking around once more to make sure none of the gunmen were still standing—none were—I headed toward the office and the door to the lower level. In actuality, I limped toward it.

The metal door had a card reader next to it. After briefly considering trying to find an entry card—I'm sure none of the gunmen had one—I opted for a more tried and true method. I braced myself for the pain and then kicked the door right in the direct center. It crumpled around my foot. Once it had bent far enough, the hinges and lock tore loose and the wrecked metal spun off into a short hallway, striking another door ten feet away. That door was labeled "Lower Level." I wondered if there was an elevator somewhere or if the floor was only accessible by stairs. I was not thrilled with using the stairs feeling like I was. I didn't have time to look, though.

The second door was unlocked. I went through and found three more doors. One was locked. I ripped it off the hinges and found an empty office. Another of the doors—unlocked—was some sort of meeting room or interrogation room, holding only a table and three chairs. The last door led to a stairwell that dropped down after a small landing.

I took the stairs two or three at a time, mainly because every step caused jarring pain in my legs, so I figured fewer steps would be better. My makeshift weapon banged on the walls a couple of times as I descended. I had already made so much noise I didn't worry about it. If anyone was down there, they already knew I was coming.

At the bottom of the stairs, I swung open a lonely, unlocked door and stepped into the hallway beyond. It looked to be a central hall for the floor, with more than a dozen doors along the walls on either side. I tried the handles as I went by and found several of them open. But I didn't have time to search every room, so I followed my gut feeling and bypassed them until I got to the very end of the hall.

The door there looked different than the others. Though they were all made of steel, this one looked heavier, almost like a barricade or a door to a panic room. It took me two kicks to crumple it. When I tore it the rest of the way off the hinges, the man in the room shot me in the chest with a handgun.

25

I was so surprised I didn't even react. I felt a burning sensation high on the right side of my chest, but didn't know what was going on at first. As I spun out of the doorway—partly from the force of the gunshot and partly because my body's defense reflexes activated—I wondered if I would have the time to take this guy out before I died.

Somehow, I had maintained my grip on the metal pole. The man ran out into the hall to finish me off, obviously not thinking about my powers or the six-foot length of steel in my hand. As soon as he came around the doorframe, I swung the pole with one hand, hitting him in the shoulder. He held the gun in his left hand, but as the bones in his arm were crushed by the pole, it fell from his grasp. The force of the blow threw him back into the room.

It was my turn to chase him. In a limping, painful sort of way. I found him on the ground, blood trickling from his mouth. I saw then that his arm wasn't enough to stop the force of the blow. It had continued on and broken at least a few ribs, if the way he favored that side was any indication. I hoped none had punctured his heart or lungs, but it didn't look good. He wouldn't be attacking me again. He was fighting for his own life.

I widened my focus then. Children, dozens of children, huddled in what looked to be dog pens around me. Every last one of them had wide eyes and held each other, shivering.

"It's...okay," I said. It was hard to breathe. I only needed to hang on for a few minutes more, just long enough to get help. "I'm...one of the...good...guys." It didn't seem to help. They still looked at me like I was going to eat them.

I went over to Eduardo Peña, writhing in pain on the ground, trying to breathe through his half caved-in chest, and took his phone out of his pocket. I used it to call the police. A short, breathy explanation of the situation and the address—they had just received it from an anonymous caller; Amy, I was sure—and I hung up.

"I have...to leave...now," I said to the kids. I couldn't be caught there. The police would probably take me into custody. If I died somewhere else, my identity would still be revealed, but it just seemed better not to die while in handcuffs in a police car.

The children huddled closer as my gaze passed over them. None of them said anything, though I could hear some whimpering and crying from within the mass of bodies. They would be fine. The police would be there any minute.

It puzzled me that they weren't already there. The sirens earlier sounded as if several cars had pulled up right outside. Maybe I was in shock and wasn't remembering correctly. It was probably better if they would take a few minutes to arrive. It would allow me to leave without having to try to dodge them.

As I limped up the stairs and through the main

warehouse, I barely paid attention to the gunmen trying to rouse themselves and move. None of them were in very good shape. The most able could barely stand and shuffle toward the exit. Experienced criminals knew better than to stick around. I was halfway to the door when the soft wail of distant sirens came floating through the air. Those capable of doing so doubled their efforts to leave. I did the same.

With my dark costume, it was hard to tell how much I was bleeding. I would check the wounds after I got out of the place. I wouldn't spend the time even giving myself a cursory look until then. A few seconds could mean the difference between getting away and being surrounded by a fleet of police cars. I put my head down, focused on where to put my feet, and got into a rhythm that allowed me to move as quickly as possible without the pain making me pass out.

When I stepped through the regular-sized entry door next to the roll-up bay door, a figure stepped out of the shadows of the alley. It had on a sweatshirt with the hood drawn down to obscure the face. The baggy clothes made the intruder amorphous so that I couldn't even tell if it was a man or woman. Whatever it was, it was shorter than me.

"Oh my God, Daniel." It was Amy's voice. "Are you okay? Is that blood on you?" She put her arms around me to support me. I had almost fallen when I recognized her voice.

"Have to...get outta...here," I panted.

She nodded, turned me gently, and half carried me deeper into the alley.

Neither of us spoke for several minutes as we shuffled from alley to alley as the sirens grew louder. She had picked the perfect path, of course, and though the lights spilled over into the street near us and even saw one of the cars from the alley we were huddling in to keep from being seen, we were not noticed.

"Hospital," I said, changing our direction toward the emergency room I had brought Shelly to earlier. "Nurse said...she'd fix me...and...not report...gunshot wound."

Thankfully, Amy understood, nodding her head as we headed there at a snail's pace. The effort of holding me up was wearing her down. I tried not to lean on her as much.

Once we were moving, I didn't want to stop to check my wounds. I'd see them when the nurse did. I began to hope I might survive after all. The pain hadn't changed much, though I attributed that to shock. I felt almost as if I wasn't really there, as if I was observing someone else limping down the street.

"Did you like my trick with the sirens?" Amy asked, probably more to break the silence than anything else.

"What?"

"The sirens. The police sirens." She pointed to her backpack. "My laptop and a big battery-powered speaker." I noticed the backpack then, full to bursting with something. It looked heavy.

"You...?" I whispered, though I tried to speak at a normal volume.

"Yep," she said through her smile. Well, through gritted teeth that was supposed to be a smile. She really was getting tired. "I wasn't about to let you go and fight all those men without some kind of distraction. I hope it helped."

She took another step before she realized I had stopped. I tottered, staring at her. "You...saved my...life," I managed to get out before my legs collapsed and I hit my knees hard on the asphalt. "Maybe," I added, trying to smile to let her know it was a joke. I failed. She couldn't see my face through the mask anyway.

"Oh, Daniel, come on. We're almost there. Just a little longer. Hold on. Don't give up on me now."

She helped me to my feet, and we shuffled on.

A hundred miles, or a couple of blocks later, I saw the ER sign. I told Amy the nurse's name, and she ran ahead to get Sharon. She and two other nurses, one a man, came back within a minute, pushing a gurney. The male nurse basically picked me up and put me onto it, and then I was off and rolling. I took that opportunity to give up my fight and lose consciousness.

When I came to, the first thing I saw was Amy. Her hair was a tangled mess—even more than normal—her hoodie and the rest of her clothes were covered with blood. Mine, I'm sure. Her face was all puffy, too.

"I must have died and gone to heaven," I whispered. "What's your name, angel?"

She laughed and scrubbed at her eyes. "You're the Angel, remember? I'm just a girl."

"Never. You are never just a girl. Why are you crying? Did someone else die?" I did a mental inventory as I spoke. The pain was much less than before, and though I still felt like I had been hit by a truck, or shot many times, at least I didn't feel on the edge of death like I had earlier. I noticed there was an IV hooked up to my right arm and wires attached to different parts of my body.

"No," she said. "These are happy tears. I ran out of the other kind while they worked on you."

"How bad is it?" I asked. "Did they do surgery or anything? How long have I been out?"

As I spoke, I thought of something and almost pulled the IV from my arm as my hand shot up to my face. I felt that the mask was still in place. I breathed out loudly.

"I wouldn't let them take the cowl off," she said. "They

were going to anyway, but Sharon physically pushed the doctor out of the way when he tried, saying she'd treat you herself if she had to. The doctor finally gave in. She's a very persuasive woman."

I smiled but aborted it halfway because it made me hurt from the top of my head to my chest.

"Oh, you have to look at this," she said. She pulled out her phone and showed me the pictures she took before they treated me and bandaged me up. "The doctor wasn't thrilled with me taking pictures, but Sharon straightened him out."

I gaped. I must have been shot in ten different places. The wounds looked strange, though.

"Yeah," Amy said, seeing that I noticed something odd. "Only one penetrated your skin, the point blank shot to the chest. Well, to the lower part of the shoulder. Even that one didn't go in too far. The doctor said it looked like you were wearing a bullet-proof vest. The only other thing he'd seen like it was when some idiot played paintball wars with no shirt on and was shot point blank. You're very bruised, but none of them were life threatening. You bled some from the other bullets—they broke the skin from the impact, but the projectile didn't go in—but most of it was from the shoulder wound. Bottom line, you'll live to continue to cause me untold annoyance."

I wasn't going to die. I thought about that for a moment and then spoke. "What about the kids? Did the police get them out of that place? Were they okay? Were any injured?"

Amy eyed me suspiciously, as if trying to figure out if I had received some kind of head trauma. "I think they're fine. I've been checking the internet for news on it, but it's only been eight hours or so. Most of the reports are preliminary, and the police aren't giving the media a lot of information just yet."

"Eight hours!" I cried out, or at least tried to. The pain caused it to come out more like a sputter at the end. "My parents..."

"...know that you stayed over at my house to work on a project," she said. "They trust me so much, they didn't even ask to speak to my parents. That kind of makes me feel bad, in a good sort of way."

I relaxed a little. "Thanks. That was good thinking. But then, that's one of your super powers, good thinking."

Amy continued, "The reports I've seen have the number of kids between eighty-two and one hundred eighteen. I haven't seen anything about injuries or death, other than Shelly being roughed up."

"Oh," I said. "What about her? How is she doing?"

"She's in Child Protective Services right now until they can figure out if she has any relatives. They keep trying to get information from her, but she's obsessed with some superhero. She keeps asking if he was hurt or killed and where he is and if she can talk to him. She refuses to answer any questions until she knows. She's pretty stubborn." Amy smiled at that and winked. "I'll have to figure out how to get the news to her without compromising our identities. Her injures weren't serious, so she'll be fine."

I let out a breath I didn't realize I was holding. "That's good. I'm glad she's okay. Hey, make sure you give her one of those discs when you see her. She'll like that, I think. It will make her believe that I'm not dead."

"Aww, that's sweet," Amy said, her words dripping with honey. I rolled my eyes.

"Have the news reports said anything about Peña?" I asked. "Did he survive? I hit him pretty hard. I was kind of distracted by the bullet he put into me, so I didn't hold back as much of my strength as I should have."

"He was in surgery downstairs the last time I heard. The news hasn't really said much, but Sharon told me."

"Downstairs?" I said. "This place is probably crawling with police."

"Yeah," she agreed, "but it's not a problem. No one knows you're here. The few staff members that know will keep quiet, even the doctor. He apologized for trying to take the mask off. He's a fan of your work."

"Good thing. Well, I guess that's everything then. All the little loose ends tied up in pretty little bows. Maybe I should take a vacation or something." I was joking, but Amy didn't seem to get it.

"Yes, you will," she said. "Until you're completely healed, you're not to put that costume on. In fact, I need to make you another one anyway. For some reason, your only one has holes and tears all over it, not to mention red stuff. Imagine that."

"Yes, ma'am." I tried to salute, but pain shot through my arm and shoulder so I lowered my hand it to the bed. Gently.

26

The news reports in the following days were surprisingly accurate. The superhero who prowled around the city had found the main base for a child exploitation and prostitution ring, entered it, taken down somewhere between thirty and fifty armed men —some had escaped, so the exact number was indeterminate—faced down the leader, been shot at point blank range, and still survived to call the police from the crime boss's own phone. Then, he somehow escaped notice and fled. No one was really sure if he survived or if he crawled off and died somewhere. The name Angel was used in most of the reports.

The Angel fan club had gone nuts, and the number of members had at least tripled. T-shirts, hats, and other paraphernalia were seen everywhere in the city, though less so at night. Wearing an Angel t-shirt in a rough part of town, especially after the sun went down, was an invitation for a beating. The criminal element didn't seem to be a big fan of someone who fought crime. Go figure.

Still, the question of whether Angel was alive or dead made it seem like the city held its breath. Something would have to be done about that. I was more preoccupied with hiding my bruises from my parents, spending as much time at Amy's as possible to keep them from noticing my careful movements. It was the middle of summer break, so it wasn't too strange for me to do so.

"Okay, you can go out for a couple of hours, but nothing too dangerous," Amy told me for the fourth time three weeks after that harrowing night. I don't want you ripping this costume up before I can make spares. And I'd prefer it if you didn't get killed after Sharon and the doctor did such good work in patching you up."

"I know, I know," I said. Again. "I just want to let people see that I'm still kicking, that Peña didn't kill me."

"All right." She eyed me as if weighing my sincerity. Then the serious look left her face, and a mischievous one replaced it. "You know, sales on all the Angel apparel will probably dip when they find out you're still alive. People are ghouls that way."

"Good," I said. "It still irritates me that I can't figure out how to get any money from them."

"Ah, well, about that." Amy couldn't seem to meet my eyes, and her face became flushed. "I figured that since so many people were getting into the game, we should have a piece of it."

I narrowed my eyes at her. "What are you talking about, Amy?"

"It just didn't seem fair that we couldn't profit off your fame, too. Supplies for making the costumes and the discs and some other things I'm working on cost money, you know."

"Amy."

"Okay, I started a little business, making and selling Angel paraphernalia. I even put an Angel poster up in my room to make it look legit. Oh, and I joined the Angel fan club. Several of them, in fact. More than a month ago."

"You did what?" I said. "And you're doing what?"

"Oh, come on," she said. "I'm a teenage girl. I'm supposed to obsess over hot, superhero studs, right?"

It was my turn. My face grew warm, but I ignored it. "Okay, fine. You better not blow my cover. If people find out my secret identity, my family won't be safe. *You* won't be safe. Everyone knows you're my best friend."

"Um, girlfriend," she corrected.

"What?"

"Everyone thinks I'm your girlfriend," she said. "We hang out all the time, so they figure we're boyfriend-girlfriend. It's natural."

"Oh," I said. I wondered if it was possible for skin to burst into flames. If so, my face would be a charred ruin very soon. "Is that okay? I mean, is that a problem for you?"

"Nope." She said it so quickly that I had no doubt it was true. "I have never cared what others think of me. They can think what they want. What we have is way better than boyfriend and girlfriend."

I couldn't help it, blushing or not, I smiled so widely I thought my ruddy face would crack. "It is."

We looked at each other for a moment, and then she shook her head to clear it. "Anyway, I'm making good money with the stuff I'm selling, especially the t-shirts. We'll talk about it later. For now, take it easy, don't get hurt again, and make sure as many people as possible see you. Consider it a PR night and not really a working night. Deal?"

"Deal." I looked at her again, studying her face. "You really are awesome. You know that?"

"I do," she said with a wink, "but I think you should tell me often so I don't forget."

"That's a deal, too." I raised my hand for a high-five and she ignored it, pulling me into a hug instead. A gentle hug. She still thought I was injured, but I felt great. Her hug didn't even hurt my injuries. Much. The shoulder was still a little tender.

The night went quickly. It was busier than I expected. I stopped a mugging and a convenience store robbery within a half an hour of each other, even though I wasn't supposed to be working hard. The store had three customers in it, plus the clerk, so I figured news would spread that I was back in action. Just to make sure, I let myself be seen by no less than twenty people when I ran through a section of a fairly busy street and climbed to a roof in front of them, jumping to the next building before disappearing out of their sight. I even waved to a few, and for a wonder, they waved back.

The next morning, it was big news that I had made an appearance and foiled two crimes back-to-back. It took a while to explain to Amy that I hadn't even exerted myself. After a warehouse full of gunmen, a mugging was nothing.

In the weeks that followed, I healed completely and got back into my regular patrol pattern. There were no more serious attempts on my life, either because someone was busy planning something big or most of the criminals were afraid to try.

Another thing that happened was that the crime rate took a steep dive. I was finally making a difference. It didn't hurt that Amy made a lot of money—well, we did, because she shared it with me—on the merchandise. Things seemed to be going well again. Of course, that made me nervous.

"Check this out," Amy said to me as we went through some new things she had bought with the money from the merchandise sales. She held out a small object. It was roughly the same size as a normal flash drive, though maybe thicker and not quite as long. I took it and turned it in my hand, inspecting it.

"What is it?" I asked.

"It's something I've been playing with. I've settled on this model. It's magnetic on one side." She took it from me and stuck it to the metal support beam on one of the shelving units in her garage. "And the other side has double-sticky tape that you can use if you peel the plastic off."

I looked at her with my sternest face. "Amy, what is it?

Her face changed into the perfect picture of surprise and disappointment, almost as if she was looking at a ten-year-old child who had forgotten how to go to the bathroom by himself. "It's a tracking device."

"Really? Nice. How does it work?"

"This particular one uses GPS satellites and pings its location." She pulled out a larger object, like one of the hiking GPS units I'd seen in the local REI store. "I chose this one based on the combination of the size, its capability, and the signal strength. I've tested eight others. Most of them are pretty expensive, but I figured it would be good to use the money from the stuff we sell to help us do a better job."

"That's great thinking," I said.

"Yeah. If you would have had one of these that time you had to run to follow the Big Dog's goons, you could have just put it somewhere on their car and then followed whenever you wanted to."

"So when do we start using them?" I was on my toes, almost bouncing. I tried to settle down, but it was exciting.

They seemed like spy gadgets. It kind of made me feel like a secret agent.

"I have to work out a few things first and order some more," she said. "Probably next week."

"Okay. I can probably wait for that." I didn't want to wait, but I knew I couldn't rush her.

Amy pulled out her laptop. "There's something else you need to see, though." I sat next to her so I could see the screen. She went to the discussion boards for one of the Angel fan club websites.

"Discussion boards?" I said. "Really? What are there, maybe three posts on it? What do they talk about?"

"For your information," Amy answered, "all of the boards are very active. There are hundreds of posts a day. I'm actually thinking of monetizing the sites to get some extra money."

"Monetizing? The sites? What do you mean? How can you do that?"

She shook her head and tsked at me, but then seemed to realize something. "Oh, that's right, I probably didn't tell you. With the first money from the merchandise, I bought some domain names and set up some sites. One of them is this one, Angel Talk."

"Angel Talk? That's the best you could come up with?"

"Do you have any idea how difficult it is to find a unique domain name with angel or heaven in it?"

"No," I said.

"Very. Anyway, that's beside the point. Stop distracting me. I own this site and have access to do anything I want. I put a special private section in, sort of an anonymous tip line, but it's not really anonymous to me."

"And....?"

"And," she said, "there are at least a couple of regular

posters to the special section. They're both active in the city's criminal world."

"Wait," I said. "You mean you're allowing criminals into the fan club?"

"Sure, anyone can join. But I don't run the fan club, just the sites I created. I think they are in the actual fan club, though, or maybe more than one. The point is that they occasionally post tips that can help us. They just started doing that last week, but I think it will be useful."

She scrolled down the screen and clicked on something I didn't see. The browser shifted to another page. "Both of them have said that the contract on you has been canceled."

"That's great. I think. Why was it canceled? Are they afraid now?"

"I doubt it," Amy said. "I'm really not sure, but I am sure that it will mean something bad for us. I just don't know what yet. Be careful out there. Maybe instead of a general contract for whoever wanted to try their luck, Crusher hired someone directly. You know, a specialist. A hit man. Or maybe someone with powers."

"You're just full of good news, huh?" I ran my fingers through my hair. "Just when I was getting to the point where I could go out without being scared by every stray cat or backfiring car."

Amy patted my shoulder. "Sorry. Better safe than sorry, though, right?"

"Yeah, I guess."

"I'm just thankful that The Six are apparently out of town on a job," Amy said. "It would have been very bad if they had taken the contract."

"The Six?" I said. "What's The Six?"

Amy fixed me with another of her long-suffering looks. "They are a team of assassins, the best in the state. In the criminal world, they are famous. No job is too hard for them. I've heard that the Secret Service has contingency plans specifically for them in case someone wants them to assassinate the President. We definitely don't want them to take notice of us."

"No," I agreed, "we definitely don't."

LESS THAN A WEEK LATER, the campaign started. I was at home watching TV.

"I'm Donald Lancaster," the man on the television said. He was a good looking guy, and he looked really fit in his tailored suit. His long dark brown hair was pulled back and secured in a man bun and his eyes, narrowed almost to a squint, drilled into the camera lens. "And I want to talk to you about the biggest danger to all the citizens of Sueño. We all know that crime had gone out of control, and that it isn't safe to leave your house at night. Sometimes, even your home isn't safe.

"I have been working with the police, and we think we have discovered the root of all this evil. It's the masked villain calling himself Angel."

"What?" I yelled at the TV. "Are you out of your mind?" I picked up my phone to call Amy, and it buzzed in my hand. She had called me first.

"Did you see that load of crap on the TV?" she asked.

"Yeah, I was just watching it," I said. "Who is this guy?"

"His dad is rich. The father lives in Phoenix. I'm not sure where he makes his money. Yet. I plan on researching him thoroughly. Donald lives here, though. He's throwing money at this, making donations to the police, bribing politicians, paving the way for his private infomercials."

"But why?" I asked. "What's the point?"

"Maybe he works for the Crusher," Amy said. "Instead of getting you killed, maybe he's trying to turn everyone against you. It's even possible if people get carried away enough, some regular citizens may try to kill you."

"That's a sobering thought," I said.

27

I continued my patrols, and the public sentiment continued to sour on me. Donald Lancaster put together a very effective ad campaign to paint me as some kind of terror, a fake hero trying to gull the public into believing in him so he could carry out his nefarious plan. Mr. Lancaster didn't know what this plan was, but he assured everyone he was doing his best—along with the police, of course—to find out and put a stop to it. He was a public servant and only wanted to help.

Oh, and by the way, he mentioned—as if it wasn't important—he would be running for mayor in the next election so he could help even more. People began calling for him to be elected almost as loudly as they called for me to be executed. It was a strange world I lived in.

My crime-fighting activities continued. Whenever I would save someone from a robbery, beating, or rape, I never knew what I would get. At times, I would be sneered at or spit at, and at other times the victim would thank me and tell me they didn't believe all the bad PR. It was about half good and half bad. I always had in the back of my mind what Amy said about regular citizens wanting to kill me, and I never turned my back on anyone.

I was kind of stressed out. Paranoia was insidious that way. Then, it got even worse.

"From the available evidence," Donald Lancaster said from the TV screen during his newest spot, "it seems as if the Angel may have attempted to murder several people."

I had thought I was used to the garbage this man was spewing, but I found my mouth had dropped open.

"These photos clearly show the damage he did to one Eduardo Peña and to several of his associates. Though no one actually died, it was not for lack of trying on the Angel's part. He used his reportedly tremendous strength and tried to kill these people. I am working to convince the District Attorney to issue a warrant for the Angel's arrest, but so far I have not had any luck."

He looked into the camera as if he could make eye contact with each individual. "Please call the District Attorney's office, the police, and the mayor's office and demand that this criminal be brought to justice."

The program went on, but I stopped listening. After a short phone conversation about it with Amy, I turned the TV off. I couldn't stand to think of it anymore. It seemed I had jumped right over the hero thing and had settled squarely on being a criminal. Great.

"Ralph Kermin, known simply as Ralphie," Amy said, showing me a grainy photo she had found on the internet somehow. "He's Crusher's number one guy. I know the picture is bad, but look at it carefully. Maybe following him around will give us some clues as to what's going on."

I had been talking to her about doing something more than just patrolling and trying to find crimes in process. We hadn't targeted anyone specific since Peña. I figured it was about time. The only way we could make a real difference was to take out the crime bosses and eventually work our way up to Crusher.

"He's got a lot of stuff he oversees directly, too, so he could be considered another crime boss, I think," she continued, "but his main value is in maybe leading us to Crusher. What do you think?"

"I think you're right," I said. "As always."

"Good," she said, "because one of our tipsters has mentioned that Ralphie likes to drink at the Sunrise Club over on Eighteenth Street. Maybe you can find him there."

I was amazed anew at how good Amy was at organizing and planning. "I think you should get a raise."

She rolled her eyes at me. "Yeah from getting paid nothing to getting zero."

"Exactly," I said with a wink. "Really, though, you are awesome. I'll head over tonight and see if he's there."

I did, and he wasn't. I kept trying, though. On my fifth try, I saw a man I thought was him give his keys to a valet and go inside the club. School had started two weeks earlier, but since it was a Saturday, I could spend the night doing my hero thing.

I watched from a nearby roof, of course. I was too young to get in the club, and my costume would probably make things tough, too. It wasn't that bad. It was almost officially fall, so the weather was nice.

I was pretty sure it was him. He was a white guy with a shaved head and some piercings through his eyebrows and lip. That may not have been all that distinctive, but he also happened to be very large. Like over three hundred pounds of large. Ralphie moved as if he was much lighter than he actually was, though. Yeah, it had to be him. The criminal on the discussion boards made a point of describing how he looked and moved.

I drifted through the shadows, cape closed tight, toward the parking lot where I had seen the valet bring Ralphie's car. It was easy to dodge the young men parking the cars and then running back to the front of the club. I attached one of Amy's tracking devices to Ralphie's car, moved back into the shadows, and tested the receiver. It worked. All I had to do was to wait until Ralphie left, and I could track him wherever he went.

It was three hours until the big man left the club. In the meantime, I checked the tracker every few minutes as I did a patrol and stopped a couple of crimes. When I finally saw it moving, it surprised me for some reason.

Following the tracking device was definitely better than chasing after the Big Dog's minions in the car that other time. I could take my time, stay hidden, and not tip off my prey that I was stalking them. I wondered if there was a way to get some kind of vehicle, my own Batmobile or at least some kind of cool motorcycle. I'd have to ask Amy what she thought.

When the signal stopped moving, I had high hopes about what I would find.

I was disappointed.

The car was pulled up to a normal-sized house in the suburbs. It must have been Ralphie's house because I just couldn't imagine Crusher living in such a place. I watched for almost an hour before the last light in the house went dark. He had gone to sleep, apparently. While stretching my face with a jaw-cracking yawn, I decided it was time for me to do the same. I headed home, working through what I would do to follow him when he moved again. The next day was Sunday, so I could spend the entire day tracking him if I wanted. In plain clothes, of course. With the way the general public felt, I wasn't about to run around in the daylight with my costume on.

It seemed that Ralphie slept in on Sundays, or maybe every day. His car didn't move until almost noon. The tracking device I had put on it worked very well. I was already at Amy's house by the time he started moving, so we were sitting there in the garage when it happened. While we talked, we kept checking the portable tracking unit, but once he was in motion, she picked up her laptop and opened it up.

"Wanna see something really cool?" she asked.

"Always," I replied.

She beckoned me over to look at the screen as she clicked. A window popped up. "Check it out," she said as she typed the identification number of the tracking device into some kind of Google Maps add-on.

A small point on the map flashed. As Amy zoomed in, I could start to see street names and the point became a circle, still flashing.

"Is that real-time tracking of his car?" I asked.

"Yep. We can just sit here and watch where he goes all day. Watch this." She zoomed in even more, and addresses or names of businesses started to appear.

"That is very cool," I said.

"I know, right? It's one of the features that made me pick that particular model."

"Great choice."

"Uh-huh," she said smugly.

We watched as Ralphie went through a drive-thru burger joint, stopped at a liquor store, and made brief detours to some of his *business* locations. Thanks to Amy's research, we already knew what most of those stops were. Finally, in the evening, he went somewhere interesting.

Amy and I got bored with watching the little dot move within an hour or so, and we were watching it in one window while listening to music and checking out YouTube videos in others. It felt like a big waste of time.

"Where is that?" I asked when I noticed the little dot had stopped somewhere.

"I don't know," she said as she maximized the map window. "Let's see, 1954 West Acacia Street. That's a pretty good part of town. Let's look at it on Google Maps."

She opened another window and soon we were looking at the street view of the address in question.

I whistled. "Wow. That's a really nice place," I said.

"Yeah," she said. "I wonder who lives there. Let me check it out."

A few minutes later, she had her answer. "The internet is a wonderful thing," she said. "It seems that the house belongs to Donald Lancaster."

"Well, that's interesting," I said.

"It is. Maybe interesting enough for someone in a cape to go and check it out?"

"Yes, I think maybe it is at that," I said.

"Good," Amy said as she set the laptop down and went to one of the cabinets in the garage. "I have a present for you."

As she dug in the cabinet for something buried behind and under other things, I looked out the window and noticed it was dark. We had been at it all day. I was hungry. As if in agreement, my stomach rumbled loudly. Amy stopped her search, reached down to another shelf, picked something up, and tossed it to me. I snatched the protein bar out of the air.

"Thanks," I said. She went back to her search.

Soon, she came out with a plastic case. "I have to hide stuff so that my dad doesn't find it by accident when he's looking through the cabinets." She handed the case to me.

I opened it to find something that looked almost like a Martian ray gun. It had a handle like a gun, but the barrel widened out into a bell shape. There were headphones nestled in the foam next to the gun. "What is it?" I asked.

"A very sensitive directional microphone. There's a collapsible dish underneath it in the foam. It's for listening in on conversations or whatever."

"Will I be able to hear people inside a house?" I said.

"It depends," Amy answered. "You'll probably have to play around with it to see if you can get some good reception. Walls and distance are the big problem. If you can get close enough and find an open window, you might get lucky and hear something useful."

"Awww, Amy, you're so good to me," I said. "You're always getting me the best gifts, and I hardly get you anything. You make me feel inadequate."

"Well, I do like revealing the truth, after all," she teased.

Rolling my eyes, I lifted the gun from the foam and turned it on. I plugged the headphones in and slipped them onto my head and then pointed the gun at the garage door, toward the house. Voices jumped into my ear, startling me.

I moved the gun back and forth until I found the best sound. "Your parents are planning meals for the next week," I said. "They do that together? That's sweet."

"Yeah, it's one of their eccentricities. We have the same things all the time, but they insist on having these planning meetings. They seem to enjoy it." She quirked an eyebrow at me. "You can hear them through the garage door and the house walls? Without the dish? Nice. It works better than I thought."

"You wanna try it?"

"Nah," Amy said. "It's probably better if you get going. It'll take a while to get there, even with you running, and you don't want to miss anything. Ralphie may leave at any minute."

"You're right," I said as I turned the gun off and stowed everything back in the case. "I'll head out now, as soon as I put on my costume."

Twelve minutes later, I arrived outside the house. Ralphie's car was still parked in the circular driveway.

It took me another few minutes to identify the security cameras and dodge them. Even with the night vision the cameras used, my costume kept me camouflaged. Amy had coated it with something that made it invisible to infrared, and the colors melted into the terrain. Still, I went through the cameras' fields of vision as quickly as I could.

Once I settled into a nice sheltered spot close to the house, I started scanning for voices. I picked up on three other conversations—one of them the cook talking to herself and two pairs of servants gossiping—before I found one that was interesting. I could barely hear it, though. Moving to another spot where there was a more direct line to the people talking, I was all set.

"...I told her to shut her mouth," a voice said. I recognized it from all the TV spots. It was Donald Lancaster. "When the time comes, we'll get married, I told her. Until then, she'd just have to be happy with all the things my money can buy her. I gave her another ring, and she seemed to calm down again."

"Yeah, women," the other voice said. I figured it was Ralphie's.

"So, how you been, Ralphie? I haven't seen you in more than a week."

"I'm good. It's just really busy now. You know."

"I get it. How are things on the business end?" Lancaster asked.

"Great, just great. Everything is running like it should. That pissant Angel has caused some delays, but we're still on track."

Was Lancaster somehow involved in Ralphie's crime activities? I listened more carefully when I heard my name mentioned.

"The Angel will be taken care of soon enough. I've seen to that. No one is going to ruin the plan, especially some little snot-nosed punk who thinks he's tough because he's manifested some powers."

"I know, Crusher, but he's—"

"Don't call me that here!" Lancaster's voice snapped. "Don't use that name at all unless I'm in costume. If you get into the habit, you may slip when someone can actually hear."

"Uh, right, sorry Don." Ralphie's voice sounded weak and penitent.

Of course. It should have been clear. Donald Lancaster was Crusher. It all made sense, why he was spending so much money and doing so much work to turn everyone against me. I was surprised I hadn't figured it out. I was *very* surprised that Amy hadn't figured it out. I continued listening.

"You're my best friend, Ralphie, have been since we were kids. Don't screw up and give me away because you can't remember when to use which name."

"I know. I'm sorry. It was just a slip. It won't happen again."

"So," Lancaster continued, "we need the money to keep rolling in. I have a lot of money from my father, but what we're doing, it's going to take more than I can get from Dad. We need to generate a lot of cash."

"We're good," Ralphie said. "We have about a third of the police in our pocket, including most of the highest-ranking cops. That's making it easier to get shipments through. We've been slowly adding key people to our side, movers and shakers who will make sure you get elected mayor. The real estate end is looking good, too. We should be able to pull permits to start building the headquarters as soon as we have a few more people on the payroll."

"Good," Lancaster said. "Our crime network is going to make the gangster dynasties in the thirties look like children playing cops and robbers in the park. We'll be the first criminal city-state. Who knows, maybe we'll grow it to encompass the whole state. Wouldn't Dad be proud of me, then?"

"I think he's proud of you now, Don, but yes, it will impress him. It's a big project."

"Just make sure you keep the money coming in. You're doing a good job, Ralphie, as I knew you would. Once we get that Angel character out of the way, things will move along smoothly. I've almost got the stupid populace turned completely against him. With no one to watch his back, he'll fall like a rotted tree in a windstorm.

"There's one more thing," Crusher said. "How is Dr. Walters doing with the cultures for the treatment?"

"He's sticking with his story that they'll be finished in another six weeks," Ralphie said. "He keeps spouting some garbage about the rate of growth of the particular organisms he needs or whatever. He knows he better have the treatment ready on time or it will be very bad for him."

"Good. We're getting close. After the treatment, if others have not disposed of Angel, I'll take care of it myself. As a test of my newly enhanced powers."

I listened for another half hour, but there was no more important information. I decided I had heard enough and it was time for me to go. Backtracking to leave the same way I had come, I slipped unnoticed off the property and back toward Amy's house. I had to share what I had learned with her. Maybe she would have an idea on what we could do. I sure didn't.

28

The only thing Amy could come up with was to continue to chip away at Crusher's organization. As he said, he needed money to implement his plan to take over the city, so if I could affect his cash flow, maybe I could slow him down. In the meantime, Amy tried to find out more about Dr. Walters. She had mentioned him a few months before. He was the top researcher into the genetics of the people developing special powers. It sounded like Crusher was going to use the research to make himself more powerful.

We still didn't know what powers Crusher had, though from what he said, it was clear he had some. The only thing that could be confirmed—and even that only by the accounts of two or three criminals—was that Crusher had smashed up a car with his bare hands, reducing it to a battered heap of metal.

That meant super-strength, at the very least, but I had super-strength, too. At times I thought I should just break into his house and take him out. I would have, if I could have been sure that I'd survive the conflict. I'd keep going after the minor crime bosses, working my way up, and wait for Amy to come up with a better plan.

The mood around the city turned darker. Everywhere I went, I heard or saw anti-Angel sentiment. A few people in my fan clubs still believed in me, but the numbers were dwindling. More graffiti appeared threatening death to me —even though the contract had been canceled—and news articles were run that painted me as the worst villain since the Oklahoma Bomber. I overheard people talking about me every day. The things they said were not complimentary.

It started to wear on me. I risked my life each night, trying to stop crime, and the whole time I had to watch what was around me, watch my back, so some helpful citizen didn't shoot me or stab me when I wasn't looking.

I hadn't paid much attention to the fan club and the websites with discussion boards about me. As things seemed to get worse, with people clamoring for me to be brought to justice and the police stating that they were actively looking for me, I felt I needed a little support, so I took a peek at what my fans were saying. That was a big mistake.

Even on the discussion boards for my main fan club, the comments were overwhelmingly negative. I looked back several weeks and read messages. Back then, everything was positive, and everyone posting seemed to love me. Then, as time went by, trolls started popping up and making comments about how I was a criminal and how someone should arrest me.

At first, some of my die-hard fans defended me, telling the critics to keep their opinions to themselves. Slowly, day by day and week by week, even those fans turned on me, starting with comments about how they doubted what I was doing and who I was and eventually getting to the point where one fan in particular, angelsgirl777, not only had changed her mind, but stated plainly that someone ought to put a bullet in my head and put me out of everyone else's misery.

It was all pretty hard to take. I didn't start fighting crime so that people would like me, but that kind of hostility made me feel bad about myself. If I was so good, how could all these people feel like I was some kind of hardened criminal?

The only good post I found in two hours of searching was one by a person with the user name Angel_fan_number1. The post was simple, but almost poetic in a way.

WHAT IS A HERO? IT IS SOMEONE WHO, REGARDLESS OF DANGER OR REWARD, SACRIFICES SOMETHING OF HIMSELF FOR A GREATER CAUSE. ALL THE HATERS IN THE WORLD CAN'T CRACK THE RESOLVE OF A TRUE HERO. ANGEL WILL PREVAIL!

Criticism in general is hard to handle, but people were saying crazy things. I was Crusher. I murdered people and disintegrated the bodies with my super powers. I had a master plan that involved me acting like a hero to gull the populace so I could implement my ultimate goal of world domination. All the crimes I stopped were staged so people would trust me, all the better to take advantage of them. The things people said I did to the homeless, women, and even children made me sick to my stomach. It affected me and my mood, giving me a cynical and darker view of the world and humanity itself.

"It's easy for you to say to just ignore it," I told Amy. "You don't have to put up with people thinking you're the world's worst enemy."

We were in my room, for a change. She had come over after I repeatedly slithered out of going to our hideout in her garage.

"It's not easy for me to hear what others are saying, either, you know," she replied. "I'm not sleeping well, and my stomach is in knots all the time."

"*Your* stomach is in knots?" I snapped. "Everyone *hates* me. I don't mean that they're indifferent, and I don't mean that they would prefer I wasn't around. I don't even mean that they dislike me. They. Hate. Me. I see and hear comments all the time about how some hero should kill me. Kill me!"

"I know, Daniel." Amy's eyes dropped to her hands, which fidgeted in her lap. It *was* affecting her. She was hurting, too.

"Listen, Amy," I said. "I'm sorry for snapping at you. It's just so frustrating. And scary. I mean, there is a real possibility that someone will try to kill me, and not a criminal. What do I do if some kid tries to put a knife into me or shoot me because he thinks he's being a hero and acting for the greater good?"

"I understand," she said.

"No, I don't think you do. Do you understand fearing for your life every second of the day? I'm scared to death that someone will find out my identity. I'm kind of hard to kill, but my family? What if people decide to go after them? What can I do? I can't be with them all the time to protect them. What about you? What if they come after you? Have you thought of that?"

"Yeah," Amy said. "I have."

I scrubbed my hand through my hair. "I feel like something is alive in my belly, something vicious and wanting to get out. It feels like it's tearing me apart from the inside out. I don't know how I'm going to survive this, even if no one tries to kill me."

"Then quit."

I stared at her, mouth open. "Quit?"

"That's right," she said. "Just stop. Burn the suit, don't go out on patrol, don't ever show your cowl again. Quit."

She made it sound so simple. Walk away and don't look back.

"I can't quit," I said. "You know that. We're talking about the safety of an entire city. There's no one else who can stop Crusher. At least not here. There are other people with powers, some of whom even fight crime, but nowhere close, not who have made themselves known. I'm all this city has."

"What good will it do if you self-destruct because of the stress?" Amy said. "If you have a nervous breakdown, how will that save the city?"

"I don't know," I said. "I just don't know."

"Daniel, you have to figure out who you are and what you want. I understand feeling afraid that everyone is trying to kill you, or wanting to. I know how it feels to have everyone else against you, with no one on your side. I'm part of the Angel, too, so everything that is said feels directed at me also. Ultimately, you have to decide what is most important. Is it the job, how people see you, what any particular person thinks? You're like a brightly colored flag, or a cape, all wrapped up tightly in a bundle. Are you going to draw in on yourself, keeping the bundle tight, or will you let yourself unfurl, letting the wind catch you so that everyone can see the brilliance you have been keeping wrapped up? It's up to you, of course, but whatever you do, it has to be your decision, it has to be something you can live with."

I don't know why, but it irritated me that she took this opportunity to preach to me. Anger rose up in me like a smoldering coal coming to life. It was being stoked into a small flame and then into a raging inferno.

"Yeah," I said, more harshly than I would have liked. "Now's a great time to give me a lecture. I'm not a flag, or a cape, and spreading out only makes me an easier target. You just don't get it, do you? It's easy for you, sitting behind your computer and in complete anonymity, to tell me what to do. I'm on the front lines here. I'm the one with crosshairs on his head, with people wanting to do everything from sending me out of the country to lopping off my head. Walk a mile in my cape and then come back and talk to me about what noble things I can do."

"I'm just trying to—"

"I know what you're trying to do. You're trying to talk me into feeling better about the whole world being against me and about feeling scared to death all the time, every second of the day. But you know what? You can't. You don't understand, can't understand. Sometimes I'm sorry I ever even saw you in trouble in the park. That's when all this started."

Amy's eyes grew wide, as did her mouth. Then both slowly closed in, her mouth into a tight line and her eyes barely slits. Water filled those orbs, but she fought to keep them from escaping.

"I see," she said, voice trembling. "Well, I hope you figure out what to do. If you're going to be a super-jerk, you can do whatever it is that you'll do by yourself. You don't need someone who doesn't understand anything."

She turned, went to the door, and opened it. As she walked through, she said to the hallway outside, "I hope you work it all out, Daniel. Be safe," and she left.

My anger receded, being quickly replaced by guilt and sadness. I almost ran after her to apologize. Almost. I'm not sure what kept me from it. Probably pride, though a tiny voice inside me said she would be better off, safer, if she wasn't close to me. If anyone ever found out who I was, all my friends and loved ones would be at risk. I knew it for a lie even as I explained it to myself. The simple fact was that I was too much of a jerk and too stubborn to tell her I was sorry.

I closed my door softly, lay down on my bed, and wallowed in self-pity.

29

The next several days, I didn't want to do anything. I basically went through my normal routine without caring about what happened. I woke up, went to school, came home, laid around, and then went to bed. Day after day, it was the same thing.

School was the worst, I think. Amy and I always used to hang out between classes, and it was a given that we'd have lunch together every day. Since our fight I only caught glimpses of her going to or from somewhere. She never made eye contact with me, never said a word, never even looked my way. I was invisible to her. I mechanically made my way through the day in a fog.

"Daniel, what's wrong?" my mom asked the second day. "Are you feeling sick?"

"No," I answered. "I'm just bored, I guess."

"Oh," she said. "Why don't you hang out with Amy?"

She must have seen something on my face. "Oh, honey." She put her arm around me and kissed my cheek. "Are you guys having an argument?"

I sighed. "Yeah, kind of. I said some things that weren't nice, and she isn't talking to me anymore."

"I understand. You'll work it out. You guys are so close, it'll pass and it will seem like it never happened." She put her hands on my head and turned it so she was looking into my eyes. "You know, if you talked to her, apologized for saying not-nice things, it would go away faster."

"I know, Mom," I said. "I'll probably do that. Later. I'm not really in the mood to talk to anyone right now. I just want to—"

"—keep moping," she finished for me. "Yes, I know. Think about what I said, though, okay? You never know what will happen. You may never have a chance to make things right. You should always take the first opportunity to fix things like this. Don't let the friction build until it's too late to repair the damage. I learned that the hard way in my life. You don't have to."

I hugged her. "Thanks, mom. I'll think about it."

She left, and then I was there alone with my dark thoughts. I knew I should apologize, try to fix the thing between Amy and me. It wasn't *just* that it was hard to go and talk to her. I wasn't sure I should. Though it wasn't the main reason I said what I did, the simple fact was that she would be much safer if she didn't have anything to do with me. With all the enemies surrounding me, someone would surely find out my secret, and then my family and friends would all be in danger. I couldn't allow that. If it meant me feeling miserable, it was a small price to pay.

I had even bigger problems to think about, though. Crime was still getting worse, and most of it was being blamed on me. As if I had built an army of criminals and sent them out to terrorize the city. No sooner had that thought come into my head than I realized that's exactly what had happened. Crusher had built an organization, and the city's residents thought I was Crusher. I had to hand it to the man; it was a good plan. And it was working very well for him.

Just quit. I heard Amy's words in my head. Was she right? Was she speaking in anger when she said that, or was she serious? Should I retire from crime-fighting? Somehow, I couldn't see myself doing that. It just seemed, I don't know, cowardly. Still, cowards tended to live longer than brave men.

The way I saw it, I basically had two choices. I could take the easy way out, the safe way, and just drop off the face of the earth. At least, Angel could. I could just stop fighting, stop trying to be a hero, and live my life like a normal person. Or, I could keep battling the criminals that were popping up all around the city, possibly causing myself or others harm or death.

I sat down hard on the chair in front of my desk. The blinds on my window were open, and I could see all the way up our street. I could see Mr. Gilmore's house, three away from mine. He was a veteran and had a flag pole with the American flag flying in his front yard. He religiously hoisted it up the pole every morning and brought it down every evening.

The star-spangled rectangle danced in the gentle breeze. Unfurled. What had Amy said? Don't keep the brilliance wrapped up inside me. Let it come out, fly in the breeze for all to see? I wondered what she had meant by that. It was the thing that set me off, for some reason, when she was just trying to help. God, I missed her.

I had some decisions to make. Important ones. I would have to choose what kind of person I would be. Would I be a coward, or would I be a hero? I had always thought the decision to be easy, obvious, when I was younger and reading a story or a comic. Of course you would always choose to be a hero. That was what you did. It was the honorable thing, the selfless thing. It was the very definition of a hero, to put one's own life on the line for others, without expectation of repayment of any kind.

That last part stung as the thought went through my head. *Without expectation of repayment of any kind.* Wasn't that what had been bothering me? People weren't calling me a hero, not heaping praise on me, so I got upset. Why should it matter? If I wanted to help people, did it matter if they praised me or thanked me? Wasn't I just being selfish?

I thought back to the conversations Amy and I had about what makes a hero. Back before we even knew I had powers. What had she said? *"And just what does a superhero look like? Who's to say they don't look just like you?"* At another time, she said, *"I think that the powers are the least of what makes you super..."*

I thought about the post I had read on my fan site discussion board, the only positive one. *All the haters in the world can't crack the resolve of a true hero. Angel will prevail!* That sounded an awful lot like something Amy would say. I could hear her voice when I read it.

I wasn't acting like a hero. I was acting like a spoiled, rotten little brat. Peoples' opinions shouldn't matter at all to me, if I was doing the right thing.

I couldn't quit. That would be selfish. I had to see this through, stop Crusher and his plans, even if no one ever knew it was me who did it. Let them think I was a criminal. The only thing that mattered was that innocent people, like Mrs. Sanderson, would not be hurt.

My resolve to continue my work made me feel a little better. A little. I thought of Amy and wondered if she'd be proud of me. I hoped so. If this thing ended badly for me, I hoped she would understand and would not think bad thoughts of me. It was better to leave things as they were with her, to keep her from danger. If I was killed, there was no use in hurting my family, but maybe people would put two and two together and see that she had been helping me. Some might want to take vengeance out on her. No, it was better to stay apart. Safer. For her.

I looked at my phone. It was nearing eight o'clock. I had work to do, and I might as well start. I got up and went downstairs to eat something. I would be going out on patrol that night, and heaven help any criminal who tried to do harm to me or my city. The Angel was about to exact retribution on the predators in the city, whether anyone appreciated it or not.

30

S   even days into my new patrol routine, Amy sent a
         hyperlink to my e-mail. At least, I'm pretty sure it
         was Amy. It was from an e-mail address I didn't
recognize, and the link took me to a hidden page on one of
the Angel fan club discussion websites. Reading through it,
my eyes popped.

Dr. William Walters, the researcher she had told me
about, the same one Crusher had mentioned in his chat
with Ralphie, had a secret research facility in the city. He
was indeed creating some kind of serum that made people's
powers stronger. It was apparently some kind of biological
as well as chemical process that he used to make the serum
because a key part of it was waiting for cultures to mature.
That was what Crusher had referred to.

Previous tests on small animals had yielded some
promising results. The doctor had plans to test it on larger
animals, but when Crusher found out about the serum, he
decided he would test it on himself, warning the doctor that
it better work as planned. The villain had taken control of

the research center and was waiting for the cultures to reach the point where the serum could be made.

Everything fit into place. I don't know how Amy got all this information, or why she sent it to me when she hated me, but it gave me something to think about. I thought again about talking to her to patch things up, but decided that more than ever, she needed to be away from me. Things had just gotten much more dangerous.

I kept up my patrols, foiling small crimes, doing what I could while I tried to figure out what to do about Crusher himself.

Then, one day three weeks after Amy's e-mail, it seemed as if crime had taken a holiday. I patrolled, but saw nothing. That wasn't all that out of the ordinary, but there were even news reports stating that crime seemed to have all but stopped in the city. The police took credit, of course, as did many of the anti-Angel activists that had cropped up. They had scared me away, they said, and with me all of my minions. I was more than a little concerned.

I still didn't know where Dr. Walters' research facility was—I had been racking my brain trying to figure out how to discover it. Amy might have been able to find out, but since she wasn't talking to me anymore and I couldn't rely on her coming up with it out of the blue like the other information she sent me, that method of learning what I needed was gone. Instead, I swept the city, trying to find any abnormal activity. If none of the criminals were committing crimes, they had to be doing something, and I was sure that something was related to Crusher and his plan. All I needed to do was find out where they were and what they were doing.

I got a lucky break one night as I searched for clues. In a

run-down business area in the city, I saw a couple of guys I recognized as having committed minor offenses standing on the street smoking. I don't know why it struck me as odd, but it did. Using the shadows in a nearby alley, I moved closer to listen to them.

"I'm tellin' ya," one said. He was round and massive. He looked like he had been muscular when younger, but it had largely turned to flab. Still, he moved like he was strong and fairly agile. "I'll be glad when this thing is over. We've already been five days standing around and waiting for something to happen. What does the boss think, that the army is gonna attack?"

"I know," the other, much thinner and younger man said. "I don't like it any more than you do, but he's paying us, right? All we have to do is raise the alarm if that Angel guy comes around. Simple. Easy money."

"It feels like working a nine to five job," the larger man grumbled.

"Yeah, yeah. We'll get more action when it's all over and done. Two more days, he says, then things'll really start popping."

I backed away and, once out of range of their hearing, made my way to the roof. So, that was it. Crusher had put all his lackeys out to guard the research facility until the cultures were ready. This was the piece of information I had been missing.

Jumping from rooftop to rooftop, I made a wide circle, looking for other guards. Once I knew what I was looking for, it wasn't hard to spot them. In ones, twos, or threes, there were sentries posted throughout a three-block radius.

After making one particularly impressive jump—I thought so, anyway—and landing on another rooftop, I saw movement from the corner of my eye. Luckily, I was just going into a roll to dissipate the energy of the jump when I saw it and was able to adjust my body to go toward it. I came to my feet right in front of a man, his eyes wide and reflecting light from a light nearby.

He reached for a gun and for something else at the same time. I calmly struck the side of his neck, just under the jaw, with my fingers and he collapsed bonelessly to the ground. I'd been doing some research and had wanted to try that for quite some time. When I rolled him over, he had some sort of device in his hand. It was small, like a car alarm control, with only one button on it. I was sure it was the way they were supposed to report that they had seen me. I didn't think he had a chance to use it. I crushed it and the gun with my bare hands—that never really got old—and left.

They'd know I was there soon enough, once they found him. I still didn't know exactly where to go, though.

I spent the next hour tracking where all the sentries were, making sure to check each roof for watchers. By the time I had finished, I thought I knew where my prize lay. Crusher's minions were hidden better toward the center of the ring of guards, but they were also more numerous. I was only able to get within a block of where I was sure the research facility was, but I knew where I eventually needed to go.

One of the problems was that although the research facility had only five floors, all the surrounding buildings were a single story. The entire block surrounding it had buildings that were too short to jump to the roof of the building I needed to get into. Damn.

After backing off a few blocks, I sat on a roof and tried to figure out a plan. If I waited, the guard I knocked out would be found and everyone would go on high alert. If I rushed in, I would be going in blind, most likely into a trap, or several, that I'd never make it out of alive. According to the men I listened to, I had two more days until the cultures were done. None of my options seemed good.

Should I call the police to get them involved? They still thought I was the cause of all the crime in the city, and I couldn't be sure who was paid off and who was not. Most likely, they would just arrest me. There were no other superheroes here for me to call on. I didn't even have Amy to ask for help.

Again, I wondered if I should just leave it alone and let things happen like they would. Trying to storm a location protected by all the criminals in the city didn't seem like a smart thing to do. Then again, how could I just abandon the city when the people were in so much danger? If Crusher was bad now, how much worse would he be if he increased his powers? I put my head in my hands and squeezed. I just didn't know what to do.

Okay, I guess that's not completely true. I did know what to do, what I had to do. I had already decided I wouldn't run away, so it was between doing something right then or waiting. If I waited until someone found the unconscious guard on the roof, it would be much harder to get through all the other sentries. They would double or triple the number of people.

I had to act. It was a suicide mission, but probably not quite as much as if I waited until the next day to try. I couldn't say that I had the element of surprise at the moment, but the chances of survival were slightly better as far as I could see.

I just wished I wasn't so alone. Even hearing Amy's voice would help.

An idea struck me as I thought that last bit. I pulled out

my phone and scrolled through my voicemails. I was bad about deleting them, so I had every one I had received in the last few months. All twelve of them.

Most of them were from Amy. Okay, all but one. That one was from my mom. I should probably delete that one.

I selected the most recent, only three weeks old, and played it.

"Hey Daniel," her voice said, "just checking to see what you're up to. Are you coming over today? We probably have some stuff to talk about. Be an angel and let me know, k? Talk to you soon."

I smiled. She liked to slip in little inside jokes, using the word angel or kestrel or something else that sounded innocent if anyone else were to hear the message. I loved it when she did that. It made me feel like we shared a secret language, or just shared secrets. And that was exactly how it was. We did share secrets, secrets of the biggest kind.

I listened to her other messages. None of them was all that extraordinary, at least on the surface. They did make me think about all we'd been through, though, and what she meant to me. I missed her. I wanted to call her but resisted. It was very late—actually, it was very early in the morning—and she would be sleeping. Plus, she didn't want to hear from me. It was better that way, safer for her.

I sat there on my roof, tapping my phone against my lips —or at least against the mask over my lips—thinking. I would most likely die trying to do what I intended. That was fine. I thought I was ready. If the world I lived in was so twisted that I was hunted as a criminal and Crusher was praised as making change for the better, I probably didn't want to live there anyway. I'd do my best to change things, to end Crusher's reign, but I didn't delude myself into thinking that I had a good chance of success. My one regret was that I'd leave Amy thinking I didn't care. That part of it killed me.

Several months before, I wrote a long letter to my family and hid it where it wouldn't be found unless they took apart my room after my death. It explained that I was the Angel and how much they all meant to me. They would know how I felt and why I did what I did.

Amy wouldn't.

I started pecking away at my phone, composing an e-mail. This would probably be my last chance to tell her. Hopefully she'd understand in time and forgive me, maybe even think good thoughts of me.

Amy,

I KNOW you're mad at me, and you have the right. First, I want to apologize for being a jerk to you. The only defense I have is that running for my life, worrying about all my loved ones, and being publicized as a criminal has stressed me out, and I reacted badly. I'm so sorry I took it out on you.

I would have apologized much sooner, but I felt it was better if you didn't like me. With everything that's going on, if someone found out my secret identity, everyone I love would be in danger. There's nothing I can do about my family, but if I could distance you, maybe you'd be safe. I couldn't bear to think that you were harmed because of me. So, I left things as they were. It wasn't heroic or selfless. It was with the most selfish of motives that I did it. The thought of something happening to you would kill me; so you see, it was all about me.

Anyway, I'm about to try to stop Crusher from taking the serum that will make him more powerful. I found the research center (though, to be honest, you'd have probably found it much sooner), and it's surrounded by Crusher's minions. There's no time left if the city is to be saved. I have to act now.

By the time you read this, I'll most likely be dead. I'm not sure how far I can get through his army of criminals, but I have to try. Maybe I'll get lucky and one of my random powers will manifest and it'll be a nuclear bomb or something. Yeah, imagine that. Then I'd really be a terrorist, just like they all claim. If I can at least get far enough to take out Crusher before his henchmen kill me, I'll be happy.

I just wanted to tell you that you mean the world to me and that these last few weeks have been pure hell without you. It's not because of Crusher, not because of everyone against me, not even because I'm fighting a war I can't possibly win. It's just because I love you and miss you.

I'm going to go and fight bad guys now. I'm sure you'll hear about it. I hope that, in the end, you are proud of me. Any good that is in me came from you. You made me the Angel. The good one, not the bastard everyone believes me to be. Thank you. Despite what I said before, the best thing I ever did in my life was to meet you. I hope your life is happy and long. You deserve it. Goodbye, Amy.

Daniel

I sent the e-mail, watched the little status bar as it completed, and then shut my phone off. My heart felt both heavier and lighter for sending it. Okay, enough thought about that. I had some work to do, and I'd better get to it.

I felt a little calmer after deciding on a course of action. The problem was I also had no idea what I would do. I sat in thought for a moment. What was the smart way to go about trying to get yourself killed by more vicious criminals than you could count? I wondered if Batman ever had this problem. Probably not. That guy was crazy.

Great, I was talking about comic book characters as if they were real people. Maybe the superhero thing would drive me insane. Maybe it was better to go out in a blaze of glory.

Who was I kidding? I didn't want to die. I wanted to go home, get in bed, and pull the covers up over my head so the monsters couldn't get me. Growing up kind of sucks. Not for the first time—or the last, I hoped—I thought about how tough being a hero was. No wonder more people didn't do it.

Okay, enough. It was time to begin. I took a few deep breaths and started to think it through carefully. There were sentries for three or four blocks around the research center. At least some of them had a device that allowed them to instantly sound an alarm. I assumed the alarm didn't blow a loud horn, so I wouldn't know if it had been tripped. There were probably troops somewhere, just waiting for an excuse for action. The alarm would give that to them.

Earlier, I had infiltrated to within about a block of where I needed to go. Sure, there was that thing with the guy on the roof—I really lucked out that he panicked and didn't sound the alarm before I rendered him unconscious—but I did make it fairly close to Dr. Walters's facility. I prayed my luck would continue to hold.

The only thing I could do was to move as silently as possible on the roofs and, when I was eventually detected, try to keep from getting killed. With the odds I'd be facing, I probably wouldn't have the luxury of holding back my blows so I didn't hurt people too badly. It was them against me. The way I figured, I'd do my best to not kill anyone, but there was only so much I could do without affecting my efficiency and speed. Hopefully it would all work out.

I scanned the rooftops nearby. I was about five blocks from the research center, so there shouldn't be anyone near keeping guard for Crusher, but I was going to err on the side of being conservative.

Seeing no one, I started moving in.

I had decided it would be best to take the same path I did before. Unless they rotated the sentries, it should be easy to repeat what I did earlier, getting close to my target before running into a situation where it was not likely I'd be able to pass unseen.

The first few blocks were easy enough. I jumped over scattered men in the alleys beneath me. I even recognized a few from earlier, still in essentially the same places. That made me feel a bit more comfortable.

How was I going to do this all night? I was already tired just from the anticipation of someone seeing me. I needed to relax.

Yeah, like that was going to happen.

I was closing in on two blocks from the center when I saw a man on a rooftop two buildings away from where I had stopped to scan the streets. It was pure dumb luck that I even saw him, but he had seen me, too. There was no hiding his wide eyes and his mouth slightly open from the shock of seeing me. He fumbled for something in his pocket, fiddled with it, and ducked back behind an air conditioning unit when he saw that I had seen him. Great.

It was going to get much noisier and exciting in a few seconds.

On cue, a door on the ground floor of a building near me opened and men poured out of it. They all had guns and were looking around. Trying to find me.

I took the opportunity to jump to the next roof, one building closer to my goal. I heard a bullet hit the edge of the roof, way too close for me to feel comfortable about it. I rolled to the side and came up into a crouch. I ran hunched over until I reached the edge of the roof. I had no choice. I had to continue moving forward, even at the cost of having people shooting at me from behind. Better to try to outrun some than to get boxed in by all the groups.

Backing up a few steps, I took a deep breath, took off like a sprinter from the crouch, and left the rooftop with a jump that utilized the speed I had generated with my short run. This time, there were several ricochet noises, but I didn't feel any of the projectiles hit me. So far, so good.

Again, I was wrong. I was getting good and tired of being wrong.

As I landed on the new roof, I let my right leg collapse so my body could drop into a roll. That move always made me feel cool. As I came smoothly to my feet, the door to the inside of the building opened and what had to be a couple of dozen men start to stream out.

They all had guns. Several of them had already started shooting at me.

It's a good thing I have those super powers, or that would have been the end of the story right there. Finish. Done. Game over. Thank you for playing. But my speed-geared vision saw them before they could get a bead on me. I stomped down hard with both feet and dove toward some kind of big box with a chimney or something coming out of the top. I didn't know what it was, but I was glad it was there.

In my panic, I overshot it by quite a distance, clearing the top of it and landing—it was a much clumsier roll that time, not cool at all—on the other side. I scrambled toward it and put my back against whatever it was. It was sturdy, the metal fairly thick, not the thin stuff that a lot of air conditioning units I had seen were made of. It should at least deflect some of the bullets.

I needed to figure out how to get out of there alive. The gunmen spread out and started walking toward me.

31

I'd found that I was almost bullet proof that night with Eduardo Peña. Almost. I could withstand a few gunshots without being killed, but I was no Superman. Just because a bullet didn't penetrate my skin didn't mean it wouldn't cause damage. And if a projectile struck me in the eye or another delicate area like the throat, I wouldn't survive it. It was better if I didn't allow myself to be shot. How was that for stating the obvious?

I looked around for anything that could help me. There was the big metal box I was crouching behind, some air conditioning units, a few little pipes or smoke stack things coming up out of the roof, a garden hose—of all things—and not much else. A garden hose? Really? I wondered what that was for. They probably sprayed off the roof occasionally. A clean roof is a happy roof, right? It didn't matter. I might be able to use the hose.

There was also some sort of machine. A pump or something. Underneath it, there was a flat metal pan, like the kind that you put under a car that leaks oil. You know, to prevent it from getting oil all over your garage floor. That could be useful as well.

The men murmured to each other, and their boots scraped the roof as they moved into position. I didn't have long until I'd be caught in a massive crossfire that even my thick skin wouldn't help me survive. There was no time to delay.

I had considered briefly, and then discarded, the idea of tearing the big metal box from its supports and throwing it at the men. There were too many of them for it to hit all of them. With how heavy it looked, I'd probably kill the ones it did hit. I'd have to do something a little more subtle.

I heard the scratch of a footstep to my right, from the direction the metal pan and hose. I had to act then or never.

Things blurred as I raced the three steps toward the sound. The man was looking right at me, but he was still surprised when I reached out, grabbed his gun hand, twisted sharply and then swung him around and literally threw him toward the others on this side of the object I'd been hiding behind. Luckily, my movements caught the other gunmen within sight by surprise also. There were a few stray shots, but none came near me. The metal box still obstructed most of the others' view of me.

Committed to the course, I ducked to pick up the pan. I peeked around the box I'd been hiding behind and threw the pan just like a Frisbee, but low to the ground, only maybe six inches or so off the roof. It spun and skipped off the roof before it reached the first man. Bullets started to fly at me since I was visible. I had to keep moving.

I picked up the neatly coiled hose—it wasn't attached to a water line, thankfully—before I looked back to see the results of my Frisbee toss. I had thrown it with enough force to do some real damage to the first group of men. The pan was large, about two feet by three feet, but wasn't very heavy. With the speed and force I threw it, though, it was a formidable weapon.

The first unfortunate victim had one of his feet almost sheared off completely. He collapsed to the roof's surface. The next few in line weren't much luckier. As the pan ricocheted from leg to leg, the sound of bones breaking created a staccato beat, punctuated by a few gunshots. By the time the pan stopped moving, it was a crumpled piece of metal and at least a half dozen people lay on the ground moaning or screaming in pain.

More importantly, those left standing were not able to concentrate on shooting me, so though bullets were flying, I hadn't been hit yet. I meant to maintain that condition. I flicked the hose out, and it unrolled rapidly.

Some of the gunmen were recovering from their surprise, and in another few seconds, I'd have way more bullets coming at me than I could handle.

I leaped out into an open area on the roof, closer to the mass of gun-wielding enemies. I registered their surprise once again, their wide eyes showing more white than seemed natural.

Then I started to twirl.

When I say "twirl," I don't really mean that I myself twirled, though I did spin a couple of times to get things going. Mostly, though, I'm talking about the hose.

There was a workout that was popular with the Crossfit crowd and other cool fitness people. I had seen it on TV a few times and even saw people doing it in the park. It was a simple thing. They get a big thick rope, like the kind we used to have to climb in P.E. at school. The exerciser then shakes the rope, trying to make waves with it, violently moving their arms up and down to whip the rope. I did the same kind of thing with the hose, but faster, more powerfully, and—I have to say—a little bit cooler.

I combined the rope thing with spinning and swinging the hose around like a lasso. The result was satisfactory, if unsettling.

As it turns out, swinging something even as simple as a garden hose—with a heavy brass end, by the way—with enough force and speed can be devastating. With each swipe, several men went down, their legs literally swept out from under them.

The sound was fascinating and also sickening. As I swung the hose, it made the whomp-whomp-whomp sound, almost like helicopter blades, but then there was the thumping and cracking sounds when it actually struck someone. And there were screams. I think it's probably difficult to have your legs broken while you're standing on them without making any sound. It made my stomach flip-flop.

I soon had almost all the gunmen off their feet and writhing on the surface of the roof. Most had dropped their guns and were trying to soothe their injuries. I saw only four men left standing, all behind some kind of cover. I took two of them out by swinging the hose vertically or diagonally and hooking it around the obstructions. I dropped the hose and zigzagged toward the other two, hiding behind the metal box I had originally used as cover. Two broken arms later, I slammed the men together so forcefully they were both knocked unconscious.

I scanned the rooftop for any hazards I might have missed but saw none. Time to move on.

As I prepared to jump to the next roof, I noticed a few twinges of pain. My left shoulder, left side of my abdomen, and right thigh stung. Checking each area, I found bullet holes in my costume. The skin below ranged from a slight bruise (my thigh) to an angry red mark (my shoulder), to barely a smudge (my side). I hoped my luck held.

The distance between the building I was on and the next one was only twenty feet or so. I sprang from a standstill toward it. As I did, I felt that familiar energy sensation, though not exactly like one I had felt before. I had just made it to the air directly over the lip of the building I was jumping to when it manifested fully. I dropped like a safe had fallen on me.

I landed just inside the parapet on the roof with such a jarring impact that my teeth clacked together. My feet had punched holes in the roof, and by the time I came to rest, I could only see my legs down to the knee. The rest was embedded in the roof itself. I pulled them out of the holes and noticed that they felt strange, almost heavy.

Stepping onto the surface of the roof made a clanging sound. I reached down and rapped my knuckle on my left shin. It thudded dully, like a piece of solid iron. I pulled off the glove on my right hand and almost lost my balance. My hand was made of metal. Knocking on other parts of my body, I realized my entire body was made of metal. It looked like cast iron pans, sort of rough and dark looking.

I was still able to move, but I must be incredibly heavy. And bullet proof. I wished it had happened a few minutes earlier. It would have saved me some pain.

I needed to get moving while I was still bullet proof.

I had only taken a half step when I felt lighter and the sensation disappeared. I looked at my hand again. Yep, flesh. I sighed. What a waste. I wondered if any of the random powers were ever going to become permanent or if I'd eventually learn to control which ones manifested. But that was something to worry about if I lived through the night.

The buildings immediately surrounding the research center were only one story tall, so I came down to street level. I figured if they were waiting for me on the roofs, ground level would be an easier path.

I was wrong about that, too.

It was true that a lot of people were swarming onto roofs on some of the buildings, but as I ran toward where I ultimately wanted to go, a door opened in some sort of warehouse ahead of me and six people stepped out.

I blinked a few times and looked again, not believing what I saw. To be honest, they looked like a singing group or some kind of sports team.

The men—no, that's not right, one of them was a woman —were all dressed identically, in snug green bodysuits. They moved like athletes, but it only took me a moment to figure out who they were. The Six.

Uh-oh.

32

As Amy told it, the Six were famous amongst people who knew anything about organized crime and assassins. They were living weapons and never failed. The only silver lining I could think of was that they didn't use guns. They didn't usually use weapons of any kind, but when they did, their implements of war were old-fashioned, things like swords and knives and staffs. Yeah, those things can still kill, but for me, it seemed that they would be easier to withstand than guns.

I guess it depended on a lot of things, like the skill of the person using it...and of the target. Considering it that way, I wasn't so sure there was a silver lining at all.

We were in an alley, maybe fifteen or twenty feet across. Even with the seven of us just standing there, it didn't seem like there was much room. I could hear other attackers from behind me, up on roofs and on other streets and alleys. I couldn't retreat because I would run into them. The only thing I could do was to try to defeat the Six quickly and continue moving forward. Oh, and not die.

Well, here went nothing. I charged.

My opponents didn't have anything covering their faces —why would they, when any who saw them ended up dead? —and each one had a neutral expression on his or her face. They didn't look excited or nervous or anything else really. It was probably just another job to them.

All six looked similar, dark hair perfect physical specimens. By that I mean they were not bulky but still muscular, and their movements showed they were quick, flexible, and smooth. I had become used to watching people and judging their threat level by how they moved and held themselves. If I was correct, I was in for some trouble.

They split up to surround me, but I was at least experienced enough not to let them do that. I moved to the side as I came toward them, using a building as a barricade on one side. They shifted automatically to move around me on the other sides.

While I was still considering what to do, two of them attacked, lunging in with such speed they surprised me. I saw their movements with my speed-geared vision, but I hadn't expected them to be able to move so fast. I wondered if they had superpowers also.

One of the attackers threw some kicks at me while the other struck at me with his fists. As fast as my powers made me, I was hard-pressed to block the blows. Another surprise was how hard their strikes were. My limbs were like hardened wood because of my abilities, but I felt my teeth rattle when blocking the kicks coming at me. The punches weren't much better.

The flurries lasted less than five seconds, but it was enough time for the other four to box me in and come in for their attacks also. I did the only thing I could. I jumped straight up, over their heads, tucked into a roll, and did a flip, landing awkwardly ten feet away. I really needed to practice the acrobatics.

I turned just in time for the closest three to attack me. Again, I frantically blocked. Or tried to. I turned aside most of what was directed at me, but a few came through. They hurt more when they hit my body than when they hit my arms. Another lesson for any who might be paying attention.

I was getting nowhere. I wondered if I could outrace them to the research center, but discarded the idea when I realized there might be other groups waiting for me there. I'd have to deal with the Six first. And soon, before the other groups behind caught up with me.

I dove at one of them, body slamming him and continuing on, carrying both of us out of the circle the others made around me. If the wide eyes on the man I tackled were any indication, he was surprised at my speed and power. Just wait.

I got up before he did. I think I knocked the wind out of him, so he was slow to move again. I had some room, so I started swinging at the others, punching where I could or just using my hands as mallets at the end of my arms when I couldn't. It made them more careful about when they lunged in to try to hit me.

They were masterful. Not only were they experts individually, but they worked well together, luring me in so that the others could strike me, distracting me so that I could be attacked from a different side. I had to even the odds.

I grabbed the next kick that came in. Even with my speed and strength, I just barely snagged it, but I did.

Closing my hand around the ankle, I pulled with all my strength and then whipped the unfortunate man toward one of his companions. The sound of tearing—I hope it was cloth and not part of the man—was loud and made me queasy. It took the two out of the fight. For a moment, anyway.

The woman and one of the other men rushed in, with the other two not far behind. The closest man reached his hand over his shoulder to his back, and when he brought it down again, there was a stick in it. Great, they decided I was worth using weapons against. I tried not to take it as too big a compliment as I prepared for the fight to go to the next level.

Before the stick-wielder could reach me, though, another of the men flicked his hand toward me in a blur. My body reacted automatically—thank you, strange self-preservation power—and dipped me to my left side, almost as if my foot had slipped. Several things whizzed by my head. A second later, I heard three thunks in the wall on the other side of me and more than ten feet away.

There was no time to wonder if more projectiles would be thrown at me. Stick man had reached me and whirled his weapon, trying to crack my skull. The woman had arrived at the same time, and she threw kicks so fast at me that my speed vision could barely see them. I wasn't sure how long I could keep her strikes at bay, and the other two were only a few steps away. Worse, the man I'd hit with the thrown person was shaking off the effects of my attack and had started toward me. It seemed like a good time to run.

I didn't.

One of my favorite Youtubers I found when trying to learn how to fight quoted an ancient strategy master, saying that if you are overwhelmed, outmatched, and have no chance of winning, yet escape is unlikely, the best thing to do is to attack. So I did.

The stick came at the right side of my head with lightning speed. I moved to the left a fraction of an inch and left and dipped my left knee so my head dropped under the strike. I could feel the air of the strike passing. Immediately, I straightened and, before the attacker could change the weapon's direction, I slapped the arm holding the stick. Very hard. Not to parry it, but to redirect it. Right toward his female counterpart.

The woman was on one leg, firing several kicks at me. My maneuver to slip the stick—that was the boxing term I had learned that referred to bobbing and weaving out of the way of a strike—also moved me just out of range of her kicks. When I slapped the stick-wielder's arm, he over-rotated and lost his balance. Even better, it caused the stick to arc around and strike the woman squarely in the face. There was a cracking sound, and something white and small flew from her. Yeah, she'd be going to the dentist to talk about her options later.

I took advantage of the momentary confusion and kicked the man with the stick before he could recover completely. Unfortunately for him, my kick connected while he was twisted at the waist. Another loud crack sounded, and he flew from me, striking the wall, sliding down it, and finally coming to rest. Ribs, vertebrae, or something else was broken. Whatever it was, he and the woman—she appeared to have been knocked out—were no longer threats.

Obviously, I had decided I would not hold back with these assassins. They were too good, and if I held back, I would be killed. Turning to face the other three just as they were about to reach me, I hoped their bodies were as tough as their attacks.

More projectiles flew toward me. Knowing what to look for this time, I saw them speeding through the air. There were four, two from each of his hands, and they flew as if in formation. This guy was really good. But so was I, and his fancy throwing made it possible for me to do what should be impossible. I stepped aside, swept my hand out in an arc and scooped all four missiles out of the air. Without a pause, I turned in a circle and launched them right back at him.

The darts struck him in the chest. Now, I don't know how to throw things like knives or darts, so it could be expected that I wouldn't do it right. Lucky for my opponent, I didn't. The darts turned end over end, striking him either flat along their lengths or on the dull side. The force I threw them with, though, was enough to propel him backward, off his feet, making him do an awkward half-flip to land on his face. He didn't get up.

Two left.

The last two attacked me at the same time, opting for punching rather than kicking. I had spent too much time with the Six already. I threw my arms out and punched their strikes as they came toward me. Two more crunching sounds reverberated in the cold night air. I didn't have time to figure out if it was my bones or theirs that broke, but the safe money was on it being theirs. While the two were stunned at what I had just done, I spun around to gain some momentum and kicked the man on the right. It was so powerful that it knocked him aside like he was a blade of grass and continued on to knock the other assassin almost as strongly. They both flew several feet and landed in a heap, moaning and unable to get up. I hoped I hadn't killed any of them, but I couldn't check.

Each second I spent would be more time for the enemies to surround me.

The fight had taken a lot out of me, and I was bruised and battered because of it, but I thought it was safe to continue. As I had hoped, my toughness kept my own bones from breaking when punching the attackers' punches. I felt like I'd been hit by a truck and I was bleeding from my nose, two places on my lips, and under my left eye. How could they have hit so hard to make me bleed where bullets couldn't?

Moving awkwardly because of my soreness and bruises, I built my stride into a lumber and then a jog. I could see the research center ahead. I was almost there.

I slowed as I came up to the research center, which looked like all the other run-down businesses in the area: brick walls and a simple metal door with no signs or markings of any kind, though it was five stories instead of just one. The surrounding establishments were warehouses or factories of some kind. I supposed it was the perfect place to carry on secret research. If it wasn't for the guards I had seen there earlier, I would never have known it was the building I was looking for.

There was a little pad next to the door, one of those receivers for entry cards that you swipe the card across. I reached for the door handle, fully expecting that I'd have to use my strength to bash the door in, but my hand never quite reached it.

My body suddenly spasmed, almost like an electrical current had passed through it. I bent over backwards, almost double. I didn't even know my body could do that. While I was wondering what had just happened, what diabolical attack had been aimed at me, I heard a loud crack and the brick in front of me shattered.

Someone had just tried to shoot me, and my body's automatic defense mechanism had activated. The bullet struck right where my head had been.

Body control regained, I sped around the corner of the building at my top speed. That should keep them from being able to get a bead on me.

I looked toward where the bullet had to have come from. I didn't see anything. Was there just one, or were there several snipers out there? The delay in feeling fear ended and my hands started to shake. I had almost died, just like that. I couldn't wait for long. There were others out there looking for me besides that one sniper. I couldn't give them the time to catch up.

I scanned the area for anything that could help me. I was so close. All I had to do was to get through that door. I spotted a manhole cover in the alley behind me. That could be useful.

With a burst of speed, I zipped to the cover, reached down and put my fingers through the slots in it, and scooped it up without stopping my run. A bullet ricocheted nearby. Yeah, the sniper was still out there.

I couldn't think of anything else to do, so I ran in circles, holding the manhole cover in front of me like a shield, trying to keep it between me and where the shooting was coming from. I felt more than heard the pings of bullets hitting the shield twice. If the sniper hit my shield two times, he was either very good or I was being predictable in my running. I began to zigzag and turn randomly. Bullets still came, but none hit the shield or me. Still, I couldn't run in circles forever.

But then, I didn't need to. I had been paying attention, and I knew where the gunman was. I even caught a glimpse of some movement at the location to confirm it.

Weighing my options, I realized there was only one thing I could do. I ran as close to the building where the sniper hid as I could, changed directions twice, set myself up for the perfect angle, and then threw the manhole cover as hard as I could.

The covers they use for manholes in the street are heavy. They can weigh more than a hundred pounds, some much more than that. That's like a small person, or me.

My Frisbee flew true, thankfully. The sniper was hiding behind the parapet on the roof of the building in front of me. The manhole cover struck with such force that it tore through a four-foot section of the building. It looked like an explosion. When the dust cleared, there was a massive hole and no sign of the gunman. I stopped my frantic running and waited.

Nothing.

I'm not sure what happened to the sniper, but I didn't think I had to worry about him anymore. I turned toward the research center, down the alley a half a block. Ten more gunmen poured out the door.

I sighed. Why would I have thought it would be easy?

The men—all men this time—were dressed in tactical gear, like a SWAT team or special forces or something. They also all held what looked like assault rifles. I don't know much about guns, but I recognized these were ones I didn't want to get hit by. Even my tough skin couldn't withstand the bullets from those. As they swung their barrels toward me, I started to run. Again.

It seemed to me that I had spent the entire night running. In fact, the sky seemed to be lightening, so I think I *had* been running all night. If I survived, I'd need to work on other techniques for staying alive. I couldn't always just run and throw things. That will only work for so long before it's no longer effective. I hoped it would be effective one more time.

The constant sound of gunfire assaulted my ears. Great, they were using fully automatic weapons. Then again, why would they not?

I dashed around the corner before the swarm of bullets could hit me. There was a dumpster nearby, and another manhole cover. I didn't see anything else of much value. Wait. There was one other thing. A hasty plan formed in my mind.

I sped to the dumpster, picked it up in one motion, and hurled it toward where the men would be coming around the corner. Before it landed, I dove for the manhole, pulled the cover off, put it under my arm like a football, and jumped as high as I could to the roof nearby.

The dumpster had been full of garbage. When the container landed, it split and the refuse flew everywhere. The gunmen were more concerned with dodging shrapnel than trying to shoot me, so they hadn't noticed me jumping to the roof. So far, so good.

It wouldn't be long before they figured out what happened, so I had to act fast. I had one chance.

The men were good. They were not bunched up, so my new Frisbee couldn't take them all out, no matter how many times it bounced. Still, they were all within about forty feet of each other. It might be enough.

I waited, watching them carefully. They recovered from the dumpster bomb quickly and regained formation. They used hand signs to communicate, the leader directing them to move around the corner to where I had been before jumping to the roof.

I waited.

When the first two men got to where I wanted them, I flung the manhole cover and prayed my aim was true.

It was.

The heavy iron disc flew downward. It bounced slightly off the concrete wall of the building across the alley from my rooftop perch and struck my target: the huge pipes that carried emergency fire water to the manufacturing business within the building. The pipes—they had to be almost two feet across—shattered with the force and more water than I've ever seen before in my life started pouring out.

I was surprised at first to hear the fire alarm but then realized it probably sounded automatically when the water flowed.

And it was flowing.

The flood knocked all the men off their feet. I had thought it would just be a distraction, but the amount of water coming out swept them all through the alley as if it was a canyon and they were in a flash flood. Honestly, it worked better than I had ever thought possible.

It was a simple matter to run across the roof, jump down to ground level, and render each gunman unconscious as the flow dissipated a block or so away. It was like plucking frogs from a bucket.

I went toward the research center again, ready to go in this time. I had reached my destination, but I was so tired. I wasn't sure how many more battles I had left in me.

I noticed it was light outside. When had the sun come up? Even more importantly, people were boiling out of the neighboring buildings. More people than I could possibly fight. My heart dropped into my stomach. Well, it had been a nice try.

I blinked several times and shook my head to clear it. I was so tired I wasn't thinking straight. The people coming out of the buildings didn't have weapons. They were workers in the nearby factories and warehouses, coming out because of the fire alarm. I heaved a sigh of relief and turned to the research center door.

Crusher stood in the doorway, a wry smile on his face.

"You must be the Angel," he said. "Are you ready to go to heaven?"

33

I had only ever seen Crusher in his Donald Lancaster persona. He was very good at coming off as a respectable person wearing the clothes he wore and acting the way he did. He had charisma strong enough to turn the entire city against me. The person in front of me didn't look like the same man.

His chiseled jaw was the same, as was his long hair pulled back and the fashionable stubble on his chin, but that familiar face looked more sinister, meaner. For one thing, he had earrings in both his ears, circles of metal that somehow seemed to make him look tougher. He was also bare-chested. Tattoos covered his chest and arms, and his nipples were pierced, but even more menacing was the fact that he was really muscular. I mean, like one of those guys you see modeling underwear or swimsuits. It was intimidating.

I only had a chance to glance at the tattoos, which included swirls and colors, realistic eyes that seemed to be staring at me, a rising sun, and large, stylized letters spelling

"Crusher" across his chest just under his neck. I gulped. The whole picture made me wonder if I could outrun him.

"I have already taken the serum," he said to me, almost conversationally. "Just in case you were wondering. You fought almost all night to get here in time, and you're too late. I took it, and I can already feel my powers increasing. You were no match for me before, but you are less than a gnat to me now. So, are you ready to die, little Angel? You have been an annoying insect to me and my plans for far too long."

Gasps rose from the crowd that had gathered. As I scanned them, I saw several with cell phones held in front of them, obviously taking video.

"You just revealed that you were the villain all along," I said. "You just told all these people that it was you in charge of all those criminals, not me."

He smirked. "You don't see, do you? I only needed them to be against you so you wouldn't be in my way. It's too late for them to do anything to me now. I really thought you'd quit when everyone in the city started calling for your execution. Why? Why didn't you just quit and go away?"

I knew the conversation was doing nothing useful, but every minute I was able to distract him was one more minute I had to figure out what to do, one more minute the police or National Guard, the marines, or someone else would have to come to my rescue.

"Heroes don't quit," I said, lifting my chin and trying my hardest to look the part, even though I had to clench my legs to keep my knees from shaking. "Whether others understand or not, heroes push on."

"Oh," he laughed, "is that what you are, a hero?" Crusher cracked his knuckles and rolled his shoulders.

"Well, hero, time's up. Let's see how your pathetic powers hold up to mine."

Even with my speed-geared vision, I only detected movement just before his punch landed on my jaw. It was so fast. As I left my feet and flew through the air, trying to stay conscious, I wondered what I could do to survive.

Luckily, my body had moved just as he struck. My internal automatic defense mechanism must have kicked in and caused me to roll with the punch, just enough to keep my jaw from shattering or other potentially fatal things from happening to me. Even so, it wasn't fast enough to allow me to dodge the punch completely. That didn't make me hopeful.

I landed on top of some of the people in the crowd. I hoped no one was seriously hurt, but I had other things to think about right then. I sprang to my feet and jumped into the center of the street, where there were no bystanders to injure. Crusher walked calmly toward me, a sinister smile on his face.

"Come here, boy," he said, "and I'll make it quick. You're no match for me."

He was right, but I wasn't going to show how scared I was. Instead, I lunged as fast and hard as I could.

The attack surprised him, and I landed a punch to his face. His head snapped back. My hand throbbed like I had hit solid rock. No, worse than that. Like I had hit solid rock back before I had my powers. I'd never felt anything so hard since they manifested.

My momentum had carried me past Crusher, so I turned to see him probing his lip with a finger, holding it out to look at the blood on it, and smiling. It wasn't a friendly smile. He spat on the ground and started walking toward me again.

My second punch never came anywhere close to him. He ducked it, came back up, and hit me three times before I knew it. As the last of the three landed, an uppercut that lifted me off my feet and threw me backwards, I thought of how much trouble I was in. He actually knew how to fight, and he was stronger and faster than me.

I landed awkwardly on my back and was up again immediately. Well, if I was going to die anyway, I might as well put in a good showing. I jumped toward him, putting both feet out in front of me to drop-kick him.

Crusher casually stepped aside and plucked me out of the air. He hardly moved at all when he changed my direction and threw me off to the side. My body pinwheeled, arms and legs akimbo, until I collided with the brick side of a building. Pain shot through every part of my body, and stars twinkled in my vision. Things became dark around the edges of my sight, and I thought I might lose consciousness. I flopped out of the hole my body had made in the wall as if it was someone else's body. I came to rest finally on the concrete sidewalk.

I told myself to get up, to get back into the fight, to move. My limbs didn't pay any attention to me. If I didn't rouse myself, Crusher would end my life. I had to move.

I shook my head to try to make the ringing go away. My vision blurred for a moment and then snapped back into focus. Crusher was casually making his way toward me to finish me.

Pieces of brick lay all around me. I picked them up, one at a time, and threw them at the man. With my speed and strength, they were hardly visible. The first two surprised him—he probably figured I couldn't move at all—and they hit him in the face and the shoulder. The next five he either smacked out of the air or dodged completely.

That was fine, though. They bought me enough time to gather my senses and jump to the roof of the building. If I was going to die, I needed to make sure I hurt as few people as possible in the process. Fighting on the roof would be a better choice. As expected, he jumped to the roof as well.

I was happy to see that Crusher's powers seemed to be the same as mine. He was strong and fast, and I assumed his skin was tough like mine. No laser eyes, flying, or other crazy powers. I could be thankful for that, at least. Yeah, I'd die the old fashioned way, crushed to death by his bare hands. Much better than dying quick from a laser blast.

I had gained myself a few minutes of life but didn't know what to do next. I moved to the point on the roof farthest from where Crusher landed. The whomp-whomp-whomp of a helicopter rotor pulsed in the air. It was a news chopper. Too much to ask for it to be a police helicopter. Or a military chopper. With a machine gun. I smiled up at the cameraman and gave a thumbs-up gesture. At least I'd look good on the footage. They could show a high definition clip of my death at my funeral.

I frantically searched the roof for anything to use as a weapon. There were the same old objects I had seen on roofs all night: air conditioning units, little pipes and smoke stack looking things, and not much else. No hoses on this roof, and no big box to hide behind. They wouldn't have worked anyway. Not against this foe.

With nothing else to do, I snapped one of the little pipes off. It was only about two feet long, but it was something.

"I'm done playing with you, boy," Crusher said. "Time to go night-night." He dipped his head and charged.

I barely avoided his hurtling body, slipping aside just enough to keep from being thrown off the roof. I felt like a bull fighter. As he passed, I swung my little pipe as hard as I could at his head.

I watched in horror as the pipe bent around his skull, apparently doing no damage at all. He shook his head, pulling the pipe from my hand and tossing it. It clattered to the roof a dozen feet away, useless.

His punch came out of nowhere. It connected with my abdomen, kind of on my side, launching me twenty feet in the air. It felt like something broke or tore when it happened. I floated, weightless, for what seemed like a long time, seeing the world blur by.

I would say that the landing knocked the wind out of me, but that wasn't true. I didn't have any wind to begin with. I bounced once, noticing how I had caved part of the roof in, and then settled again with a thump. I sucked to pull breath in and then wished I hadn't. The scream I let out would have been much louder if I had any air left in my body. I figured the end was near.

Crusher wasn't messing around anymore. He started toward me, almost running. He was going to finish me. I was scared, of course, but I was satisfied that I had given it my best shot. The simple fact was that I was outmatched.

Still, I rolled over onto my stomach and did the most pathetic push-up ever seen to limp to my feet. If I was going to die, I was going to do it with the last shred of defiance I had left in me. I put my left foot forward, into as close to a fighting stance as I could manage. I raised my arms— another mistake with the broken ribs Crusher had just given me—and waited for the end.

As I waited for a punch powerful enough to crush my skull, I saw a flash of movement and suddenly my foe wasn't there any longer. I blinked, shook my head, and blinked again. Where had he gone?

A noise to the left drew my attention. Crusher was peeling himself out of what was left of an air conditioning box, shaking his own head. What had happened? I looked at my hands. Maybe it was one of those random powers that came up occasionally, or maybe it was my automatic defenses. Whatever it was, I wasn't going to argue with it.

I took a few deep breaths—okay, they were shallow breaths, but they hurt like deep ones—and prepared myself. Maybe if I could do that again, there could be a chance I'd live through the night. Well, day now.

Crusher was looking around for something, focusing on looking up. He climbed from the twisted metal and glared at me. "It won't save you," he said.

He moved toward me, still looking around. There was another flash of movement, and he turned quickly, turning as if to dodge something. Still, he was struck by something —someone?—and slid across the roof. All I had seen was a flash of green. Maybe I had been hit harder than I thought if I was hallucinating.

Crusher spit curse words like I had never heard anyone do before. He jumped to his feet quickly and turned in a circle, scanning the sky again. When the green flash came again, I noticed it. But so did he. He dodged it, striking at it as it zoomed past. Hitting it right toward me.

I still wasn't at a hundred percent, so I couldn't have reacted if I had wanted to. However, my automatic defenses were on high alert, it seemed. Something else controlled my body and I twisted while catching the speeding object, lessening the force of the bodies colliding but also making me feel like my insides were tearing apart. I screamed, or grunted—no, I scream-grunted—and finally came to rest after having spun completely around. I was holding someone in my arms.

"I got your note," she said, blue eyes staring into mine.

34

I put her at arm's length to get a better look at her. She was dressed all in green with a big stylized K in the middle of her chest. The costume was very tight, making me uncomfortable at having her so close. Her raven hair was drawn back into a ponytail coming out of the back of her cowl, which did not hide the fact that she was probably the most beautiful woman I had ever seen. Unlike mine, hers only covered half her face, leaving the bottom unobstructed. I felt my face flush for several different reasons, not the least of which was that I had a dream in my arms, and I should have been concentrating on fighting Crusher.

"Amy?" I whispered.

She nodded. "I prefer Kestrel when I'm dressed like this, if you don't mind."

"How—" I started, but she put a gloved finger to my lips.

"We'll talk later. We have a bigger problem right now." She nodded her head toward Crusher, who was coming toward us.

"Right," I said. "Any plans?"

"Don't get killed," she said. "I'll think of something."

She kissed me on the cheek and flew up and out of my arms. I goggled. When did she learn to fly?

Crusher came at me, but only part of his focus was on me as he scanned the skies. He was no longer taunting me, however.

Before he got to me, a shadow passed nearby on the roof.

Crusher disappeared as a trash dumpster suddenly appeared where he was standing. Part of the roof caved in from its weight, but it didn't fall all the way through. He heaved the dumpster off. As he climbed out from the hole, hatred burned in his eyes.

Before he could react, I doubled up both fists and swung as hard as I could at his jaw. I had mixed feelings when it connected. I felt elated that I had landed a good, solid blow, but I was also in agony from my broken ribs. As I watched him fly across the roof, it occurred to me that I might be bleeding internally. Even if Amy—Kestrel—and I could defeat him, I might still die. Beating him and dying was much better than I had hoped, though. I'd take it. It beat losing and dying.

Crusher had no sooner gotten to his knees than Kestrel walloped him again. This time, I saw that she wasn't hitting him with her fists but with some objects she held in her hands. Yeah, we'd definitely need to talk. If I survived.

We had Crusher on the run, and he actually showed signs of injury. He bled from several locations on his face, and bruises developed in others. There were no cuts from the things he'd been hit with—or had dropped on him—but he was looking more mortal all the time.

Kestrel and I worked well together. I would try to hit Crusher so she could blindside him, and when he was paying attention to her, I would hit him, kick him, or throw any piece of wreckage or something else at him that was close at hand. He was actually looking nervous.

Kestrel misjudged one of her passes, and he struck her a glancing blow, sending her spinning off. I lunged in—okay, it was more of a pathetic hobble—and tried to hit him, but he almost disdainfully slapped my attack aside. He grabbed at me, but I dodged his grasp. I counter-grabbed and pulled him toward me.

If he hadn't been dazed still from his last knock, I never would have been able to do what I did. I still don't believe it. As I pulled him toward me, I punched toward his face as hard as I could with the other fist. The pulling and punching at the same time snapped his head back when the strike landed—I think I was as surprised as he was—and his eyes rolled back for just a moment. I thought I might have knocked him out.

I didn't.

He fell backward, and I lost my grip on him. The villain landed awkwardly on his back and rolled to a stop on his hands and knees. Shaking his head to clear it, he directed his unfocused gaze to me again. There was murder in those eyes, even more than before. I started to move toward him anyway. We were both in bad shape, so maybe if I got lucky, I'd be able to actually knock him out.

I never had the chance to get to him.

Kestrel streaked out of the sky. I thought she would hit him again, but she had something different in mind. She grabbed Crusher, hugged him to her, and flew off with him.

"No!" I yelled to her, but she was already too high to hear me. What did she think she was doing?

I watched as Kestrel rocketed up into the sky. After a moment of stunned immobility, Crusher started to fight back. He was much bigger and stronger than Amy, and he broke her hold on him easily. They were so high, I could hardly see what they were doing, but it was obvious it was some kind of scuffle.

Kestrel still flew upward, dragging her opponent with her. He wriggled and maneuvered his body, and then I saw what he was going to do.

"Kestrel!" I called. "Push him away. Drop him. He's going to—"

I never finished my sentence. Not that she probably heard me anyway. Before I got the words out, Crusher did as I knew he would. He held onto one of her arms with his left hand, drew his other arm back, and fired a punch at her. Luckily, hanging by one arm made his movements awkward, and his fist only struck a glancing blow on the side of her head. It was enough to make her let him go completely.

The force of his blow, and trying to pull her at him with his other arm, caused him to lose his grip. He was too far up for me to see his face, but I could imagine it as he realized he was suspended in mid-air, the instant before he began plummeting toward the ground.

They had gone at least twice as high as the tallest building in that part of the city. I'd been on all those buildings, some of them reaching more than twenty floors into the sky. Crusher was falling that distance. The news chopper flew nearby, the camera no doubt recording every second of it.

It was a horrible sight, but I was more concerned with Amy. She had spun off from the force of the blow and was still trying to right herself. At least she didn't seem in danger of falling out of the sky, but if she didn't recover within the next second or two, there was no way she'd be able to swoop in and save Crusher's life. If she even wanted to. I found myself hoping she could save him and at the same time hoping she couldn't. Would she be able to make it in in time?

I, and all those around me, had our answer soon enough. Crusher dropped out of the sky, hit the parapet of the roof I was still standing on with a sickening crunch, striking it crossways with his side, and then continued downward, spinning wildly to strike the concrete below head first. From my vantage point, I watched his head make a crater in the pavement. His skull, toughened by his powers, was no match for gravity and reinforced concrete. It was crushed like a melon dropped from a rooftop. I felt like I was going to throw up everything I had ever eaten.

Amy had regained enough control to fly toward Crusher, but she had been too late. She was only ten feet from him when he hit the roof. It might as well have been a hundred. She had tried, though.

I swallowed hard a few times until my stomach settled. Looking up, I saw Amy—Kestrel; I needed to remember to call her that when in costume—flying toward me, her face pale and sickly. She had seen, too. She landed next to me.

"I tried to get to him," she said. "I wasn't fast enough."

"I know," I said softly. "I know. It's not your fault."

"I was just trying to bring him high enough so that he couldn't breathe," she told me, "so he would pass out. For some reason, I don't have trouble breathing no matter how high I go. Once he was unconscious, I figured we could give him to the police. Why did he fight? He had to have known he would fall."

"I don't know," I said. "I think he panicked. It's over now."

"Yeah."

I looked at her. She was frazzled and still a little

unsteady standing there, but I scanned her, looking for injuries and, honestly, just enjoying the sight of her. She looked amazing. Her costume showed every line and curve of that perfect body of hers, and her face—even with the cowl—was so obviously beautiful that, even after a battle like that, she could have been the cover model on any magazine I could name. In fact, if I saw a girl like that on the street, the first thing that would come to mind is, "she is so out of my league."

"What?" she asked, noticing my eyes skimming over her and stopping to look into hers.

"You...you're gorgeous," I said. "I mean, I still prefer how you always look, but, wow. They're going to make posters of you, you know. You really look like a superheroine."

She blushed and a wave of heat rushed up and down my body. "You're the hero. You fought all night, knowing you couldn't win. You knew you'd die, and still you did it. I'll say it again, you're my hero."

It was my turn to blush. We stood there, eyes locked, for what had to be several minutes before I blinked and realized where we were. I started to say something, but she interrupted me by pulling me close, peeling my mask halfway up, and kissing me.

I resisted at first, surprised, but only for a half a second. Then I put my arms around her and kissed her back, stroking her ponytail with one hand and pulling her tight against me with the other. It hurt my ribs, but I was willing to put up with a little pain for this. I felt her arms wrap around me, too. The world swirled, and when we pulled apart, I saw that we were thirty feet above the roof of the building we had been on, in plain view of everyone. The news helicopter hovered nearby, camera pointed at us.

I smiled at her. "Thanks for the help, Kestrel." Putting

my mouth near her ear, I whispered, "Maybe we should leave. I have to go tell Amy how much I love her."

She leaned in and whispered back, "I have a feeling she has a few things to tell you, too." She replaced my cowl and kissed it over where my ear was as I noticed the sirens and lights far below us. The police had finally arrived.

35

Amy took us directly to the hospital where my friend Sharon was. After a full examination, it was determined that I had cracked two ribs but was in surprisingly good shape for having been shot and beat up and basically manhandled all night long. Amy had some bruises and a fair sized lump on her head but didn't have a concussion and was in much better shape than me. Much better shape. I saw the way the two male orderlies in the emergency room looked at her. They thought her shape was good, too.

After being patched up and given instructions on how to heal properly, we left, Amy flying us to our training area hidden in the trees where she had stashed some street clothes. She thought of everything. She was the best.

We were soon in her garage, our secret hideout. It was only mid-morning, and though I just wanted to sleep, there were some things we had to discuss.

"How long have you had super powers?" I asked.

"Not long. Maybe a month"

"You seem to have gotten the hang of them."

"Yeah," she said. "There are only really two things, though. I can fly, and I can make anything I touch weightless so I can pick it up and fly with it."

"Really?" I said. "That's awesome. Is there a limit to what you pick up? A weight or size limit?"

She shook her head. "I don't think so. I haven't picked up really big items, though. That dumpster I dropped on Crusher, that was about the biggest and heaviest thing I've tried so far. I wanted to talk to you so badly when I realized I had powers. I had my phone ready to dial your number at least a dozen times, but I forced myself not to. You had things to work out, and I had to let you.

"It was only two days after we fought. I don't know, maybe it was the strain of losing you, the emotions of feeling like you didn't care, like I had let you down, that caused them to activate. It makes me wonder how many people have latent powers waiting to be activated if they were put in the right situation."

"Well," I said, "I'm sorry I caused you so much pain. I'm glad that you developed those abilities, though. You saved my life. And now maybe I can test you and scratch things in a notebook." I winked at her.

I looked her over. She was back in her ill-fitting clothes with her hair in a mess of mismatched pigtails. He oversized glasses hid some of her face, too.

"You know, you are so beautiful, it's hard for me to think around you," I said.

"Aw, thank you. It shouldn't be a problem when I'm like this, though. You should be able to think well enough when I look like I normally do."

I looked her in the eyes, this time without getting too nervous. "Amy, I mean how you look now. You look amazing in your costume, and you're as beautiful as a supermodel with your hair coming through the back of your cowl and everything, but how you look normally, how you look now, I think you're even more gorgeous like this."

Her eyes went wide for a moment, and then her eyebrows drew down and her eyes narrowed at me. She must have seen something in my eyes that told her I was telling the truth, and she wrapped her arms around me and kissed me. This one was even better than our flying kiss. "You really think so?" she said when she pulled away enough to look at me.

"Definitely."

After a few more long kisses, she settled her head against my chest. We stayed like that for several minutes, until I almost fell asleep. It was so comfortable. I didn't want it to end.

She had other ideas, though. Tilting her head to kiss my chin, she sighed and sat back into her chair. Reaching down, she picked up her laptop from the floor and started clicking away.

"What are you doing?" I asked.

"Just checking on what folks are saying about us," she said. "There should be lots of news reports about it by now."

We spent the next hour looking at news reports, including footage of the fight, of Crusher's death, and of our mid-air kiss. I made her freeze the video on that last part so I could burn it into my memory. Too bad I couldn't take the image and make it the background on my phone without seeming like a superhero-stalking creep.

"What's that hot woman doing with that skinny boy?" I asked.

"Falling in love, by the looks of it," she answered without a pause.

"God, I hope so." I was giddy.

"Oh," she said, making whatever I was thinking go right out of my head.

"What is it?"

"I just checked the discussion boards for the fan pages," Amy said. "There are hundreds of posts already this morning. It seems that you're famous again and in favor. Look at all these posts about Kestrel. I guess someone should leak her name, huh? No one seems to know it."

"I guess that someone ought to start a Kestrel fan club," I said as I stepped behind her and hugged her as I looked at the screen over her shoulder.

"Um, too late," she said as she tilted the screen toward me. There was a full-length picture of her in mid-air, snapped perfectly during a pause in her action.

"I'm sure all the guys will leave me and join your fan club. I would. Look at you. My God." Her blush was adorable.

"So," she said, "partners? Angel and Kestrel, the city's crime-fighting team."

"Absolutely," I said. "It's about time you get equal billing. I couldn't do any of it without you. I never could."

36

The heavily muscled man watched the news report. There had been some type of epic battle, a supervillain against a couple of superheroes, in the city of Sueño. The villain lost, and the community was fully behind the heroes. There was a massive investigation into the police department, and several high-ranking members were already being taken into custody. He watched with a detached interest, as if it was of little concern. Only the muscle popping out on the side of his face as he clenched his teeth showed it was not so.

He was dressed in a sickly gray-green costume, a tight, long-sleeved shirt tucked into snug pants, which were in turn tucked into boots. He had a biohazard symbol emblazoned on his chest, identifying him as a powerful supervillain and crime lord. The people called him Pestilence.

As he continued to watch, his fists clenched, and the muscles in his forearms quivered. When the grisly image of the body that used to be the villain called Crusher finally flashed onto the screen, the man's eyes widened and a murmuring boiled from his throat. Before it developed into a full scream, he choked it back. No, he would retain control.

He breathed in and out three times, forcing himself to be calm. Though he wanted to break something, he slowly used the remote control and turned the TV off, putting it down gently and then folding his hands in his lap. He took a few more breaths and raised his eyes to the ceiling.

"The Angel," he said to the air, "and that flying girl, Kestrel. They are the ones who did it, who not only ruined all the careful planning, but also killed Crusher. The Angel. And the girl. Payment is due. The bill must be paid."

Frederick Lancaster, publicly a billionaire and not so publicly the supervillain called Pestilence, leaned back on his couch. He didn't know how two upstarts had been able to kill his son, but he did know one thing. They would not live long. He had the resources and the power, and he would turn them toward these *heroes*.

"Charles," he said to the empty air. "We have a new project. Come in here, please."

The door opened, and a shadow entered the room. Pestilence didn't even look up, only recited instructions on how these two would be taken care of.

PREVIEW REMINDER

Be sure not to miss the sneak peak of Unmasked, the second book in the Unlikely Hero series (at the very end of this book).

THANK YOU...

...for reading my book. **Please consider taking a moment to post a review** where you purchased the book. Reviews are important in helping other readers find exciting books and help authors to continue to write them, as well as providing valuable feedback for the author. Your honest review would be very much appreciated.

If you would like to get information on upcoming books, such as the next book in the Unlikely Hero Series (titled *Uncovered*), please visit my web site at **pepadilla.com** and join my mailing list.

I also appreciate any comments I receive, so please feel free stop by my web site and comment on the site itself or to send me an e-mail at pep@pepadilla.com.

ALSO BY ERIC PADILLA

Adventures in Gythe (under pen name P.E. Padilla):

Vibrations: Harmonic Magic Book 1 (also available as an audiobook)

Harmonics: Harmonic Magic Book 2 (also available as an audiobook)

Resonance: Harmonic Magic Book 3

Tales of Gythe: Gray Man Rising (also available as an audiobook)

The Unlikely Hero Series:

Unfurled: Heroine is a Tough Gig (Unlikely Hero Series Book 1) (also available as an audiobook) (This book)

Unmasked (Unlikely Hero Series Book 2)

Undaunted (Unlikely Hero Series Book 3) (out early 2018)

The Shadowling Chronicles:

Shadowling

Witches of the Elements Series (under pen name P.E. Padilla):

Water & Flame (Book 1)

Song of Prophecy Series (under pen name P.E. Padilla):

Wanderer's Song

.

ABOUT THE AUTHOR

A chemical engineer by degree, air quality engineer by vocation, certified dreamer by predilection, and writer by sheer persistence, Eric Padilla learned long ago that crunching numbers and designing solutions was not enough to satisfy his creative urges. Weaned on classic science fiction and fantasy stories from authors as diverse as Heinlein, Tolkien, and Jordan, and affected by his love of role playing games such as Dungeons and Dragons (analog) and Final Fantasy (digital), he sometimes has trouble distinguishing reality from fantasy. While not ideal for a person who needs to function in modern society, it's the perfect state of mind for a writer. He also writes epic fantasy under the pen name P.E. Padilla, and lives in Southern California, though he would like to be where there are more trees.

PREVIEW OF UNMASKED:

UNLIKELY HERO SERIES BOOK 2

1

The alien invaders were unstoppable. Try as they might, the people of Earth couldn't stand up to the technologically superior weapons of the extraterrestrial attackers. It looked like the end of life on the planet as we knew it.

Fighter jets screamed across the sky. The pop of ignition and the whoosh of rockets speeding toward the alien ships mingled with the explosions nearer and the faint screams of people who were blasted by the alien weapons. The rockets had no effect, bouncing off the crafts' sleek armor. It was like a child hitting a tank with a stick.

"Daniel!" my mom called.

Amy paused the movie—*War of the Worlds*, the newer version with Tom Cruise.

"Yeah?" I yelled back.

My mom came into the living room where Amy and I were sprawled on the couch, feet on the coffee table, big bowl of popcorn between us. Amy elbowed me, and we both pulled our feet off. With my super speed, mine hit the floor and I was sitting up straight before hers had even cleared the table top. Sure, her flying abilities were cool, but in this situation, my powers had definite advantages over hers.

My mom looked at Amy and narrowed her eyes. She had told us not to put our feet up there. Many times. Amy swallowed, not able to meet Mom's eyes.

I looked more like my mother than my father. We both had sandy brown hair and blue eyes, and while I would be considered skinny, she was slender. Those words meant the same thing to me, but other people seemed to think they were different. Amy had told me more than once that meeting my mother's eyes was nearly like looking into my own, except for times like now when Mom's seemed to have fire behind them.

"I need you to put the trash out," she said, "and then go pick your brother up from the skate park. Here are the keys."

"Okay." I jumped up but tried to keep the excitement from my voice. I didn't want her to know how much I liked to drive, even on little errands like this. Someday I'd need to negotiate for use of the car, and I wanted her to think she was in my debt. "You wanna come, Amy?"

"Oh, you're so romantic," she said. "Always taking me to the most exciting places."

"Yeah, whatever." I pulled her toward me and kissed the side of her face, scrunching up her eye. She laughed at me.

"But yes, my Romeo, I'll go with you."

I waved toward the paused movie. "We can watch the rest later."

"I already know what happens anyway," she said.

"You do?"

"You don't?" Her look made me feel three or four years old.

"Um...I've never seen it before," I said.

"You haven't seen the original? You haven't ever read the book? You don't know how it ends?"

"Nope. Should I?"

"Come on." She looked at my mother, who shrugged. "It's important modern history, part of pop culture."

"Sorry," I said. "But I don't know."

"You better watch it, then. You can finish it without me. I've seen it, read it, seen the original."

"Fine. I'll do my homework." I puffed out my lower lip. "Do I need to write a report on it, too?"

"Don't tempt me," she said, wagging a finger at me. Then she broke out in the beautiful smile that always made me sigh.

I sighed.

Amy wasn't what most people would consider a fashionable person. Her over-large clothes, clunky shoes, messy brown hair in a tangle of uneven pig tails, and huge glasses drew attention away from how absolutely stunning she was.

Her bright blue eyes pierced the glare of her glasses, and her perfect beauty hidden by those spectacles filled my vision. Others saw a nerdy, awkward, unkempt girl. I saw a goddess. She was definitely the best thing in the entire universe.

"Come on, my angel," she said, taking my hand. "Let's go pick the little trickster up. I can tell you how the movie ends if you want." I loved it when she worked *angel* into normal conversation. Of course, it was much easier than me working *kestrel* into my regular speech. We did that a lot, drop little inside jokes about our superhero identities. It made me feel like we were sharing secrets behind everyone's backs. Which of course, we were.

I let her lead me out the door, looking back over my shoulder at my mother as we left. I grinned at her, and she smiled and waved back, shaking her head.

I jogged around the passenger side of my mom's old Honda Accord and opened the door for Amy. She smiled at me as she slid into the seat.

"Why, thank you, sir," she said.

"Of course," I replied as I closed the door, then went around to the driver's side.

"So..." she said as we headed toward the skate park. "You really have no idea how that story ends? *War of the Worlds*?"

"Nope. Consider it a hole in my education."

"Do you want me to tell you?" she said.

"Sure. Who knows if I'll ever watch the rest of it."

"Okay." She settled into the seat and twisted her torso toward me as if she was going to tell me some long tale. "You see—"

Traffic ahead stopped suddenly. I noticed the red lights out of my peripheral vision as I was looking at Amy, and slammed on the brakes. Well, I actually didn't slam on them. If I had done that, I would've punched the brake pedal through the floorboard of the car with my super strength. I only lightly tapped them. I'd been practicing using a soft touch in everyday life so I didn't destroy everything around me.

The car jerked to a halt. I whipped my arm out across Amy's collarbones to slow her down instead of letting the seatbelt do the work. Things happened fast, but to my speed-geared vision, it was pretty slow. She looked down at my arm and hand, dangerously close to her chest. I pulled it back as if burned.

"Sorry," I said. "I didn't want you to get hurt."

She smiled. "No problem. Thank you for the placement of your arm, even though lower would have been more cushioned." She rubbed where my arm had been.

I swallowed. I started to sweat. Maybe it was the excitement from almost getting in an accident.

"I wonder what's going on up there." Amy sat up in her seat and craned her neck, trying to see past the cars in front of us. "It doesn't seem like a normal traffic jam. Look at all the people."

Motorists had gotten out of their cars and were walking forward. What *was* going on? "You wanna check it out?"

"You bet," Amy said, stepping out of the car.

I joined her, scanning what was now a parking lot, with people standing around us. Other people were doing the same thing, leaving their vehicles and going with the crowd. No one was going to be driving anywhere anytime soon, so Amy and I joined the throng as they shuffled toward whatever had captured everyone's interest.

Long before we saw the fire, a black plume spiraling away from us caught my eye. I hadn't noticed it before because the wind was blowing the other way, but as we got closer, I could smell the burning and see the black plume angling off away from us.

It was a big one.

The building was six stories tall, the bottom three of which appeared to be on fire. People waved frantically from balconies on the top two floors, and even more were behind windows, banging to get out. There were no fire escapes visible on the outside of the building, meaning the only escape would be through internal stairwells. Right into the burning floors. Things didn't look good.

I met Amy's beautiful, cool-blue eyes. She nodded. We

both ran for the nearest alley after a quick stop at the car for our backpacks. I carried mine with me everywhere, and Amy had adopted the habit. Actually, it was her idea to begin with, but whatever.

The first alley was full of people trying to bypass the crowded street to get a better look at the fire. The second and third were less busy, but still had too many observers. I shook my head at Amy.

"Too bad you don't have super speed like the Flash or Superman so you could just get into costume right in front of people so fast they wouldn't notice," she said.

"Yeah." I felt time passing, could almost hear a ticking clock. People in the building were going to die if we didn't get into costume and take action.

We ducked down another alley, a dead end between two buildings and blocked off by a third. There was barely room for a garbage truck to get in, and dumpsters crowded the back half. It would have to do.

I used the speed I did have, much faster than a normal person but not comic book fast. I was already peeling off my clothes as Amy came around the dumpster I had ducked behind.

We had started wearing our costumes underneath our other clothes. It was easier for her because she normally wore really baggy pants and shirts, whereas hiding a costume under my normal jeans and t-shirts was a tougher proposition. Amy had remade my costume so the fabric was thinner and somehow tougher at the same time. She had also modified the hood so it could be detached. The cape and boots had to stay in the backpack, though with the new material, they could collapse to the size of a paperback book in the compression pouch she gave me.

In no time, we were suited up and ready to go. Amy—I

mean Kestrel—took us up to the roof of one of the buildings to stash our clothes, and then we zoomed off into the sky toward the fire.

Kestrel was handy to have around. Her ability to fly was cool enough, but part of her power allowed her to carry just about anything. We hadn't figured out the upper limit yet. Whenever she grabbed something and exerted her power, it became weightless to her, allowing her to fly off with it and move it wherever she liked.

I didn't weigh much to begin with—barely over a hundred pounds—so it was no problem for her to grab my shoulders and tow me toward the burning building.

At first, I thought it would be uncomfortable, being snatched up and tugged through the sky by one part of my body, but it wasn't like that at all. I barely felt her touch, as if I were floating and she guided me with her hands. I'm pretty sure she could have carried me with a couple of fingers.

Over the noise of the fire hoses and the roaring of the fire, I heard oohs and ahs as we flew. Amy's—I really needed to remember to call her Kestrel—costume was a striking green, somewhere in between lime and forest. The material stretched tight over her to show off her fantastic body. My charcoal-colored costume, while great for sneaking around in the dark, was drab in comparison with her bright clothing.

It was okay. All eyes were drawn to her anyway when we worked together. She was gorgeous—even with a mask on—and shapely and perfect. I might as well have been invisible. But like I said, that was fine with me.

"Are you ready?" she asked. Another odd facet of her power was that no matter how fast we flew, we could speak to each other in normal, conversational volume. There was no windrush noise to deaden our hearing.

"Check," I said, tensing up for my part.

"Okay. Drop-off in three, two, one." She let go of me and pulled up as we approached the building. I free fell toward it.

2

At the last moment, I turned, aiming my feet toward the window on the fifth floor. With a crash and a spray of shattered glass, I plummeted through and into the building, tucking into a roll as I made it to the floor. I came to my feet and traveled a few steps before stopping, and looked around.

In a short hallway, the metal doors of two elevators gleamed to my right, and a heavy wooden door with fancy carved designs and a brushed brass knob stood closed to my left. Straight ahead, another door, not quite as large and ornamental as the other, faced me. Behind me, near the shattered window, was the door to the stairwell. No fire, but the air was slightly hazy with smoke wafting up from the lower floors.

I had found, in some of the research sessions with Amy, that I could hold my breath for a long time. I mean a long, long time. I came close to ten minutes once, though that was remaining still. Amy said something about my cardiovascular system working more efficiently, too, so I used less oxygen. I could run super fast and not breathe that heavily, so I guessed she was right.

I might be taking advantage of that very soon.

Kestrel flew past carrying a man who did not look all that comfortable floating through the air held by a girl's small hands, regardless of how secure he was or how she looked in that costume. She must have been taking people who had made it to the balconies to the ground.

A man and two women burst from the door in front of me, eyes wide and motions jerky. When they caught sight of me, they slid to a halt on the tiled floor. The man looked around as if he was trying to escape, and one of the women made a strangled cry.

"Is anyone hurt?" I said, trying to calm them with my voice. "I'm here to help."

The other woman's mouth dropped open. She took in my costume in an instant. "You're him," she said. "You're that superhero guy."

"Yes. I'm Angel. My partner is helping to evacuate people. Stand over here near the window, and she'll get you out of here before the fire reaches this floor."

"The flying woman?" the man said, suddenly more interested than scared. "The one with the tight green suit?"

I eyed him, but didn't have time to deal with the feelings of jealousy wriggling around in my belly. "Yes. Her name is Kestrel. I need to look for others. Are there more people in the area you came from?"

"No," the man said. "We were the only ones there when the alarm went off. I'm not sure about the other offices, though" He pointed toward the other door to my left. "It's a different company."

"I'll check," I said. "Stay here and wait for Kestrel to take you to safety."

I nudged the door with my fingertips. The door exploded off its hinges and flew ten feet before striking a wall and then settling onto the floor. I guess I needed more practice at the soft touch.

"Oops," I said to the three people, and then I headed into a maze of cubicles and offices.

I rushed through the area looking for anyone who needed my help. The place seemed to be deserted. Were there no people here today, or had they all escaped already? If they left, where had they gone? The fire was too dangerous to go through the lower levels.

The building groaned. Had I just sensed a movement in the floor, as if the entire structure was beginning to sway? I gulped.

I came around yet another cubicle wall, gray cloth covering it and slogans pinned to the surface. "Make today your best day." "No one can stop you unless you let them." "Stoke the fire inside you." That last one made me chuckle. An office door on the other side of the cloth-covered box was open, and something moved inside.

A man in a shirt and tie sat at the desk, focusing on his keyboard and monitor. He had headphones on, nodding his head to the beat of whatever he was listening to. I could hear the music from the doorway but didn't recognize it.

"Hey," I said. "The building is on fire."

There was no response. The music pouring out of the headphones nearly drowned out the clicks of the keyboard.

I waved my arms, but the man didn't seem to have good peripheral vision, so I walked up to him and pulled the headphones off. The music blared as I dropped them on the desk.

The man jumped and swiveled toward me. He looked like a victim in one of those horror flicks where everyone overacts. He scrambled back, eyes darting and limbs twitching, like I was going to eat him or something.

"Sorry I startled you," I said calmly, "but the building is

on fire. The first three floors are in flames. You need to get out of here."

"What?" he said. "Fire? Are you sure?"

"Uh, yeah. Can't you smell the smoke that's filtering up into this floor?"

"I have allergies. I can't really smell anything right now."

"Go to the window near the elevators," I told him. "I need to look for others." I started to walk away.

"There isn't anyone else," he said. "The office is closed today. Everyone is at a company retreat. I came in to get some work done. I'm the only one here."

I wondered if I should take his word for it. He would have still been sitting there when the flames engulfed the building. Oblivious. "Okay, thanks. Get to the window." I ran from the room, making a quick sweep of the entire area. I didn't try to get into closed office doors. It seemed that he was right. There was no one else here.

I made it to the elevator lobby before he did and headed to the stairwell. Kestrel would have gathered all those on the floor above. I had to check the floors below.

As I went down the stairs, it became hazier, smoke infiltrating the space. I wondered how fireproof my skin was as I burst through the door to the third floor. It was smoky, but not too bad. I breathed shallowly, thinking that might help. I didn't see any flames, but it was warmer than the floor above.

The large reception desk right in front of the elevators was flanked by three doors. One of them was open, so I went through it first. Desks and cubicles were spread out across the main open area, but this floor had more offices. I caught movement off to my left and headed toward it. Four people were crowded on a small balcony, looking down at the firefighters trying to battle the blaze. Three men and one woman.

Amy—I mean Kestrel—flew by on her way up to the higher floors, and I yelled for her. The people jumped as they spun toward me. After recognizing me, Kestrel zipped toward the balcony.

"Sorry to startle you," I said to the group. "I wanted to get her attention. She'll take you down to the ground safely."

Kestrel caught the last of what I had said. "Yes, I can take two of you at a time." She reached toward the woman and one of the men and tilted her head at me, as if in question.

"I'll search the rest of this floor," I said. "I haven't found anyone else here yet. I'll probably go down one more floor to see if anyone is trapped there."

She nodded. "Be careful." To the other two men, she said, "I'll be right back for the two of you. It won't even take a minute." She addressed the woman and the man she would take. "You're probably going to want to close your eyes." She lifted them over the balcony railing and then sank toward the ground. All four people's mouths dropped open.

"I've got to look for others," I told the men. "Do you know if anyone else is here on this floor?"

"No," one of them responded, still watching as Kestrel lowered his coworkers to the throng waiting below. "Some others went upstairs to try to find another way out, but I don't think there's anyone else here."

I sped around the floor anyway, checking in every office I could find. There was no one else.

I only debated for a moment before going to the stairwell again. It would be dangerous on the lower floor, but I had to try. If anyone was trapped there, they wouldn't survive long. I would make a quick check and then get out of there.

I felt the door leading from the stairwell into the second floor of the building like all those videos in school told me to do. It was warm. No, it was actually pretty hot. My skin was thick and insulated well. If I had done what I'd always been told to do, I would have not opened the door.

I opened the door.

Okay, it was really more a case of me kicking the door off the hinges and hoping fire would not shoot out at me.

It didn't. I breathed out in relief.

The air did look bad in there, though, full of smoke with the glow of fire coming from around the corner. The floor had two doors, both open, barely visible in the haze. I couldn't see beyond the doorway into the offices.

"Hello," I called, coughing as I breathed in. The smoke was pretty bad. "Is anyone here? I'm here to help." I ducked my head into the stairwell and took another breath of cleaner—and cooler—air.

I heard what sounded like a cough inside the left door. I breathed out slowly, emptying my lungs completely, then breathed in as much air as I could hold. Then I charged into the smoky area. I'd really test how long I could hold my breath this time.

A weak, strained voice sounded, barely louder than the groaning of the building and the hissing of the fire. There were no flames visible near me, but they were close. The place was going to go up soon.

I went around a cubicle and finally saw flame. One of the offices on the far side of the floor was on fire, and the others looked to be ready to go themselves. Warmth played across my skin like stepping out of a shadow on a cool but sunny day, only magnified a hundred times. My skin was resistant to the fire's heat, but parts of my costume seemed to be curling up like when you leave an iron on a polyester shirt. I actually experienced that once, but I don't really like to talk about it.

I blinked, rubbed my eyes, and blinked again. A man stood a few feet from the fire as if he was patiently waiting for someone. He wore a full-body suit that looked like it was made out of fireproof material. Really, it looked like he had clumsily sewn together dozens of those silver-colored oven mitts. The hood kind of thing he had draped over his head, eyeholes crookedly cut into it, didn't help the image.

I didn't speak—I was still holding my breath after all— but I grunted my surprise. The man turned to me, eyes widening.

Then he threw a fireball at me.

Made in the USA
Columbia, SC
22 November 2018